"*Nenemoosha.*
The Chippewa word for sweetheart."

"*Nenemoosha,*" she repeated. Then more slowly, softer, "*Nenemoosha...*" with a wistful sigh.

He leaned toward her, unable to resist the word said so sweetly. "Say, *metea.*"

"*Metea?*" she asked.

"Do not say it like a question," he instructed.

"*Metea,*" she repeated.

He leaned the rest of the way across the little tea table and deposited a kiss on her lips.

"Again?" he asked.

"*Metea.*"

Again he kissed her, deeper, fuller.

When he sat back, she smiled. Ah, she understood that the word was an invitation.

"*Metea, metea, metea,*" she said.

Tugging her into his arms, he took intense satisfaction in the feel of her against him. God forgive him, it did not matter if she was telling the truth. He wanted her. And that was all that mattered at this moment.

"You owe me, Mrs. Forbush," he said against her lips. "And I want payment...!"

* * *

The Missing Heir
Harlequin Historical #753—May 2005

Praise for Gail Ranstrom

Saving Sarah

"Gail Ranstrom has written a unique story with several twists that work within the confines of Regency England....If Ranstrom's first book showed promise, then *Saving Sarah* is when Ranstrom comes of age."
—*The Romance Reader*

A Wild Justice

"Gail Ranstrom certainly has both writing talent and original ideas."
—*The Romance Reader*

DON'T MISS THESE OTHER TITLES AVAILABLE NOW:

#751 THE DUCHESS'S NEXT HUSBAND
Terri Brisbin

#752 ROCKY MOUNTAIN MAN
Jillian Hart

#754 HER DEAREST ENEMY
Elizabeth Lane

GAIL RANSTROM

THE MISSING HEIR

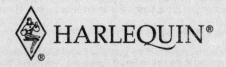

HARLEQUIN®

TORONTO • NEW YORK • LONDON
AMSTERDAM • PARIS • SYDNEY • HAMBURG
STOCKHOLM • ATHENS • TOKYO • MILAN • MADRID
PRAGUE • WARSAW • BUDAPEST • AUCKLAND

ISBN 0-373-29353-4

THE MISSING HEIR

Copyright © 2005 by Gail Ranstrom

This edition published by arrangement with Harlequin Books S.A.

® and TM are trademarks of the publisher. Trademarks indicated with ® are registered in the United States Patent and Trademark Office, the Canadian Trade Marks Office and in other countries.

www.eHarlequin.com

Printed in U.S.A.

Dedicated to The Hussies,
for their unfailing friendship,
nurturing and support.

Special thanks to Eileen G., Lisa W. and Suzi S.—
the Wild Writers. Thanks for keeping me
focused, writing and laughing.

Prologue

Wednesday, May 24, 1820

"But there was something relentlessly methodical in the way my brother was fleeced, and that is why I suspect cheating." Miss Laura Talbot sat primly on the edge of her chair, an air of expectancy hovering about her like a storm cloud. "Can you help me?"

Grace Forbush glanced at the four other women in her parlor. Annica Sinclair, Lady Auberville, merely blinked. Charity MacGregor arched her eyebrows and tilted her head to one side. Lady Sarah Travis shook her head in sympathy, and Dianthe Lovejoy shot a worried glance back at Grace.

Grace delicately cleared her throat and set her teacup aside. "Before we undertake any case, Miss Talbot, you must understand that the Wednesday League is devoted to obtaining justice for women. Justice. You must be completely candid with us, and you must accept that, should we discover your brother's gaming debts are honest, we can do nothing to help you. We cannot alter the truth, merely uncover it." And Grace more than half suspected the debt was honest. Who, after having lost his entire fortune, did *not* cry "foul"?

"Yes, of course." Miss Talbot nodded eagerly. "I have been candid, and though I would not like the consequences, I am willing to abide by them."

"What *are* the consequences to you, Miss Talbot?" Lady Annica asked. "Aside from reduced circumstances?"

"Two and a half weeks hence, on the tenth of June, I am to wed Lord Geoffrey Morgan. You see, I was a part of my brother's last desperate wager."

"Lord Geoffrey Morgan?" Lady Sarah frowned and shot a glance at Grace. "He must have been desperate, indeed."

Grace nodded. Her own experience had been remarkably similar to Miss Talbot's, down to the blend of old and new bruises on Miss Talbot's arms, and likely other, less exposed, places. And, like her own brother, Grace saw this as evidence that Miss Talbot's brother delighted in the infliction of pain and complete domination. Unlike Miss Talbot, however, she had found marriage to a stranger an escape rather than an unacceptable fate.

"I gather Lord Geoffrey is not a choice you would make for yourself?" she asked.

"Heavens no!" Miss Talbot gasped. "I've met him only once, the day after my brother's losing wager. He is a gambler, and when I asked my friends about him, I learned that he has a very murky reputation. The very idea of marriage to such a man is abhorrent to me."

The Wednesday League knew Geoffrey Morgan. He had been close to Constance Bennington, a member of their group, before her death. He'd disappeared for several years after her death, and then returned under a rather dark cloud. Grace studied Miss Talbot closely. The girl was perhaps ten and seven, and very pretty in an ordinary sort of way. She had a lovely complexion, even features, wide brown eyes and a trim figure. Grace could only imagine what marriage to a man who had to gamble for a bride would do to an innocent like Laura

Talbot. Well, not while *she* breathed! Laura would have the chance that Grace never had.

Grace leaned forward and patted Miss Talbot's hand. "If Lord Geoffrey has been cheating, we shall discover it, my dear. Meantime, I would like you to think about simple refusal of your brother's debt. It is his debt, after all, and not yours. I do not think the courts would look kindly on this sort of thing."

Miss Talbot glanced down at her lap. "If this were taken to the courts, the scandal would ruin what is left of the family reputation. Regardless, my integrity and reputation would be stained. I cannot decide which I dread more at the moment, Mrs. Forbush—my brother's wrath or Lord Geoffrey's attentions. I suspect my brother has the capacity to make my life exceedingly more unpleasant than Lord Geoffrey. And, since I have not reached my majority, I am obligated to my brother."

That, too, was familiar territory! But Grace had not been gambled away by her brother. She'd been arbitrarily bartered for land adjoining their estate.

Charity MacGregor stood and went to glance out the parlor window at the park across the street. "Strategically speaking, Grace, how are we to accomplish this task? We cannot march into gaming hells and demand to see betting books, nor can we cast dice or bet on the turn of a card."

They couldn't, it was true. But she, as an independent widow of spotless reputation and high social consequence, would have a certain immunity in these matters. Society would watch her for any misstep, but they would allow her more latitude than a spinster or married woman, believing she would soon tire of it. And she would—within two and a half weeks.

Squaring her shoulders, she said, "I shall lead the investigation. I am certain I can persuade Lord Barrington to introduce me to the appropriate persons." She turned back to Laura

Talbot and smiled. "Do not worry, Miss Talbot. I promise that I will do everything within my power to prevent your marriage to Lord Geoffrey. And I shall begin tomorrow."

Chapter One

Adam Hawthorne turned his face upward and breathed deeply of the warm spring rain before entering the imposing graystone building at precisely ten o'clock. He turned the collar of his fringed buckskin jacket down and shook the raindrops from his hair. Such niceties as hats and greatcoats had been sadly absent in the northwest wilderness and, after four years, deuced difficult to even remember.

Barely one day back in England and he was already feeling out of place. He supposed the buckskins didn't help. How long would it take him to think and feel like an Englishman again? A week? A month? Ever? Ah, well, at least he'd remembered to do his duty first and leave personal concerns for later.

He strode up the stairs to the second floor, down the hall to a door at the end, and announced himself to a slender young man wearing wire spectacles. "Adam Hawthorne to see Lord Barrington."

The young man's gaze swept Adam from head to toe and curiosity registered behind the pale blue eyes. That glance brought home to Adam just how starkly foreign he must look in a London Ministry building. He supposed he should elevate finding a tailor and a barber to the next item on his list of things to do. But that would depend on what he found out here.

"His lordship is expecting you, sir. Please go in."

Adam rapped sharply on the frosted-glass pane of the door before opening it and stepping through. Lord Ronald Barrington glanced up from a stack of papers.

"Hawthorne! By God, 'tis good to see you." He gestured at a leather-upholstered chair in front of his desk. "Sit down, man. When I got your message earlier, I was dumbfounded. You were reported dead four years ago."

"So I've heard, my lord."

"Why are you here, Hawthorne? You're a diplomatic attaché, so I am not in your line of command."

"Yes, sir, but I was attached to the military at Fort Garry. I reported to Lord Craddock the minute I got off the ship and, once he'd taken my statement, he suggested I see you as a courtesy. He thought some of the intelligence I gathered might be of interest to you."

"Indeed?" Barrington looked intrigued as he called the clerk into his private sanctum and instructed him to take notes. "Well, give over, man. I'm always interested in what's happening in the northwestern reaches."

It was well into the afternoon before Lord Barrington sat back in his chair and nodded, dismissing the clerk with a wave of his hand. "Thank you, Hawthorne. Your information should prove useful. Despite the Treaty of Ghent five years ago, I do not delude myself that the French influence in Canada is over."

Adam nodded. Now that business was out of the way, he could pursue his personal agenda—the one that had driven him for the past four years, and the real reason Lord Craddock had referred him to Barrington. "I need a piece of information from you, Lord Barrington."

"Ask. I'm much in your debt and I'll be pleased to answer anything."

"I'd like the name of the military attaché at Fort Garry four years ago." Indeed, he wanted that name more than he wanted breath and life. Finding the name of the bastard who'd given the order to decimate the Chippewa tribe he'd been lodged with was the only thing that had kept him alive through long, frigid winters huddled in wigwams, through deprivation and starvation and homelessness.

"Any particular reason you want that information, Hawthorne?"

Adam affected nonchalance. He softened his expression and offered a smile. "Just curious who reported me dead, sir."

"I believe it was a party from the local fort. They rode out on patrol and came back with the news that everyone, to the last woman and child, had been murdered in warfare by a rival tribe."

Idiots! Bloody damned idiots! Had they even investigated the attack? Likely not. It had only been made to *look* like tribal warfare. Was Barrington covering the truth, or was he foolish enough to believe that neighboring tribes simply attacked each other without reason or provocation? He couldn't be that naive. But with Barrington's help or not, someone would eventually talk—even if it was at the point of Adam's knife.

His long years in the Diplomatic Corps came to his aid. Slipping into his English skin, he buried his anger and gave Barrington a bland smile. "I'd like to tell him in person that there were a few survivors. I'd think that would ease his mind."

"Yes, but how *did* you survive? The word we received said that not a single living thing was left. Given the savagery of the attack, it was believed no prisoners were taken."

Adam nodded. "None were, my lord. I'd gone out with a small hunting party the day before the attack. There were eight of us, and when we returned to the village and found… well, believing the English were responsible, and rather than kill me, my hosts took me hostage and we rode south to…to a place the Indians call *Chick'a gami*. You've heard the rest, sir."

"Aye. Well, I'll have to search through the records for his name. It may take some time. Will you be in town?"

Tension drained from Adam's shoulders. He stood and smiled. "Yes, sir. I still have some business here. Lord Craddock said he would have me reinstated and secure my back pay. I'll need it to repair and stock my cottage and lands in Devon. Since I was reported dead, I imagine the stock was sold off, but I pray the cottage is still in the family."

"Family," Barrington repeated. He looked thoughtful.

"Well, only Uncle Basil and I remain, unless that young wife of his has given him heirs."

"You've not gone there?"

Adam recalled the expansive home on Bloomsbury Square and smiled. "I wanted my business finished so that I could relax and enjoy the reunion. I've never met my new aunt, you know. Uncle Basil said he met her while selling a parcel of land to her brother. She was in the country when I was last in London on my way to Ghent, but I saw the portrait of her in Uncle Basil's study."

And what a portrait it had been! It had kept his blood humming for weeks afterward, and many long winter nights since. Dark, sultry eyes gazed out of a face of sheer perfection. Her expression had been self-possessed and confident, and Adam found himself envious of his aging uncle for the first time. He'd suspected the wife was a fortune hunter, since a woman like that could have married someone considerably higher in station. And considerably younger. He wondered if there'd still be fire in those dark eyes.

Barrington heaved a deep sigh and wouldn't meet Adam's gaze. "Damn it all, Hawthorne. Craddock should have told you. I'm afraid I've got bad news. Your uncle expired immediately after we'd had word of your death. Everyone said it was the grief, but it went beyond that."

Adam sat again, trying to comprehend this last in a chain of bitter disappointments. "How…."

"He hadn't been well. He did his best to hide it from you on your last visit. Didn't want to worry you, he said. When we got the news of your death, the spirit went out of him. I helped his widow make the final arrangements and put his business in order. The last thing he did was change his will to leave everything to her."

Adam nodded, registering the logic in that. He had already discovered through his earlier visit to his bank that his uncle had closed his bank accounts and taken his assets, but he had been confident they would be returned to him. Ah, but now everything was in the possession of his widow, and it was anyone's guess what she would do. "Well, there appears to be some matters we will have to sort out. Did she and my uncle have heirs?"

"No," Barrington admitted.

"Has she remarried?"

"She seems quite content to be a widow."

A niggling suspicion grew from his hunch that she'd been a fortune hunter. Had she sped her husband's demise once the competition for his money was gone? No. Barrington just said his uncle had been ill even before his last visit.

"She lives quietly," Barrington continued. "Her reputation is of the highest order. Not a breath of scandal."

"Discreet, then," he concluded.

"There is nothing to be discreet about. She's blameless."

Adam glanced up at Lord Barrington. His reaction to the implied criticism was telling. All the signs were there. Damned if Barrington wasn't in love with his widowed aunt! He cleared his throat and stood. "Good to know," he said, heading for the door. "You'll let me know when you find the name of the military advisor at Fort Garry?"

"Where shall I send word?"

He smiled, an idea taking root. There was only one way to get to the bottom of his uncle's death. "I'll let you know when I'm settled, sir."

The sound of a bell downstairs announced a visitor. A quick glance at the little enameled clock on her bedside table urged Grace to haste. Ronald Barrington must have come early. He was not supposed to pick her up for another hour. Mrs. Dewberry, her housekeeper, would put him in the library with a glass of port, but she did not like to leave him alone so long. He had a propensity to snoop through her private correspondence.

Glaring in her mirror, she fussed with a few stubborn strands of hair. She always wore the dark mass smoothed back and contained in a tidy chignon due to its unruly tendencies and she never felt completely groomed until it was perfect.

"Really, Aunt Grace, I think you should snip half of it off and leave the rest in curls." Dianthe shook her own blond ringlets and laughed. "I've never seen hair so long you could sit on before. And I think you'd look younger with it down."

Yes, that was half the problem. Grace did not want to look younger. Though less than ten years older than Dianthe, she had learned to act twenty years her senior. She smiled. "If I cut it, I'll never gain control of it again."

Grace met Dianthe's gaze in the mirror. She was lying across the bed and resting her chin on the heel of her hand. It was generally acknowledged that Dianthe was one of the reigning beauties of the Season. With her pale blond hair and petite figure, she drew admiring glances wherever she went. What an observant young woman she was! Perhaps that was why she was so adept at maneuvering through complicated courtships and unwanted entanglements—she saw them coming and avoided them, much as Grace had done since Basil's death.

"Yes, I suppose it is," she finally admitted.

"Why have you never considered Barrington as a potential husband?"

Should she give her niece the easiest answer, or the truth? *Heavens, not the truth!* That was too humiliating to admit. "It is not that I think he would be cruel or unkind, but he occasionally smothers me with his condescension and his attempts to mold me into his ideal. And I do not love him the way a wife should love a husband." There. That much was true.

Dianthe's china-blue eyes twinkled. "You mean, like my sister loves the McHugh?"

"Yes. Like that," Grace said. "McHugh's passions are very close to the surface. One look at him and Afton and there can be no doubt that they are made for each other."

"That kind of love is very rare." She sighed and pushed herself into a sitting position. "I am certain I would not be comfortable with something so fierce. Better a man I can manage. And you can manage Lord Barrington quite nicely, Aunt Grace. That should be an advantage."

Oh, if Dianthe only knew! She fastened a crystal-studded snood over her chignon and stood. She smoothed her gown, a deep burgundy satin that lent her an air of mature elegance—an image she was constantly striving to achieve. If anyone should guess what lay beneath the surface, she would be finished in society.

"Enough about me, Dianthe. Shall we discuss you instead? What are you doing tonight?"

"Nothing so interesting as you. Are you certain I cannot come with you and Lord Barrington?"

Grace laughed. "Positive."

"Hmm. Then I suppose I shall have to go to Hortense and Harriet Thayer's dinner party with Lady Sarah and her husband. Not nearly as much fun as you will have, I wager."

"Wager? Very amusing, Dianthe. This is but the first step.

I doubt I will do much wagering tonight. I only intend to accustom myself to the atmosphere and the customs—perhaps learn a game or two before I pit myself against Lord Geoffrey so that I will not look like a complete novice."

"Has dear Ronnie asked you about your sudden interest in gambling?"

"He did indeed. It required a little more persuasion than I had anticipated to elicit his help. I simply told him that I wanted to do something new."

Dianthe laughed. "I think he consented just to keep you from asking one of your other admirers to escort you. Still, it must have sent him into a tizzy."

More like a rage!

Grace's bedroom door flew open and Mrs. Dewberry stood there, looking for all the world as if the sky had fallen.

"Oh, Mrs. Forbush! There's a man downstairs—a Red Indian! He wants in. I've tried to send him away, but he will not go."

Dianthe stood and glanced toward the corridor, her eyes round with excitement. "A Red Indian? How very intriguing. I wonder what he could want."

"I cannot imagine." The last thing Grace wanted to deal with at the moment was a confused foreigner. Well, she'd simply have to give him directions and send him on his way. "Where did you leave him, Mrs. Dewberry?"

"In the library, Mrs. Forbush. Couldn't very well leave him on the stoop, could I? What if the neighbors saw?"

Grace sighed. She was less concerned about what the neighbors would say than she was with the stranger himself. A Red Indian could be dangerous. What if she could not make him understand her, as Mrs. Dewberry had been unable to do? She composed herself and hurried down the stairs. She wanted to be rid of the man before Lord Barrington arrived.

Dianthe followed close on her heels. "I've never seen a Red

Indian before," she whispered. "I wonder if they are as fierce as I've heard. Should I fetch a pistol?"

"Of course not," Grace said, bracing to open the library door. "But if he begins to make trouble, fetch Mr. Dewberry. I believe he is in the coach house." She lifted her chin and opened the door silently.

A man, tall and lean, stood at the side table with his back to her, holding a brandy bottle and a glass. He was dressed in buckskin leather breeches, a jacket with fringed arms and yoke, and moccasins that extended to his knees and, above that, a long, lethal-looking knife strapped to his right thigh. His hair, long and bound back with a leather thong, was a medium brown with glints of light playing through it from the firelight. The set of his shoulders shifted almost imperceptibly and Grace knew he was aware of her presence.

Behind her, Dianthe drew in a soft breath and touched Grace's arm as if she would pull her back. Grace shook her head to warn Dianthe to silence. She sensed that she could show no weakness or uncertainty.

Taking two steps into the library, she affected what she hoped would pass for a pleasant but firm countenance. "Good evening, sir. Is there something I can do to assist you?"

He turned to her and she nearly gasped. He was definitely not an Indian. He appeared to be perhaps four or five years older than she, his skin was deeply tanned but his eyes were a greenish hazel. He had a strong, straight nose—an aristocratic nose—and full sensual lips. A shadow of whiskers darkened his jaw and, when he moved toward her, the brandy in his glass scarcely shifted for the smoothness and grace of his gait. He moved like an animal, silent and steady. His chest, bare beneath the loose laces of his jacket, was strongly muscled and Grace found her gaze riveted there. She *wanted* to look away, but she just couldn't. She was mesmerized.

He smiled and the flash of white teeth completely disarmed her. Her heart pounded wildly and her breathing deepened. He extended one large hand to take hers and bowed over it. His lips were firm and cool, and the contact made her head swim. Heavens! What was wrong with her?

When he straightened, he flashed another of those startling smiles. "Hello, Aunt Grace."

Chapter Two

From her quickly hidden look of astonishment, Adam gathered that she had no idea what to do with the savage in her library. Interesting, the reactions he'd gotten from people who, four years ago, would have entertained him gladly. He surmised by the manner of her dress that he'd interrupted her as she was preparing for an evening out. She was every inch as stunning as her portrait—sultry, lush, distant. Untouchable?

She blinked and a guarded look settled over her perfect features. "I fear you must have me confused with someone else."

Ah, that was good. Very smooth. Not a single gesture betrayed anything other than a natural confusion beneath the surface. Even her voice was calm. Admiration filled him at her aplomb. He'd known many ambassadors with less self-possession.

He released her hand reluctantly. She was the first Englishwoman he'd touched in four years, and he was startled by the suppressed hunger that surged in him. "My name is Adam Hawthorne—your husband's nephew. Perhaps he mentioned me?"

Her dusky-rose lips parted slightly, as if she were struggling to say something but couldn't think how to put it in words. "Adam?" she finally managed to say. "I…we were told that you were killed in an Indian attack."

"The news of my death was a bit premature." He grinned.

"Oh, dear." She pressed one finger to the bridge of her nose in a gesture of distress and her eyes welled with tears. "I—I do not know quite how to tell you this, Mr. Hawthorne, but your uncle…my husband…is dead."

Her sympathy caught him by surprise and he held his own grief inside. He would deal with that later, and in private. "Would that mean that I am not welcome here?" he asked.

"Oh! Of course you are welcome. You were Mr. Forbush's only relative. He spoke of you often."

"Did he?" She referred to her husband as *Mr.* Forbush? That did not exactly tell of an intimate relationship. Had all the fondness been on his uncle's part?

"In glowing terms. He was very proud of you."

He held up his brandy glass and said, "I hope you do not mind that I helped myself. It has been many years since I've had strong drink."

"Of course not. You must make yourself at home."

Oh, he planned to make himself very much at home. "Thank you, Aunt Grace." He paused to give a self-mocking grin. "I am sorry if I sound flippant, but it seems awkward to call someone obviously younger than I 'Aunt.'"

She gestured toward the sofa in front of the fireplace. "I am afraid this whole situation is a bit awkward, Mr. Hawthorne. To say I am surprised is somewhat of an understatement."

"No less surprised than I to find my uncle had died in my absence."

She glanced over her shoulder at a lovely blond creature who looked to be pinned to the spot. "Mr. Hawthorne, may I present my niece, Miss Dianthe Lovejoy."

He bowed, noting that the girl was staring at his laced buckskins. She stepped a little closer to her aunt. For protection?

Grace took a few more steps into the room. "May I prevail upon you to tell me the details of your...arrival here?"

He hadn't the heart to go through that another time today. An abbreviated version would have to do. "Not much to tell," he said, sitting on the edge of the sofa. He was tempted to see if his worn buckskins had stained the silk damask. "I was taken hostage by a small band of Chippewa four years ago and when I was free to leave, I found there were compelling reasons to stay. I've only just come to a point where returning was imperative."

"And here you are," she finished, taking a chair across from him.

She folded her hands in her lap and Adam used the moment to congratulate himself on his assessment from the portrait he'd seen all those years ago. His uncle's wife was, indeed, all cool composure on the outside. Cool enough to kill his uncle? Ah, but there was something else there, something the artist had been unable to capture with brushstrokes on canvas. A hint of fire and depth was carefully banked beneath the icy exterior. It was a smoldering heat that could clearly bring a man to his knees with desire, but not many would have the courage to penetrate her intimidating demeanor. But he had seen enough of the world to know that Grace Forbush was a woman who barely held herself in check. She was hiding more than that smoldering sexuality, and he would not leave London until he discovered what it was.

"I'd have written," he said at length, "but there was nowhere to post a letter."

She smiled and nodded, and a small shift of her shoulders indicated a decision. "How long will you be in town, Mr. Hawthorne?"

"Not long. I have a few business matters to conclude, and I'd like to contact some old friends, then I shall go to Devon. Or, depending upon the answers I get here, back to Canada."

"Have you decided to make your home there?"

"No." He glanced down into his brandy. Home. He'd traveled the world in search of it, but he'd never found "home." Even England felt foreign now. He gave himself a mental shake and looked up again. "But there is a matter still pending."

She looked curious but she was too well bred to ask the question. Instead she changed the subject. "Have you found comfortable accommodations in town, sir?"

He'd stayed in a flash house last night after debarking. He'd lain awake, waiting for one of the thugs who'd sized him up to steal the leather pouch with all he had left in the world. But no one had bothered him—likely because he'd slept with his knife in his hand—the deadly razor-edged knife that had become his constant companion in the last four years. "My ship docked late so I found a room near the wharves. Then, of course, there's the money. As I've been reported dead, I imagine my accounts were closed?"

The lovely widow knit her brow and pressed an index finger to her forehead again. He wondered if she realized that she was betraying emotion with that gesture. "Mr. Hawthorne, you must stay here, of course."

"Very kind of you, Mrs. Forbush, but—"

"No. I insist. You see, Mr. Forbush closed your accounts and, in the absence of another heir, absorbed your assets."

Adam managed to look surprised. "I see. Well, that is the logical thing for him to have done."

"Yes, but it poses a complication now. I will need to go through the accounts and separate your assets from his and attribute any interest that would have been yours had your accounts remained open. I have made some investments with the funds, and those will revert to you, of course. I am afraid the accounting will take a little time. Or, if you would prefer not to stay here, I could advance you a portion and—"

"I'd be pleased to lodge with you." If he gave her another

moment to think of alternatives, she'd probably withdraw her invitation. It suited his purposes much better to stay here. "Truth to tell, Mrs. Forbush, I shall enjoy feeling a part of the family again," he hastened to add. That much was true. He longed for a sense of belonging, but had never found it. That emptiness had led him to the Diplomatic Corps. Perhaps he'd thought he'd find "home" in his travels. He hadn't. Just more solitude.

Adam smiled as his hostess requested her niece's assistance. "Dianthe, please find Mrs. Dewberry and have her prepare the guest suite for Mr. Hawthorne. And ask her to send up a bath and…and the trunk in the attic that has Mr. Hawthorne's name on it." She turned back to him and tilted her head to one side as Miss Dianthe hurried from the room. "Perhaps there is something there that you can wear until you have time to see a tailor, Mr. Hawthorne, but we shall have to air them out. They are likely to smell of camphor and dust. Have you had your dinner yet?"

How efficient she was. There appeared to be nothing that could shake her composure for long. She'd have made an excellent diplomat's wife. "I'm afraid not."

"I shall ask Mrs. Dewberry to bring you a tray."

Was he to be banned from the table? "I wouldn't want to be any trouble."

"No trouble at all, sir. I regret that Dianthe and I will not be able to join you tonight. We both have previous commitments. But tomorrow we shall take some time to become better acquainted. We shall look forward to hearing tales of your adventures."

The only tales he had to tell were not fit for civilized ears, Adam thought. But they would most definitely become better acquainted while he took the woman's measure. Was she a fortune hunter? Might there be something odd about his uncle's death? He intended to find out.

* * *

As their coach drew close to an infamous hell near St. James Square, Grace finally spoke. "You knew? Why did you not warn me? I was so astonished that I must have looked an utter fool."

At least Ronald Barrington had the good sense to look shame-faced. "I had no idea he would come to see you today. I thought he'd settle in somewhere and—"

She pulled her green silk-lined pelisse closer around her and clutched her beaded reticule tighter as the dank air seeped through the coach window. "He *has* settled in—at *my* house. Not that I begrudge him hospitality for a single second, but this was hardly a good time for it."

"'Twasn't in my plans, either, Grace. This has caused some damned inconvenient problems for me, as well."

She glanced sideways at her escort. In his late fifties, slightly overweight and with a florid complexion, he could still confound her with his pomposity. "What inconvenience has it caused you?"

"Ah, well, 'tis business, m'dear. No need to worry your little head about it. I only wonder what the ton will say about his presence in your house."

"No one will gossip. I rather think there would be a greater scandal if I refused him shelter. And, despite his rather eccentric appearance, he seems to possess the requisite manners to get along in society."

"Send him on his way, Grace. He's older than you, you're both unmarried and people will speculate. Do you want your friends peddling your business behind their fans?"

"My friends would never peddle my business. And I've done nothing improper." Still, gossip regarding her sheltering a single man could cause a problem. If word got back to her brother.... Lord! He'd come to London and drag her back to Devon by her hair!

Barrington gave her a speculative look. "And now we are on the subject of improper, why have you suddenly taken an interest in gaming?"

Grace was prepared for the question. She disliked telling half-truths, and she loathed the necessity, but Ronald Barrington was not, and would never be, privy to Wednesday League business. That was always strictly confidential. She sighed and glanced out the coach window. "I've told you, sir. I am bored half to death. I crave something different. Something more exciting."

"I could give you something more exciting, Grace," he intoned meaningfully, leaning closer and squeezing her arm.

What in the world had gotten into Lord Barrington? He'd never pressed her thus before. They'd always been clear that theirs was a platonic friendship, though they'd allowed the ton to think otherwise. And anyway, it was completely beyond her imagination why men thought a sweaty, uncomfortable coupling in the sheets was such fun. For her, it had been—no, that was well-traveled territory. She would not go there again. She hadn't put herself through that since Basil had died.

What was wrong with her? Why had all these ghosts risen to haunt her? Adam Hawthorne's sudden resurrection must have upset her more than she'd thought. He'd looked almost savage in his buckskins and long hair, and something deeply disturbing inside her had answered that primal pull. The sight of his leather breeches snug over strongly muscled thighs, the jacket straining against his shoulders and chest, and the raw masculinity he exuded had stolen her wits.

She took a deep breath as she prepared to exit the coach. She needed to put thoughts of Mr. Hawthorne behind her. He was a distraction from her goal. Tonight she would learn at least two popular games and the rudiments of placing bets. She must be prepared before she took on Lord Geoffrey at his own game.

* * *

Well past midnight, ignoring the looks of suspicion and wariness from the other patrons of the Eagle Tavern, Adam stepped up to the bar and fastened the publican with a steady gaze. "Fast Freddie?" he asked.

The barkeeper gave him a long look. "Who wants t' know?"

"Hawthorne," he answered, without any real hope that would grant him access. Adam realized his appearance was a disadvantage—anything that called attention in this part of town was a disadvantage.

The man blinked once, then nodded toward the stairs. "Upstairs," he said.

Good God. Four years later and Freddie Carter still kept "hours" in an upstairs room of the Eagle Tavern off Red Lion Square. He could scarcely believe his luck. He climbed the stairs, his moccasins silent on the treads. He rapped twice on the solid door and stood back.

A deep voice called, "Yes?"

"I'm looking for Fast Freddie," he answered.

"Is that Hawthorne?" the voice called from within. "Good Lord, man! I heard you were back scarce an hour ago!" The door opened wide and Freddie clapped a meaty hand on Adam's shoulder and dragged him inside. "I heard you'd gone native, but I wouldn't believe it until now. Aye, but you're a sight for sore eyes."

Adam grinned. "And I scarce dared believe you'd still be holding court in a seedy tavern. Shouldn't you have saved the world by now?"

The man laughed and pulled him nearer the fire. "Got thrown off schedule when you left, Hawthorne, but now you're here and we'll get back on track." Freddie pressed a tankard of stout into his hand and went to lock the door.

"Have I interrupted business hours?" he asked.

"Just wrapping things up for the night, Hawthorne. Anyone who had a private commission for me would have come by now. Do you have something to occupy me?"

"Not at the moment."

"Something to do with your travels, I warrant." Freddie leaned back in his wooden chair, tipping it onto the back legs.

Adam grinned but said nothing. Fredrick Carter had always been perceptive. That was his gift, and it was what made him one of the best investigators in England.

When they'd been in their final term at Eton, Freddie's father had been killed by street thugs for his watch and wedding ring. Adam had gone on to Cambridge, but Freddie had been forced to support himself, his mother and his three brothers. He'd devoted himself to bringing his father's murderer to justice, he'd collected the reward and his course was set. Now he craved the excitement and danger of being a thief taker. Couldn't live without it, he'd told Adam. He'd even persuaded Adam to work with him on a few cases before Adam was posted to Toronto.

"Come then," Freddie said as he took a deep swallow from his tankard, "and tell me about your adventures. What did you do to get yourself reported dead?"

Adam emptied his tankard, savoring the dark earthy flavor of the stout. He launched into the story he'd already told Craddock and Barrington but added detail he'd only share with a friend. Freddie's eyes widened as he concluded. "Then, when they realized I could not be guilty of the massacre, I'd become so mired in tribal warfare and retribution that I couldn't leave."

"Four years with Indians," Freddie mused. "There's even more to the story than you've told, Hawthorne. Does it have anything to do with that thing on your arm?"

Adam glanced down at the intricately beaded band on his left wrist. "Everything," he admitted.

"A gift?"

"From Nokomis, a beautiful Indian maid. I found her gutted and scalped when we returned to the village."

"You loved her," Freddie said softly.

Nokomis, Daughter of the Moon, had been infinitely sweet and funny, and she'd owned his heart completely. "Nokomis was eight, the chief's daughter, and like a daughter to me. I've seen war before, Freddie, but this…this was different."

"So it took you four years to find the sons of bitches? Time well spent, I'd say."

"We hunted the warriors down one by one, but we never found the one the Indians called Long Knife, for the sword he wore. That man, Freddie, was an Englishman and British soldier. I'd wager my soul he was the one in command of that attack."

Freddie whistled softly as he tipped his chair forward and went to stir the fire. "So that's what brought you back. Can't say as I blame you. Only promise you will not gut an English soldier on a London street. I'd hate to have to bring you in."

Adam stared into the glowing embers, remembering how Nokomis had thrown her arms around his neck and begged him to wait for her until she'd grown up. So sweet, so innocent, she'd sworn she would marry no one but him.

When he'd found her in the mass of putrid bodies, she bore cuts that could only have come from an English blade. Adam prayed he had retained enough of a grip on his decidedly English values to restrain himself from killing the man who'd done that. It would be a near thing, though, in view of the fact that he hadn't exercised much of that restraint lately. "I think I can safely promise you that I will not *gut* the man, Freddie."

"Good. Meantime, what are your plans?"

Adam ran his fingers through his long hair. "Find a barber and a tailor. I've reported to my superiors and, until I am officially declared alive, I'm on my own. Craddock said I'd be reinstated, but I wonder if that's a good idea. Another assignment like the last could end me."

"Do you not have property in Wiltshire or Devonshire?"

He nodded. "Devonshire. But since I've been declared dead, there are a few complications."

"Ah. But it will all be yours anyway, now that your uncle is dead."

"Barrington said he'd left everything to his widow."

"Bloody hell," Freddie murmured. "I gather that's the complication?"

Adam nodded. "My uncle's widow has claimed his fortune and mine. She's young, beautiful and, now, very rich. There were no children. I'm wondering if she could have…"

Freddie sighed. "Greed makes people do strange things, Hawthorne. I won't lie to you—there were whispers to that effect. But the gossip died and suspicion was dropped. Where can I reach you? Where are you staying?"

"With my aunt, Grace Forbush. Bloomsbury Square."

Freddie's laughter followed him down the stairs. "Watch your back, Hawthorne."

Chapter Three

Mrs. Dewberry snapped the heavy ivory velvet drapes open, keeping up her steady stream of chatter. Grace winced as the early morning light streamed through her bedroom window and struggled to sit up.

"'E ate everything on the tray, I'll give 'im that. Good appetite for someone so thin, that man."

Grace rubbed her temples, picturing the lean form of Adam Hawthorne. She doubted the hollows in his cheeks were natural. He had the look of a man used to a Spartan existence and heavy physical activity.

"And I could've been wrong about the man," Mrs. Dewberry admitted—a rarity for her. She placed a breakfast tray across Grace's lap and shook out the napkin. If Grace did not take it quickly, Mrs. Dewberry was sure to tuck it beneath her chin. "'Is manners are quite lovely when 'e uses 'em. The mister says 'e inquired if 'e could stable a 'orse 'ere. Said 'e'd be glad to pay the mister, 'e would."

"Of course he may have a horse here. And Mr. Dewberry is not to accept anything from Mr. Hawthorne. He is our guest. I shall see that there is extra in Mr. Dewberry's envelope for the inconvenience."

"That's very considerate of you, Mrs. Forbush."

Grace poured herself a cup of strong breakfast tea. Her head ached and she needed to clear the cobwebs before she dealt with her solicitor and factor. Barrington had taken her to two gaming hells last night, infamous smoke-filled places where her eyes stung and her head throbbed. But she had to admit that she'd felt an edge of excitement when she'd won a small wager playing vingt-et-un.

One more night to learn, then she'd be ready to set herself up as an easy mark. If Morgan gulled her, she'd find out how, and then she'd expose him. The Talbot name would not need to come into it at all. His debt would be void and Laura Talbot would have a second chance to make a happy match.

She was spreading butter on a muffin when Dianthe burst into the room, tying her robe at her waist. "Aunt Grace! I just saw Mr. Hawthorne leaving."

"Oh, yes," Mrs. Dewberry said. "'E said 'e 'ad some things to do and that 'e'd join you for dinner." She paused at the door and smiled. "I'm 'aving Cook make a nice roast of beef and Yorkshire pudding."

"And strawberry tarts for dessert?" Dianthe added.

"Aye, miss. I'll tell Cook."

Dianthe jumped on the bed and sat cross-legged. "I wish you could have heard the talk last night, Aunt Grace. It couldn't have been midnight yet when the news began to circulate that you had gone to a gaming hell with Barrington. It was all the buzz."

Grace laughed and shook her head. "That did not take long. What are they saying?"

"That you must be bored. Only Mrs. Thayer said that you'd bear watching lest you get yourself into some trouble."

"Hmm." Grace sipped her tea, beginning to feel better. "Well, by the time anyone has the least bit of concern, I shall be done. Nothing to worry about, Di. The Wednesday League has taken on much more difficult cases than this. *This* will be a mere stroll in the park."

"All the same, I wish I could help you. I really do not like the idea of you going alone to such…unwholesome places. I asked Mr. Thayer about Geoffrey Morgan last night, and he said to warn you rather strongly about him."

"Is the news out that Mr. Hawthorne has returned?"

"No. I thought that odd, but I gather he has not been out in society since his return. I will be amazed if there are not whisperings by tonight. Are you going out after dinner?"

"Barrington has agreed to take me to another hell. I've heard the Pigeon Hole is an amusing place."

"Will you take Mr. Hawthorne with you?"

Grace pushed her tray aside and stood. "I think he would frighten fully half the population of London."

"You are ashamed to be seen with him," Dianthe accused.

Absolutely not. Yet, when she tried to imagine walking into the Auberville ballroom with a man in buckskins, she almost laughed. She could not begin to comprehend the gossip that would cause. But then she thought of where he *would* look at ease, and she glanced at her bedroom door. She imagined him there, late at night, holding a candle, that insouciant smile on his face, making himself as comfortable as he had in the library. Her mouth went dry and her chest constricted.

"Aunt Grace!" Dianthe exclaimed. "I have never seen you blush before. How interesting."

She went to her dressing table and looked in the mirror. Delicate pink stained her cheeks and neck. "I must get dressed, Dianthe," she said. "I am going to the bank and my factor's office. The sooner Mr. Hawthorne has the resources to leave us, the better."

Mr. Evans tapped a sheaf of papers on the surface of his desk to straighten them. Moistening his index finger, he began to leaf through the heap. Page by page, he separated the stack into two piles. "You realize this will considerably diminish your assets, do you not, Mrs. Forbush?"

Considerably? "I dare hope it will not impoverish me?"

"Nothing so severe as that," her factor said, glancing above the rim of his spectacles. "But the bulk appears to be the investments of Mr. Hawthorne's assets. If you insist that he should reap all the benefits—despite the fact that they were your investments—then your accounts shall suffer."

She sighed and shrugged. An honest debt was an honest debt. Her gravest concern was that the news of her reduced circumstances would affect her ability to make Morgan take her seriously as a deep player. Oh, blast the timing! She would have to hold Adam's funds until after dealing with Morgan. Now he would have to depend on her hospitality for another fortnight. "Mr. Evans, take your time in separating the assets and attributing the interest. I would not want you to make any mistakes because I had rushed you. We need not conclude this matter for two or three weeks. Mr. Hawthorne is staying with me and his needs will be taken care of. No need for unseemly haste."

"As you say, Mrs. Forbush."

Grace smiled. She employed Mr. Evans to act in her best financial interests, and he was certainly doing so now. "I wish Mr. Hawthorne to have the interest. If he'd been here, he would have made his own investments."

"If he'd been here, you'd not have had anything to invest," Mr. Evans muttered as he continued his separation of the papers.

"I'd still have had my husband's estate," she corrected.

"Likely not, Mrs. Forbush."

Grace frowned. What did the man mean? Her solicitor had made some veiled reference to the same thing earlier this morning at their appointment. She'd asked to see Basil's will, and he had told her it was "unavailable."

"*Likely not?* What do you mean, Mr. Evans? Explain yourself."

He finished sorting the stacks and looked up at her, concern creasing his forehead. "What? Oh…I, um, meant there would not have been as much to invest, Mrs. Forbush."

Grace sat back in her chair. She had the uneasy feeling that people were keeping things from her. "I want Mr. Hawthorne to have everything that should have been his, Mr. Evans. Mr. Forbush was always generous with me, and I can be no less with his nephew. That is what he would have wanted."

"If you are certain." Mr. Evans looked over the rims of his spectacles again. "Your integrity is admirable. Shall we meet a fortnight hence to sign the papers and complete the separations?"

"I shall mark my calendar, Mr. Evans."

Adam tied his cravat for the fifth time. He'd gotten rusty in the particulars of refined dress. There were no cravats in the wigwams of the wilderness. Finally satisfied on the sixth try, he shrugged into his jacket and headed down to dinner. He'd taken several items of his better clothing to a tailor for the alterations he would need to make himself presentable in society, and had kept these few clothes out for use in the meantime. New, currently fashionable items would have to wait until his reinstatement and the pay that went with it.

When he entered the dining room, he found Grace and her niece waiting for him. "Sorry," he said. "Had trouble with my cravat."

Grace looked up at him and blinked. A slow smile warmed her face and her expression turned sultry. She stood and came toward him, extending her arms. When she was close enough for him to smell the delicate floral scent of her perfume, she lifted her graceful hands to tighten the knot and arrange the folds. He watched her fingers work through the fabric and felt a swift visceral reaction. How would those fingers look against his bare flesh? How would they feel closing around his—

She looked up, smoothing the fabric and meeting his gaze. "There. What do you think, Mr. Hawthorne?" Her voice was slightly breathless.

That it's a damn good thing you don't know what I'm thinking! He stood frozen for a moment while he gained mastery over his rioting blood. "Well done, Mrs. Forbush."

She returned to her place at the table and even the rustle of her blue-gray gown caused him to catch his breath. He'd been too long without a woman. But his uncle's widow was more than just any woman. She was Salome incarnate—a natural seductress.

A moment later he took the place set for him at the opposite end of the table, Miss Lovejoy between them. "Feel free to correct my manners, ladies. I've been so long away from utensils and china that I may forget myself and use my hands."

Dianthe laughed. "I think you will adapt quite easily, Mr. Hawthorne. Aside from your native clothing, I've seen nothing of you that is unpolished. Though your barber could have cut a little closer."

He acknowledged her compliment with a smile, but turned to Grace for confirmation, given with a single nod. "I rather think the length becomes you as it is, Mr. Hawthorne."

They were silent as Mrs. Dewberry served dishes laden with roast beef, Yorkshire pudding, tender vegetables drowning in rich butter and what seemed like a myriad of condiments and confections after the simple fare he was accustomed to eating.

"Are you coming out tonight, Mr. Hawthorne?" Dianthe asked him at length.

The question startled him. How long had it been since anyone had cared or questioned his comings and goings? Odd, how the careless question made him feel a part of something larger. "I do not have plans, Miss Lovejoy, but I think I am ready to make an appearance in society. Must be done sooner or later and there's no sense putting it off."

"Marvelous," she said with a smile. "Then you must accompany me to Charity MacGregor's little reception. She is a delightful hostess, and all the most amusing people will be there. The Aubervilles are picking me up on the way. You could come along if you wish."

He'd met Lord Auberville years ago when he'd been a diplomatic advisor to a military contingent suing for peace with Algiers. "I would like to pay my respects," he mused. He looked at Grace for her consent.

"I have other plans for tonight, Mr. Hawthorne."

"Aunt Grace is going gambling," Dianthe volunteered.

Surprised, he looked at his hostess in a new light. He hadn't suspected she had an adventurous side. Who was this woman with such an odd blend of innocence and experience? Everything about the woman was contradictory. "Gambling, eh? What is your game of choice?"

She shrugged and gave him a listless smile. "I think I prefer vingt-et-un, sir. Hazard and faro are diverting. I enjoy whist, but I do not like being dependent upon a partner."

He nodded, unsure what to make of this news. "I suppose it would depend upon the partner," he allowed.

By the quick flicker of her eyes, Adam knew that she had read the veiled meaning in his words. It would be interesting to match wits with Grace Forbush. Subtlety was her hallmark and she only gave herself away in the slight lift at the corners of her luscious mouth or the blink of an eye. She was so tightly contained that he could not help but wonder what she might do if she actually lost control. He'd like to find out.

"Do you gamble often, Mrs. Forbush?"

"There are more ways to gamble than laying counters upon a table, Mr. Hawthorne, and the stakes need not be money."

Now this was interesting. Where else might the lovely widow gamble, and for what stakes? "I shall remember that, Mrs. Forbush. Perhaps we will have occasion to make a wager."

Dianthe regarded them suspiciously. "What have I missed?"

Adam smiled at Grace and then turned to Dianthe. "I've been puzzling all day how to address everyone. If Mrs. Forbush is your aunt, and she is mine, would that make us cousins, Miss Lovejoy?"

Dianthe smiled. "I suppose it would, though Grace is not actually my aunt. She was my mother's cousin. My sister and I came to live with her only recently so that she could sponsor our coming out. Afton has married, but, alas, I have yet to find a husband."

He laughed at her ingenuous admission. "I would guess that has been your choice. But since we are family, we should not stand on formality. You may call me cousin or Adam, whichever suits you best."

"And you must call me Dianthe or Di. But I cannot imagine what to do with Aunt Grace. I know her nickname was Ellie when she was younger, but no one has called her that in ages. And every time *you* call her Aunt Grace, it sets me on a giggle. Mrs. Forbush sounds like an ancient governess, and I think she is far too stunning for that. Would you not agree?"

He nodded. Far too stunning, indeed. "Ellie? Where did that come from?"

"My father," Grace admitted, shooting a stern look in Dianthe's direction. "Grace Ellen York was my name before marriage. Papa thought Grace too drab a name for a young girl."

He tried to imagine her as a rosy-cheeked child with a long dark pigtail. He wondered if she ever wore her hair down now. "I agree with your father," he said.

"I left that all behind years ago, Mr. Hawthorne. You may call me Grace, but Ellie makes me feel absurdly young."

"Very well, Grace," he said. Judging the time to be right for a question that had been bothering him since his arrival at Bloomsbury Square, he asked, "Do you mind telling me whatever happened to Bellows? And Mrs. Humphries?"

"They've retired," Grace said with no further explanation.

Retired? Or gotten out of the way? Had she not wanted his uncle's servants to be around to talk about what went on in the house? Or about any suspicions they might have had? His uncle's widow was beginning to look very suspicious indeed.

Grace allowed Lord Barrington to take her wrap and hand it to a footman as they entered the Pigeon Hole. After his rather mild introduction to gambling the night before, she was not prepared for the raw undercurrents running through the rooms as he led her deeper into the establishment. The air was heavy with smoke and tension. An occasional shout of laughter or collective moan punctuated the steady drone of conversation.

"I could have taken you to some smaller private clubs, Grace. Much more suitable for a woman of your station. Why you selected this one is beyond me. 'Tis reputed that one of the owners is the abbot of a notorious nunnery. I do not like to think of you rubbing elbows with the likes of him."

"Could I catch something from elbow rubbing?" she asked, keeping her expression neutral. "Aside from a soiled elbow?"

Barrington looked slightly confused and she knew he hadn't caught her teasing. Honestly, sometimes the man was so stodgy that it amazed her. But looking back on the past several years, she could see that *she'd* become rather stodgy. But why should that occur to her just now? Because she had just broken that mold? Or—

Adam Hawthorne, again. Barely a few years older than she, every line of his body, every movement, every smile, told of an energy and enthusiasm for life that she'd forfeit for safety.

His strength and vitality were a stark contrast to her own blurred ennui. Heavens, she was envious of him!

Barrington harrumphed. "Perhaps you wouldn't catch something, Grace, but you are apt to acquire some nasty habits or bad language."

"I shall guard against that," she promised.

"Why risk it at all? Why put your reputation under scrutiny when there's no need? I cannot fathom why—"

She cut him off. "We've been over this, m'lord. I weary of discussing it. If you'd prefer not to take me, I will not beg or pout. I shall simply ask Mr. Phillips to escort me. He has often said that he'd be—"

"Now, now. No need for that. If you're determined to do this, I would rather be close at hand in the event that…you need assistance."

How diplomatic of him. She'd have sworn that he was about to say "in the event she got herself into some trouble," but had stopped himself in time. "Thank you, my lord. I shall do my best not to impose upon your kindness."

He harrumphed again and guided her toward a table where vingt-et-un was being played. A footman circulating with a tray of wineglasses came by and Barrington claimed two. "Have a care not to drink too much, Grace. 'Tis one of the ways the house leads you to play deep and reckless."

Needless advice, but Grace nodded. She actually wanted to gain a reputation as a "high flyer." Did she dare tip her hand to Barrington? No, she could only risk one bland question. "I was discussing my interest with Sir Lawrence this afternoon, and he said I should watch someone named Geoffrey Morgan play. He said the man was a genius at games of chance."

"Sir Lawrence? When did you see him?"

"He came to see Auberville when I was calling on Lady Annica. We chatted for a few moments in passing. When I told him that I was going gambling tonight, he was all enthusiasm.

Perhaps we shall run into him." She glanced around, trying her best to look bored. "Is Lord Geoffrey here tonight?"

Barrington peered into the hazy air, squinting through the curtain of smoke. "Don't see him, but it's early yet. And I don't much fancy you making his acquaintance, Grace. He is not the sort one wishes to count among one's friends."

Grace smiled patiently. "We were introduced years ago, and I was not seeking to make the man my friend. I merely wanted to watch him at the tables. Sir Lawrence said I would find it educational."

"Hmm," Barrington replied noncommittally.

For the next hour Grace placed small wagers at various tables, trying her hand at faro, picquet and rouge-et-noir. She encouraged Barrington to find his own entertainment at the hazard table. Though the other players regarded her with curiosity, they were all willing to take her money. The two other women present were vivacious females who were dressed in colorful gowns with daringly low décolletages. Grace had never seen either of them at any of the events she regularly attended and suspected they might be of the demimonde.

"By God, Morgan! You have the devil's own luck!" a portly man at a picquet table said.

Grace moved closer to study the other man. So here was Lord Geoffrey Morgan. He'd changed since she'd last seen him four years ago. Still handsome, to be sure, but harder, more cynical. What had happened to him in the interim? If Lord Geoffrey was so attractive, and possessed of a fortune, why could he not find a wife in the ordinary way—courtship? Could his murky reputation include mistreatment of women?

Morgan was a man of above-average height and trim build. His dark hair was threaded with stands of silver now, but he did not look old. To the contrary, the silver was premature and simply made him look distinguished—a stark contrast to his smooth, unlined skin. His features were pleasant and the grin he gave his companion was not in the least bit smug. But his best feature—at least the one that caught her attention—was his hands. Long elegant fingers caressed the deck of cards almost like a lover, riffling the edges in a confident, bored manner. Those hands were the only things about the man that spoke of his inner restlessness.

He grew still, as if he sensed her attention. In a slow deliberate manner, he glanced toward her and caught her eye. He studied her from the toes of her slippers upward to her face, and then his lips drew up in a smile. Did he remember her?

She dropped her gaze, then lifted it again in a soft, almost seductive greeting. With a little lift of her chin, she turned and walked away, feeling the heat of his gaze follow her. She stopped at the vingt-et-un table and placed a small bet, knowing he would still be watching. When she glanced over her shoulder, he grinned again and she did her level best to look worldly and as bored with the scene as he. When Barrington joined her and took her arm to lead her away, she noted a small look of irritation on Lord Geoffrey's face.

Oh, it was good to know your enemy's weaknesses.

Chapter Four

Adam, having left his newfound "cousin" in the care of Lord Auberville and his wife, found himself climbing the stairway at the Eagle Tavern for the second time in as many days. He hadn't expected to see Freddie again quite so soon, but circumstances warranted. The more he learned about Grace Ellen Forbush, the more suspicious she appeared.

Privately, he asked several men about her. They all smiled regretfully, saying that, after a protracted mourning period, Grace's name had been linked to several powerful men. Then Barrington claimed the exclusive right to escort her to various functions. It was generally accepted amongst the ton that they had been lovers for the past three years.

Adam's mind revolted when he tried to imagine Grace's slender, delicate frame pinned beneath a sweating, heaving Barrington. Or his uncle, for that matter. To complicate matters, the whispers of her new interest in gambling had begun to spread, and men were speculating that if she was restless, she might be looking for a new lover. Adam was hard-pressed to believe the amount of interest the topic was generating. Was every man in London queuing up to vie for that honor?

He hesitated only a moment before knocking on Freddie's

door. When it opened, a furrow-browed dandy exited, nearly running over Adam in his haste.

"Come in," Freddie called.

Adam closed the door behind him and gave Freddie a smile. "Bad news?" he asked, nodding toward the departing dandy.

Freddie nodded. "His wife is meeting privately with his best friend. I wouldn't want to be either of them tonight."

Lord! Was all of London taking lovers?

Tipping his chair onto the back legs, Freddie grinned. "So, did you just miss me, Hawthorne, or do you have a use for me?"

"Could be both."

"Are you going to help me with this one?"

"As much as my time will allow."

"Let's hear it. As luck would have it, I'm between jobs."

Adam sat by the fire and sighed. "Find my uncle's valet and housekeeper. I'd like to have a chat with them."

Freddie nodded, studying his face. The man was trying to get a "read" on him, and Adam smiled. "And keep an eye on my dear aunt Grace. There's something odd going on there. I'm wondering if there's any truth to the rumors that she hastened my uncle's death."

"Report to you daily or weekly?"

"I'll find you when I want to talk," Adam said. "If you have something you need me to know sooner, you can find me."

"And what will you be doing?"

"My best to keep an eye on the winsome widow." He stood and moved toward the door to put his plan in action.

Freddie grinned. "Careful, Hawthorne. Bad manners, not to mention the possible risk to life and limb, to tup the hostess."

Adam finally found Barrington's coach waiting on a side street around the corner from the Pigeon Hole on St. James Square. Though he wasn't a member, he slipped the doorman a guinea with the promise to speak to the proprietor about buying a subscription.

The main salon was lavishly appointed, well lit with a crystal chandelier in the central area, and darker around the edges of the room. Adam kept to these shadows as he watched waiters circulate with wineglasses and hors d'oeuvres. The proprietors, two savvy men who'd won the establishment from the original owner in a high-stakes game of whist, did not want their guests to have any reason to leave the tables. Any delicacy, any desire, was fulfilled. Deep play was encouraged, and when a man's counters were spent, it was only a matter of a signature to acquire more. A few women dressed in scandalously low gowns circulated with glasses of wine and would occasionally disappear with a guest for short periods of time.

He caught sight of Grace's slender form gliding from one table to another, a low buzz following in her wake. It was true, then—her presence in the gambling world *was* causing a sensation. And if speculation was running rampant, he would know the gist of it by morning. A small group of men stood near the hazard table, talking in muffled tones. Every few moments one or the other would turn to look in Grace's direction. Did she quite realize how widely she was drawing attention? Or was she so accustomed to attention that she scarcely noticed?

Barrington said something to her and she turned to him and smiled. Even in profile, she stole his breath away. The sweep of her neck, the delicate hue of pink that tinted the curve of her cheek, and the demure knot of dark hair at her nape all beckoned him, and he found himself taking a few steps forward before he could check himself.

He realized with an angry tweak that he was no different than those men who stood in line for her. When she'd repaired his cravat earlier, and stood so close to him that he could feel the heat of her breath against his cheek, he'd been a mere blink from pulling her into his arms. Had it not been for Dianthe's presence, he might have done so. Was she sublimely unaware that she was a natural seductress? No, she had to know. She'd been married. She'd had numerous affairs. She would have to know the power she held over men. The banked fire in her eyes spoke what words could not. She was a woman made for love.

A burst of laughter floated from the hazard table and Grace turned to Barrington, clapping her hands with delight. A glow of excitement lit her face as she collected a small pile of counters. Perhaps it was true, then. Perhaps she craved excitement and risk.

He could think of far more interesting ways to excite and challenge his enigmatic hostess.

"La! Es-tu folle, chère?" Madame Marie asked.

Was she crazy? Grace wondered. She studied herself in the trifold looking glass in the back fitting room of La Meilleure Robe. No, she looked quite sane. She smoothed the fabric of her new icy-violet gown over her hips, delighting in the fluid sensation and drape of the fabric. The gown would move with her, not act as a cage to hide her form. She sighed with the realization that sensory perceptions were important to her. If anything was wrong with her, it was that she was far too earthy.

"No, madame, I am not crazy. It is the only solution." She turned on the little stool as Madame Marie marked the hem and glanced over her shoulder to entreat Francis Renquist, Madame Marie's husband and the Wednesday League's investigator. "Tell her, Mr. Renquist."

Renquist sat forward in the delicate chair and studied the toes of his boots, clearly wishing himself elsewhere. "I'm not certain it *is* the only solution, Mrs. Forbush."

Grace was a little surprised by his reply. "If I had not suspended my Friday salons until autumn, I could ask him to tea. If you have another, please tell me. I am all ears, sir."

"Let me put more men on the problem. If Geoffrey Morgan is a cheat, we will uncover it. Aye, we could have results twice as fast."

Grace nodded. "By all means," she said, making a tiny turn for madame's marking. "Put more men on it. But can you guarantee you will have the required proof and be able to neutralize Lord Geoffrey within two weeks?"

"Well, I couldn't actually guarantee—"

She nodded, suspecting as much. "Then surely you can understand why I am willing to risk everything, even my reputation, Mr. Renquist. Miss Talbot will be quite literally sold into marriage to a man she does not even know if we are unable to acquire evidence of his cheating. I have the resources as well as entrée to the hells Morgan frequents. Meanwhile, I would like you and your men to find other men who have lost heavily to Morgan. I want to know how many of them suspect him of trickery, and if they have any idea how he might have done it. Furthermore, I would like any information you can uncover about the man himself—who his friends are, how he spends his time when he is not gambling, where he goes—"

"It is precisely because of Lord Geoffrey's reputation that I would urge you to distance yourself," Renquist interrupted.

"His reputation is not my concern unless it affects Miss Talbot's case." She sighed, thinking of the man she had seen last night at the Pigeon Hole. When Constance had kept his company, he'd been well-mannered and polite. Geoffrey Morgan had an air of banked vitality that society women would find vaguely unsettling—the same vitality that lay beneath Adam Hawthorne's smooth grace. She found that vigor curiously attractive in both men. What might they be like beneath the surface, if they chose to unveil themselves?

She gave herself a mental shake and made another quarter turn on the stool. "I merely mean to observe the man to determine if he is cheating, and then, if he is, to think of the best possible way to expose him, thus rendering the markers he holds null and void. Simplicity itself, Mr. Renquist. Not in the least dangerous or complicated."

Renquist was watching her with apprehension. "My blood chills when I hear those words from the ladies of the Wednesday League," he murmured. "Do you promise to come to me if you are in any danger, Mrs. Forbush?"

She laughed at Mr. Renquist's needless concern and shrugged, drawing an annoyed cluck from Madame Marie. "I am not tracking a murderer, sir, but you have my oath."

Stealing a few minutes before the dinner bell that evening, Grace slipped into the library and sat at the massive mahogany desk. Withdrawing a sheet of paper and a pen from the center drawer, she began to make a list.

The Pigeon Hole, the Two Sevens, Rupert House, Thackery's, Belmonde's, Fabrey's and the Blue Moon—a new and very popular hell. Those were the establishments she knew Morgan frequented. As for the games he favored—*hazard, faro, vingt-et-un, rouge-et-noir, E.O. and picquet.* Though she hadn't chosen the hell for their encounter, she picked the game. It would have to be picquet. It was one of the few games that allowed her to wager Morgan directly without the intervention of a dealer or banker and did not require a partner. The house would be due a percentage of the wager, but that should not present a problem.

She tapped the end of the pen against her cheek as she thought. Morgan was not likely to risk cheating for an inconsequential wager, so she must think of a way to make the wager worth the risk. "How much would be enough?" she mused out loud.

"The eternal question," a deeply masculine voice answered.

She looked up and found Adam standing in the doorway. He grinned and stepped into the library, closing the door behind him. Impeccably dressed, he exuded an aura of easy self-confidence as he went to the sideboard to pour himself a glass of sherry. He was obviously planning to go out for the evening and she was pleased to see that he'd found something to fit him.

With a glance in her direction, he poured a second glass. "You look as if you could use it," he explained as he brought it to her and sat across the desk from her.

She smiled. "Oh, please won't you come in and join me, Mr. Hawthorne? Do sit down."

He laughed at her teasing, and the easy sound made her laugh, too. "Have I been impertinent? I forget to be formal. I practically grew up in this house and I forget that circumstances are different now."

"You must make yourself at home," Grace told him truthfully. "I was not aware that you'd spent so much time here. You and Mr. Forbush were close, I gather?"

"Quite. My mother—his sister—died of consumption when I was still at home with a governess. My father was killed riding to the hounds when I was at Eton. From that time forward, Uncle Basil and I were all we had of family. I came here for most holidays, and in summer we would spend a few weeks at the cottage in Devon."

Grace nodded. Basil had told her as much. It was part of those lands in Devon that Leland had traded her for. "I've asked my solicitor to go over Basil's will and determine what should have been yours. You may well be entitled to this house, and then Dianthe and I would have to prevail upon *your* hospitality until we could find accommodations elsewhere."

"Which I would give as gladly as you have," he said, raising his glass. After drinking, he regarded her through those deep hazel eyes. "Did I interrupt your calculations on 'how much would be enough' to settle with me?"

"No, I…" Grace stopped. Had there been a note of suspicion in Adam's voice? "Do you think I would cheat you, Mr. Hawthorne?"

"I barely know you, Mrs. Forbush. How would I know what you might or might not do?"

She felt his suspicion like an insult. "I suppose you wouldn't, sir." He stood and came around the desk to look over her shoulder. She fought the instinct to cover her list, knowing that would only make him more suspicious.

"Hells and games of chance? Is that what you were calculating?"

"I…um, yes. I have not been able to determine if there is a maximum wager at any particular game. I wondered how much would be enough to make the house declare a limit."

"Are you such a deep player that you want to wager the limit?"

"I merely wish to know what it is." *And how much it would take to tempt Lord Geoffrey into cheating.*

"That would depend upon the hell."

"I see. Well, thank you for the education, Mr. Hawthorne."

"Why hasn't Barrington undertaken your, er, education, Mrs. Forbush?"

She shrugged. "We are going again tonight, but he does not approve of my new interest. He barely tolerates my attendance at some of the hells. I fear he may refuse to escort me at any moment."

Adam moved to the fireplace and rested one arm on the mantel. "I believe that may well be the best decision."

She took a deep sip from her sherry and stood. "Because you disapprove of a woman engaged in a male pastime?"

"Because anything could happen to a lady at a hell. Men are not…at their best in such circumstances."

"And who knows where it all would end?" she asked archly as she went to the sideboard to refill her glass. "What next, sir? Women's clubs? Women in taverns? Unescorted to restaurants? Frequenting brothels?"

He laughed. "Aside from the last, those prospects do not alarm me in the least. But how can a man indulge his baser nature with a wife or daughter looking on?"

"Ah, then mankind is safe, since I am neither any man's wife or daughter." But she was Leland's sister, and that could be a problem unless she concluded this matter quickly.

"I daresay you would be shocked at what men do outside of female observation."

She smiled. After all the cases the Wednesday League had taken, she doubted she was capable of shock but the notion intrigued her. "Would you even have any idea what it would take to shock me, sir?"

Adam left his glass on the mantel and came toward her, an enigmatic expression on his face. "I believe I would, madam."

Before she was aware of him moving, he was standing mere inches away. She had to tilt her head upward to see into his eyes. Then his intent was clear. He was going to kiss her, and the small pause gave her the opportunity to escape. To her own surprise, she didn't take it. How long had it been since she had seen a kiss coming and welcomed it? Ever?

Adam slipped his arms around her and pulled her firmly against his chest. The heat of his body seeped into hers, drawing an answering warmth from her. Heavens!

She dropped her lashes and waited, breathless, for the contact of his lips, but Adam dragged the moment out. His lips, soft and relaxed, parted slightly as he bent to her. He seemed to be in no hurry, as if he were relishing the moment, committing it to memory. She was not disappointed. The sweetness of the first touch of their lips was all the more intense for that slow, deliberate anticipation.

Softly insistent nibbles gave way to deeper, longer contact, eliciting a strong involuntary response from her—a soft sigh, a faint moan. She rose on her tiptoes to press closer and parted her lips a little, a thing she'd never done of her own accord before.

Clinging to the square set of his shoulders, she was acutely aware of Adam's large hand splayed at the small of her back, pressing her closer as his other hand slid up her spine to caress the stretch of her neck. Chill bumps sent a delicate shiver through her and her breasts firmed in response.

Slowly, almost reluctantly, Adam lifted his head enough to look into her eyes. A lazy smile curved his mouth. He cupped her head as he lowered to her lips again. This time the kiss was subtly different, no longer asking but insisting. This time his tongue, tasting faintly of sherry, made contact with hers. The depth of intimacy in that touch shook her to her very core. She was experiencing Adam in a way that she had never experienced any other man. This intimacy felt more intense to her than all the nights of Basil's clumsy and ineffectual fumbling or Barrington's sporadic attempts to woo her.

It was just a kiss. *Just…*a kiss? How could it feel like so much more? He broke contact and she sighed in protest.

"Shh," he whispered. "Patience." He trailed a path of tiny kisses to a spot just beneath her ear, where he hovered for a moment, his lips barely brushing her flesh as he spoke. "I feel your heart beating," he said, then nibbled and tugged gently at her earlobe.

She closed her eyes and her knees nearly buckled. Adam continued to give attention to the spot while the hand that had cupped her head moved downward, then around to brush her breast. Oh, how sweet a sensation that was coupled with the tingle of his kiss!

The dinner bell shattered the moment and Adam straightened, looking heavy-eyed and exceptionally annoyed. He released her, keeping one hand at her waist to steady her.

He studied her face and gave her a teasing grin. "I…concede that I may not have shocked you, Mrs. Forbush, but I collect that I've managed to surprise you."

Grace took a steadying breath, confused thoughts and emotions running riot through her muddled brain. Where had those feelings, those *yearnings,* come from? She glanced down at the floor and smoothed her gown, trying to cover her perplexity. "Surprise? Why, yes. You did."

Adam turned away and went back to his sherry. With his back to her, he took a long drink and squared his shoulders before saying, "Should I say I am sorry?"

"Only if you mean it, Mr. Hawthorne."

The silence dragged out for a moment before she realized he was not going to apologize. He was not sorry he'd kissed her. She paused, giving time and distance a chance to restore her composure. "Nevertheless," she murmured, "if we are to keep close quarters—"

"We'd do well to guard against a reoccurrence of that sort," Adam finished for her. He turned to face her again, looking as shaken as she felt.

She nodded, her mind in turmoil. This was an intolerable complication! Everything she held dear was at risk. She couldn't allow herself to feel this way. She just couldn't. It would complicate everything!

The library doors opened and Dianthe peeked in. "Oh, here you are. Did you hear the dinner bell? I'm famished and Mrs. Dewberry has made her poached salmon and a lovely aspic." She looked at Grace, then Adam, and smiled. "But ignore my interruption, please."

"Quite all right, Miss Lovejoy," Adam said, going to take her arm to escort her to the dining room. He glanced back at Grace and winked. "I am famished, as well."

Chapter Five

Despite the gilt elegance of the main salon, there was something about the wholly masculine atmosphere of a gambling hell and the men who inhabited it that intrigued Grace—a coarseness and baseness that seemed to contradict their underlying dignity. In one corner, she watched as a man celebrated as a great naval hero, and reportedly happily married, cursed roundly as he threw his cards on the table. He pulled the young woman next to him into his arms, swearing that if he could not win at cards, he'd damned well win at love. She giggled as he led her out of the main salon and down a darkened corridor to the rooms kept for such purposes. If this was the sort of activity men preferred, it was a wonder to ever find them at an afternoon garden party.

Barrington whispered, "There, Grace. I warned you what sort of thing goes on at these places. Are you ready to throw it in?"

She thought of the bruises on Laura Talbot's arms. No, she could not "throw it in." "Really, my lord, do you think me so delicate that I cannot withstand a little smoke and the demimonde?" From the corner of her eye, she saw Lord Geoffrey Morgan come through the arched entry to the main salon.

"Why would you want to? That is what I'd like to know," Barrington muttered. "Never would have suspected you'd have a taste for the low life, Grace."

Low life? "Do you think I have sunk low just because I wish to play a few games of chance?" she asked as she watched Morgan's cool gaze sweep the room.

"Er, no, Grace. Nothing of the sort. Just don't think this is a suitable place for a woman of your...your social standing and exceptional reputation."

"Perhaps it is *just* the place," she said with a little shrug. "I have been thinking, lately, that I've become a bit stodgy."

Morgan glanced in their direction and smiled. Grace wet her lips. He was coming toward them and, by the length of his stride, he would be upon them before Barrington noticed. When Barrington did notice his advance, it was too late.

"Barrington," Morgan greeted him. "I haven't seen you here in a while. Where have you been keeping yourself?"

Barrington affected a look of surprise. "Oh, Morgan. Nice to see you again. I've been keeping busy. Always a war somewhere, you know."

Geoffrey Morgan laughed and Grace was struck by the sound. Though she suspected it was polite and social, it had the ring of sincerity. Was he enjoying Barrington's discomfort?

"Well, I am glad to see you back. I've always said you are an excellent player."

"Yes, well..." Barrington paused awkwardly. "I, uh, I suppose you've met Mrs. Forbush?"

"A lifetime ago, it seems, although I was simply Mr. Morgan then." Morgan turned his full attention to her. "It is nice to see you again, Mrs. Forbush."

"Lord Geoffrey." Grace smiled in acknowledgment. "I was sorry to hear about your father's passing."

"Thank you, Mrs. Forbush. Are you enjoying yourself?"

"Very much." She smiled, her excitement rising now that

she'd finally made the first contact. "I had no idea such exciting entertainments were only moments away from Almack's."

He laughed and nodded. "And now that you've been here, you are not likely to be invited back to Almack's."

"Then, since I will have the spare time, you are certain to see more of me." She tilted her head slightly and gave him an innocent smile.

He lowered his voice and said, "I pray that is so, Mrs. Forbush."

Barrington cleared his throat. "Grace is just playing at gambling, Morgan. She'll soon tire of it and—"

She patted her escort's arm and smiled up at him. "Lord Barrington is always kind enough to indulge my whims, whether he understands them or not."

Her escort looked down at her, momentarily confused. "Why, uh, I do my best."

"As would I," Morgan said, "were I fortunate enough to have the attention of so lovely a woman."

Barrington bristled. "But Grace, er, Mrs. Forbush, wants to take more risks than she should. A little reckless, if you ask me," he continued, just warming to the subject.

"Reckless, eh?" Morgan asked.

Grace could almost see his speculation. Was he assessing her to determine if she'd be an easy mark? Or just wondering precisely *how* reckless she might be? She felt the need to explain. "Lord Barrington is only out of sorts because I asked him to take me to the Blue Moon tonight."

Now Morgan laughed outright. "The Covent Garden hells are *déclassé,* and well beneath your notice, I promise you. They call it the Blue Moon for a reason. Their clients only win once in a blue moon."

Barrington nodded. "Quite right, Morgan. There, you see, Grace? I told you it wasn't the place for you."

She merely returned Barrington's grin. She'd only wanted

to go because she'd heard that it was one of Morgan's favorite haunts. "Nevertheless, I should like to go there sometime."

"Perhaps you will be able to persuade someone to take you," Morgan said. "But come. Have you learned faro, Mrs. Forbush? Allow me to teach you if Barrington has neglected that part of your education."

"I tried my hand last night, Lord Geoffrey, but I do not seem to have a grasp of the game. I lost miserably."

He took her arm and led her toward the faro table with Barrington at her other side. Whatever the man was, he was not lacking in social graces.

The afternoon sun was still high when Adam checked the slip of paper that had arrived by messenger that morning from Freddie. He glanced at the gray ivy-covered cottage again. Yes, the St. Albans address was correct if a bit surprising. Retired valets and household servants most often shared quarters in retirement, if not entered a home for the infirm. This small cottage was set back from the street, had a vegetable garden and was well kept and in good repair. He knocked twice, wondering if Freddie had gotten the address wrong.

A balding man opened the door and blinked rheumy gray eyes in surprise. "Mr. Hawthorne! I…we…."

"Thought I was dead," Adam finished for the speechless valet. He was startled at how much the man had aged since he'd last seen him. He would not have recognized Bellows on the street. "But, as you can see, I'm hale and hardy."

"Come in, sir. Come in." The man stood aside to allow Adam to pass. "What a pleasure to see you, sir."

The main room had a low ceiling and was small but comfortable. Surprised, Adam recognized a few nice pieces from his uncle's house mingled with other good but worn furniture. He removed his hat and shook Bellows's hand. "I heard you'd retired, Bellows, so I came to pay my respects."

The man flushed with pleasure. "Please sit down. May I offer you a cup of tea?"

Adam took one of the chairs by the fireplace and shook his head. "No, thank you, Bellows. I can't stay long. I just wanted to reassure myself that you are well and happy."

"Very kind of you, sir." Bellows sat opposite him and smiled. "Quite a shock, finding you alive all these years, sir. If I was rude, I apologize."

"Not at all," Adam assured him. "But you cannot have been more shocked than I to learn that you'd retired. I somehow thought you'd work until you were senile."

Bellows laughed and rubbed his bald head. "And I would have, too, if Mrs. Forbush had not insisted. But once your uncle was gone, there didn't seem much point in staying on. He'd already begun to fail but after we had the news about you, well, the end came quickly. He did not suffer, sir."

Adam nodded and said nothing. Barrington had said Uncle Basil had been ill since before Adam's last visit. According to Grace, he began a decline after the report of Adam's death. Now Bellows reported he'd been ill only shortly before the report of Adam's death. Which was the truth?

"Aye, sir. And when our mourning was done, Mrs. Forbush asked my help in putting Mr. Forbush's things away. We had nice long chats while we worked, and 'twas when I mentioned that I'd worked for Mr. Forbush for forty-five years that Mrs. Forbush insisted I should retire. Said I done more than faithful service and deserved a rest. I was that shocked, I was."

"I hope you are not suffering financially."

"Nothing of the sort, sir." Bellows straightened in his chair and smiled. "I've been pensioned off. First of every month, I get an envelope from the missus. More than enough to pay my expenses, sir. In fact, the ladies in the village think I'm quite a catch. I can tell you, Mr. Hawthorne, that I do not lack for companionship."

Was the pension a bribe for not talking? Adam wondered. If his uncle's end had come quickly, perhaps it had been assisted. "Tell me, Bellows, was my uncle ill when I was here last and just neglected to mention it?"

"That was just before you went to the colonies, was it not? No. He'd been fit as a fiddle. He did not decline until just before the news of your death came. Then, of a sudden, he went very quickly, sir."

"Did you think that odd, Bellows?"

"Odd? No, sir. After all, he was near sixty and five."

"Then I gather it was not his heart that gave out?"

"No, sir. A quick wasting illness of some sort. The doctor couldn't quite put his finger on it. He thought it might be the grief of losing you, sir. Wouldn't eat, and then purged when he did. No Forbushes left now, but for the missus."

Adam puzzled this out. Why had Uncle Basil given up— especially when he had a woman like Grace Ellen York to share his life? That didn't make sense. "Apart from the report of my death, was my uncle happy, Bellows?"

"Yes, sir. His business was doing well and the missus always brought a smile to his face. She was a blessing to him. Real gentle, she was, even though he was sometimes short with her and said hurtful things. Told her she was a burden and had been a bad bargain. He said he had expected more of her, but I cannot imagine what, Mr. Hawthorne. The missus was diligent and did more than most wives. You know how mean-spirited he could be sometimes. But she took good care of him at the last. Wouldn't leave his side. I feared we'd lose her if she didn't rest. Heart-wrenching, it was."

"They were in love, then?"

Bellows sat back in his chair and frowned. "Well, sir, when she first came to London as his bride, I assumed she was a part of his business dealings with her brother. But, as time went on, I saw a certain fondness grow." He paused and lowered his voice confidentially. "You know how these things are, sir—older husband wants an heir and gets himself a young bride? Then a year or so later, the wife quietly takes lovers? Never happened with Mrs. Forbush. She was devoted to the mister, though I cannot say if it was the kind of love you mean, sir. More like friendship. She cried for weeks after he passed, and quarreled fearsome with her brother when he came to take her home. Said she wouldn't leave the only peace she'd ever known. Lord Barrington had to intercede for her."

Adam tried to picture the serenely self-possessed Grace crying for weeks. Or calling upon anyone for help. There was something quite odd about this account. "Well, I gather that since she's still here, she won her way."

"With conditions, sir," Bellows said.

"What conditions?"

Bellows blinked. An indiscreet servant was the bane of an employer's existence. Had he realized he'd said too much? "Oh, uh, I wouldn't know about that, sir. That happened behind closed doors."

Blast! He should have been more circuitous in his questioning. Certainly less obvious. If he pressed now, Bellows was sure to deny everything. He stood and clapped the valet on his shoulder. "I should be going. I just wanted to stop in and make certain that all was well, Bellows. My uncle was always fond of you."

Bellows nodded again as he walked Adam to the door. "I'm a lucky man," he said. "Most valets do not retire in the style Mrs. Forbush has provided. And Mrs. Humphries, too."

Adam paused. "Ah, yes, Mrs. Humphries. Could I trouble you for her address? I'd like to assure myself of her good situation, as well."

Grace stared at the envelope on the silver tray for a several minutes while she weighed the consequences of burning the contents unread against the consequences of reading it. The letter, from Leland, had arrived an hour ago. When her brother took the time to write a letter, it could not be anything good.

She glanced at the clock on the fireplace mantel. She should be preparing for another evening at the hells instead of dawdling in the library. Would the letter wait until morning?

No. The dread of it would taint her entire evening and she was certain not to sleep. She'd best have it over with and know what was afoot. First, though, she went to the sideboard and poured herself a draft of sherry. She suspected she'd need the fortification.

She sat at her desk, took a sip, and slipped her silver letter opener beneath the flap. She took one deep, bracing breath, and then unfolded the single sheet and began reading.

Mrs. Forbush,

I am distressed to hear that you are engaging in unsavory pastimes and have made some ill-advised decisions, thus exposing yourself and your family to scandal. My name and reputation as your brother and only remaining male relative could be affected, thus it is my duty to recall you to your senses.

You will recollect that our agreement in the wake of your husband's death permitted your continued residency in London, provided that you did nothing to invite scandal. Alas, I do not consider sheltering an unmarried man who could be the instrument of your destruction and cavorting at gaming hells and wagering your inheritance to be acceptable behavior.

Grace gasped. It was not as if Leland's behavior had always been completely circumspect. He'd had his fair share of scandals, not the least of which was the way he treated his sister and his wife. Pricilla, though, never complained because she was too frightened or did not know any better. Instead she would take to her bed pleading a headache or some other malady.

> *Either you cease your activities at once, or you will compel me to come to London and remove you to Devon—forcibly if need be. Do not think you can refuse me, sister, since I know and will use your disgraceful secret to ensure your compliance.*
> *I remain,*
> *Yr. Brother, Leland York*

Grace dropped the letter on the tray. How did Leland find these things out so quickly? And why did his demands and threats still devastate and infuriate her so? All she had to lose was…everything. And the worst that could happen was that she would end up back at her childhood home under her brother's heavy hand. Unacceptable. Completely unacceptable.

But even more unacceptable was abandoning Miss Talbot to a similar fate. It was too late for Grace, but there was yet time to save Miss Talbot. Despite Leland's threats, she had to go on. Striking a decisive blow for Miss Talbot had taken on the proportions of striking a blow against Leland's abuse. She would continue because she had a moral obligation to help anyone who shared her fate, and anyone without the strength to stand on her own. "Damn him," she muttered when tears welled in her eyes. She picked up her glass and lifted it to her lips.

Passing the library on his way upstairs, Adam heard a muffled, "Damn him!" He peeked in to see Grace looking quite distressed, her attention fastened to an open letter. How unlike the unflappable Mrs. Forbush to curse. He didn't want to interrupt her, but neither did he want to leave her in distress.

He leaned one shoulder against the doorjamb and waited for her to finish.

When she lifted her wineglass to drink, she noticed him for the first time. He was surprised to see tears welling in her eyes. He'd stake his life that she was not the sort to cry without a reason. "Bad news?" he asked.

She blinked to clear those dark sultry eyes and glanced away as if embarrassed to have been caught in a genuine emotion instead of the carefully constructed impression she fought to maintain. Her shoulders squared and the social mask fell into place, shutting him out as effectively as a snub.

"A letter from my brother." Her voice was tight, and she looked down.

He crossed the library and stood across the desk from her, not knowing what to do. There was something indefinable in her expression, something touchingly vulnerable. She frowned and pressed a spot in the center of her forehead, as she'd done the day he arrived. He'd learned it was a thoughtful gesture. One she used when puzzling a problem or fighting a headache.

"I-is there something you needed, Mr. Hawthorne?"

Her words were a reproach—a dismissal at the very least—and he bristled. "No," he admitted. "You looked as if you needed a friend."

She glanced up at him again, little creases forming between her eyes. "I did not mean to be short with you, Mr. Hawthorne. You surprised me. I hadn't realized you were standing there."

"I heard a sound when I was passing," he explained. Their stilted conversation was awkward and he turned to go.

"Mr. Hawthorne, please wait." She stood and came around the desk to face him. "I apologize if I made you feel uncomfortable. I fear I am so used to keeping my own counsel that I have become unfit company. Forgive me?"

"Of course." He'd have forgiven her anything when she

looked at him so earnestly. She was close enough that she had to look up to meet his gaze, and he found himself leaning toward her, drawn almost against his will. "Does your brother often affect you in this way?"

"Always, I fear." She sighed. "He knows just what to say to bring me to a boil."

He laughed, relaxing. "I gather that is ordinary for brothers."

"I wouldn't know, sir. I only have the one, and we have ever been at odds. He thought Papa favored me and has always found ways to make me pay for it."

"And he has found another way?" Before he could think better of it, he reached out and touched her shoulder. She flinched and then caught her breath on a sob, as if the human touch had been more than she could bear. He'd only meant to comfort her, not devastate her.

She turned her face away and murmured, "I…I am sorry, Mr. Hawthorne. I don't know what has gotten into me."

Selfishly, because he wanted to feel her against him, he tugged her into his arms and held her tightly, half expecting her to pull away. Instead she fit against him perfectly. The tension drained from her shoulders and she gave a shaky sigh.

There was something shy and uncertain in her surrender. Grace, for all her composure, was human, after all. He regretted his suspicions. She could not possibly be guilty of murder. "How long has it been, Grace, since someone offered you comfort?" he asked.

"Since…since Mr. Forbush," she whispered.

"Mr. Forbush," he repeated. "Did you always call him that? Was he never 'Basil'?"

She sniffled. "He always called me Mrs. Forbush, and so I returned his courtesy. I believe he preferred it that way."

Adam struggled with that for a moment. Could his uncle have been blind? How could he not have invited—even welcomed—informality between himself and his lovely wife?

Unforgivably, but needing to know, he asked, "Even when… intimate?"

He felt her stiffen and pull away. "Really, Mr. Hawthorne, I do not wish to discuss such things."

"I've offended you."

"I…it is not appropriate for you…for us, to have a conversation regarding my…your uncle's…at all," she finished, more at a loss than he'd ever seen her.

The calm mask that drove him insane fell into place again and she moved toward the door. "I would appreciate it, Mr. Hawthorne, if we could avoid a repeat of this scene. I find it disturbingly inappropriate considering our…connection."

"We have no connection, Grace. You might have been married to my uncle, but you were never my aunt."

She paused at the door, her back to him. "Nevertheless."

"Nevertheless," he agreed.

When the door closed behind her, he lifted the forgotten letter on the desk and scanned the lines. Though he was not a snoop by nature, if there was anything here that would help him solve his uncle's death, he'd better know it now.

The first disturbing item came early on. Her brother evidently wanted Grace to tell Adam to leave the house. And what the hell had he meant that *he* could be the instrument of Grace's destruction? He read on, appalled at the arrogance of Leland York.

Good God! Who was this prig? Even more disturbing than the order for Grace to evict Adam was the veiled threat. York knew Grace's secret and would use it to blackmail her? What secret? Adam could only think of one thing dire enough to warrant such a threat and connect him as the "instrument of her destruction." That she'd had a hand in his uncle's death and that he might discover and expose her.

Chapter Six

The scene with Adam had Grace on edge and impatient when Lord Barrington arrived to escort her to Belmonde's in Pickering Place. By the time they were inside and Grace had purchased her counters, Barrington was wearing on her nerves to a high degree. He had done nothing but complain about her "ridiculous new diversion" and the "insane chances" she was taking with her reputation during the entire drive. It was eerily like listening to her brother.

The main salon of Belmonde's was decorated in shades of deep green and gold, the lighting was dim, and the tone was more sedate and the crowd of a higher social class than at the Two Sevens. A low hum of voices played against a background of a single pianist. Feeling quite comfortable in this venue, Grace seized the first opportunity to divert him to happier matters. "My lord, I see Mr. Elwood by the vingt-et-un table. I think it would be an excellent idea for you to congratulate him on the arrival of his heir. I understand the birth went well. The baby is the picture of health and everyone is completely over the top about it."

Barrington looked toward the group across the room. "Yes? Well, if you think I should…"

"Oh, I do," she sighed, anxious for any respite from his complaints. "Take your time. I shall find a nice little game and settle in."

"I dislike leaving you on your own, Grace. You're bound to encounter trouble."

"I swear I will find you if I should need the least little thing," she said, straightening his cravat and sending him off with a little push in the direction of the vingt-et-un table.

She hoped to find a game of hazard. She wanted to learn it quickly, but she really must remember to ask Miss Talbot the game her brother had been playing when he lost his fortune. If she could watch Morgan at that, she might be able to determine whether he cheated or not. Though men of experience had been unable to catch him, she expected to have better luck. Morgan would not be so cautious in dealing with her, since she was a mere woman. And, she smiled to herself, she had always been of the opinion that women had the superior intellect.

Holding her wineglass in one gloved hand and her counters in the other, she circulated, watching the activity at one table and then another. She was engrossed in studying the intricacies of betting at hazard when she felt someone leaning close to her left ear.

"I wouldn't advise it, Mrs. Forbush. The odds are heavily in favor of the house."

She turned and smiled at Geoffrey Morgan. Had he done that deliberately? "From what I've been able to determine, sir, the odds are heavily in favor of the house no matter the game."

"Precisely why I prefer to play games that pit my skills against other players instead of the house."

Now this was interesting. Grace sighed and gave him a sidelong glance. "Few men will allow a woman at their table, Lord Geoffrey. What would you suggest I do?"

"Play with me," he said in a low, husky voice.

Grace smiled and dropped her gaze to the silver embroidery at the hem of her gown. "Do you recommend a particular game?"

"Whist. Do you know it?"

"Quite well," she admitted. She had learned it at a country house party many years ago where the ladies had played for pins, and she had played it frequently since. "Are you asking me to be your partner, Lord Geoffrey?"

"I've come looking for one. If I bring you to the table, Mrs. Forbush, no one will say you nay."

"I am surprised that you are willing to link your fortunes to my skill when you really haven't the slightest idea what my proficiency might be. My misjudgments could cost you dearly."

He laughed and took her by the arm to lead her away from the main salon. "All of life is a risk, Mrs. Forbush. The greater the risk, the keener the excitement."

She tilted her head to look up at him again and found a small smile playing at the corners of his mouth. She laughed. "Then you should be very excited right now, Lord Geoffrey."

He returned her smile. "You have no idea, Mrs. Forbush."

Grace had a momentary flash of fear. She took a deep breath at the suggestiveness in that comment and hoped things had not just slipped out of her control. "Who are our opponents?"

"Reginald Hunter and Adam Hawthorne."

Heavens! This had not been in her plans. Adam! Even in the midst of all these men, she could only think of that extraordinary kiss in the library and how she wished it could happen again, despite what she'd told him. She willed her breathing to even and her heartbeat to slow. There was nothing for it but to brazen it out. "Lead on, sir," she said.

Laughter trailed off and conversation stilled as Lord Geoffrey led her into a small side room. Just the appearance of a woman could, evidently, make men feel awkward. She was entering a male domain—one that few women ever saw. It would take all her resources to ignore the fact that she wasn't wanted here.

Lord Geoffrey led her to one of the three tables in the room and announced, "Mrs. Forbush, may I present—"

"Mrs. Forbush, how are you?" Reginald said, rising, extending his hand and smiling widely.

"I'm well, thank you, Lord Reginald." She turned to Adam, standing, too, and appraising her with a speculative gleam in his deep hazel eyes. "I see you are fitting quite comfortably back into society, Mr. Hawthorne."

Adam bowed and when he straightened he gave her a crooked smile coupled with one raised eyebrow. "Parts of it," he said laconically.

He was the polar opposite of the man in buckskins she had met for the first time—now elegantly attired in sober black with a deep green waistcoat over an impeccably tied cravat. He had evidently not needed assistance with that tonight. How would she ever be able to sit across the table from him and keep from watching the way his eyes sparkled in a jest or thinking of how those lips felt on hers?

Lord Reginald, looking puzzled a moment before, began to laugh. "Ah, yes. Now I recall. Mrs. Forbush, you and Hawthorne are somehow related, are you not?"

Lord Geoffrey turned to her in surprise. "How so, Mrs. Forbush?"

"Through marriage. My late husband was Mr. Hawthorne's uncle."

He glanced from her to Adam and back again. "Life never ceases to amaze and delight me," he said. He held a chair for her before taking his own across from her. "May I assume you are not in league with Mr. Hawthorne to relieve me of my ready?"

Adam leaned back in his chair and gave an easy smile but did not rise to the bait. Grace could not tell if he was insulted or amused by the gibe.

She merely laughed and turned to Reginald. "Forgive me Lord Reginald, but may I assume that you and Mr. Hawthorne are not in league to take advantage of a novice?"

"Touché, Mrs. Forbush," Lord Geoffrey acknowledged.

With a glance and nod in the direction of a house monitor whose duty it was to observe the activities at each table, Lord Geoffrey began to shuffle the deck. Grace noted how nimble he was, how adept at handling the cards. And how quick. He slid the deck to his right and Adam cut them before Lord Geoffrey began the deal. The last card, dealt face up, was a heart, declaring the trump suit.

When Grace opened her hand and sorted her cards, she was pleased to find seven hearts. She looked up at her partner, wondering if he had somehow known and manipulated the cards. But how could he? Even if he'd known the bottom card was a heart, how could he have dealt her hearts from the middle of the deck? He was studying his hand with rapt concentration and nothing in his expression or bearing indicated that cheating was afoot. Her hand must be a happy coincidence.

Lord Reginald led and the play began. At one point she glanced up to find Morgan studying her over his hand. He raised his eyebrows as if asking a question. She smiled, realizing he was flirting with her. Rather effectively, too.

When she took the last trick for a total of ten, Lord Geoffrey smiled. "Well done, partner," he said.

"Well dealt," she answered.

Lord Reginald, completely unperturbed, gathered the cards and began to shuffle. "As it is my turn to deal, I shall try to give *my* partner likewise good cards."

Grace shot a quick glance at Lord Reginald. Was he intimating that he suspected Lord Geoffrey of cheating in the deal? There did not seem to be a challenge in his eyes.

"Excellent!" Adam said, cutting through the tension. "Mrs.

Forbush made rather short work of us, did she not? I'll relish the chance to even the score."

"Nothing like a little competition," Lord Geoffrey said. "It always sharpens the senses and adds excitement, wouldn't you agree, Mr. Hawthorne?"

Meeting Lord Geoffrey's gaze, Adam gave a half smile, one that only lifted one corner of his mouth. "If the stakes are high enough," he said with a hint of challenge.

Lord Geoffrey nodded and returned his attention to the cards. Was there some sort of history between the men?

The next several hands went more slowly than the first, but Grace wasn't aware of the passage of time until she felt Barrington's hand on her shoulder.

"Here you are, Grace. It is time for us to go. Let's fetch your wrap."

"Come now, Barrington," Lord Geoffrey protested. "I've scarce had such good luck with partners before."

"Too bad, Morgan. Grace is coming with me."

Grace looked over her shoulder to see Barrington's face. He was completely serious! She lowered her voice to a conciliatory tone. "As soon as I finish this hand—"

"Now."

A hush fell over the table as the men looked from her to Barrington and back. She folded her cards and took a deep breath. Every instinct she had told her to avoid the scene—to do whatever she must to smooth this over and keep the peace, as she'd done with Leland her whole life—but she'd finally had enough of Barrington's subtle bullying.

"After I finish this hand, my lord. If you will fetch my wrap, I will be done by the time you return."

Barrington gripped her elbow and pulled her to her feet, tipping her chair backward in the process. She was so stunned by this maneuver that she was rendered momentarily speechless. Players at the other tables stopped to look in their direction. Barrington seemed oblivious to the attention they were drawing. She heard chairs at her own table scraping backward but kept her eyes riveted on Barrington and prayed for restraint.

"My lord, it would be unforgivably rude of me to leave the game in progress. I am not the only one to consider here."

"Well, you are the only one I am considering, Grace, and you are coming with me." He tightened his hold on her arm and pulled her away from the table.

Adam, Morgan and Lord Reginald all stepped forward as if they would intercede. She lifted her hand to them, trying to avert the pending disaster. She must avoid a scene at any cost. All she could think of was her brother. Leland had always gotten what he wanted by bullying, demeaning and embarrassing her. She thought she had escaped that ugliness, and that she'd never be at any man's mercy again, but here she was. She knew she should face him down, but still…

But still the fear of Leland and of calling his attention was controlling her, forcing her compliance—at least in public. Choking on the words, she said, "Gentlemen, please excuse me. Allow me to—" she tried to open her reticule, dangling from her wrist, to withdraw the remainder of her counters "—to reimburse you for your losses, Lord Geoffrey."

"No need, Mrs. Forbush," he said, a frown knitting lines between his eyes. "Our winnings far exceed our losses. In fact, I will owe you—"

Barrington tugged at her arm and Adam took a step forward, his intent clear. Lord Reginald, too, gave Barrington a hard look and made a move forward. Panic threatened to overwhelm her. *Be calm,* she counseled herself. *Softly. Breathe.* When she spoke, her voice was so serenely controlled that she scarcely recognized it.

"Thank you for a lovely evening, gentlemen, but I really must be going. I have just recalled that Lord Barrington is quite right. We are long overdue for an appointment."

* * *

Though it was the deepest part of night, traffic along the main thoroughfares did not stop. Drivers called to one another and the sound of hooves on cobblestones filled the air. The moment Barrington's coach stopped moving, Grace did not wait for a footman, but threw the door open and hopped down. She had not spoken the entire ride, not trusting herself to remain rational. Mrs. Dewberry had waited up and stood just inside the foyer. She handed the housekeeper her pelisse and reticule. "You needn't have waited up, Mrs. Dewberry."

"I like to be sure everyone is all tucked up for the night, Mrs. Forbush. I don't mind in the least."

Before she went any further, Grace needed to be certain she and Barrington would not be interrupted. "Is Dianthe home yet?"

"Aye, Mrs. Forbush. Retired an hour ago."

"Thank you, Mrs. Dewberry. Now please get some sleep."

"Shall I fetch more brandy for his lordship, Mrs. Forbush?"

She headed for the library, peeling her gloves away as she went. "He will not be staying long. Now off to bed with you."

"Yes, Missus." The woman hurried toward the coach house where she and her husband had separate quarters.

"Grace—"

She was already pouring herself a glass of brandy by the time Barrington caught up with her.

"Grace, talk to me," he pleaded.

Grace had wanted to be safely home and out of the reach of society gossips and Leland's informants before she gave vent to her anger. Her back to him, she gulped the brandy and braced herself as the fire seeped downward, relaxing her clenched stomach muscles and stilling her trembling. She rarely drank anything stronger than sherry, but this occasion called for it. The next few minutes were going to be extremely unpleasant and she would need fortification to get through it.

"Damn it all, Grace," Barrington snarled, red-faced. "I won't have it. I won't have you cavorting at hells and flirting with every man there. It cheapens you."

She straightened and turned to him, ready to deliver the conciliatory speech she had devised on the coach ride home. "I am painfully aware that this is my fault, Lord Barrington, and I accept responsibility. I allowed this to go on far too long. Despite your assurances, I have, of late, begun to suspect your feelings for me were more than they should be. Certainly more than we agreed upon for our friendship."

Barrington harrumphed and straightened his jacket. "I know how you dislike displays of emotion, Grace. I did not want you to feel uncomfortable or have any reason to…to—"

"Any reason to end it?" she finished. *How could she have been so blind? How could she have been so naive to believe the assurances that he expected nothing from her and that he'd only wanted a hostess and occasional companion?* "But you must see that has only caused more problems. I do not, and will never, have those feelings for you, my lord. Now I am in the loathsome position of asking you to cease calling on me. I hope we shall be able to be cordial when we meet in public, but I will understand if you cannot."

"You think I don't know?" Barrington scoffed, advancing on her. "You kept me around because I was convenient, Grace. Because I was safe. You didn't want any messy entanglements, and you thought I would not press."

Was that true? She felt the sting of guilt. After Basil's aborted attempts at lovemaking, she had sworn she'd never put herself in that position again. Had she been too eager to believe Barrington's assurances to question them—she, who had observed such things so easily in others? Her only defense was that, "I thought you would not press because you didn't care. You swore you only wanted a hostess, a companion for the many functions and state dinners required of your position. I served a purpose for you, as well, my lord. I am sorry if you had any further expectations of me, but I was always careful not to give you any reason to think there could ever be more."

"You have always known—"

"That's just it, sir. I did *not* know. I was so certain you understood that—"

"Three years, Grace. Three years I've been keeping your company. Three years of waiting."

"Three years of knowing that I never intend to marry again, and that I do not want a lover," she interrupted. "Three years of saying that was acceptable to you. Three years of swearing this was all you wanted of me."

"You let me think there was a chance," he shouted.

"You will *not* make me guilty!" she cried. When all else had failed, Leland had used guilt to control her, and she would not go down that path with Barrington. She turned to pour more brandy into her glass.

"You should thank me, Grace," he said, seizing her arm and whirling her back around to face him. "If I hadn't stopped you, you'd have made a spectacle of yourself."

"Have you gone mad? *You* are the one who made the scene tonight, Barrington! You are the one who called attention to us and will be the cause of talk tomorrow."

"Precisely why you will continue to see me. The ton must know that all is well."

She tried to pull away, but Barrington tightened his grip on her arm. "All is *not* well," she said as calmly as she could manage. "Nor will it ever be. Our friendship is over. I shall never accompany you again, nor are you welcome here."

"Society will say you have found a new lover. Who is it, Grace? Hunter? Morgan? Or is it Hawthorne? Is that why you refuse to put him out? How convenient to have your lover living under your roof."

She had never seen this side of Barrington. His eyes were hard and his lips were drawn back in a sneer. "Are you outraged because I am defying you, or because you are afraid you will look like a cuckold to society?"

He pulled his hand back and slapped her face, still holding her firm in his grasp. "I *am* a cuckold, damn it! You are flirting and whoring all over London, making yourself look ridiculous! If I cannot control you, how shall I keep the respect of my peers?"

Control me? She touched her cheek where it stung. Something darkly primal fired deep in her soul, a volatile blend of fury and panic, making her insensible to her vulnerability. How many years had she suffered these arguments with Leland? How many times had she swallowed her pride for the sake of peace? Yet the arguments and rage had only grown worse. And if she gave in to Lord Barrington now, she would never be free again. That sort of abuse only escalated, never ceased. Lord Barrington would simply take Leland's place as her master.

It must end now, no matter the cost. Her voice was low and deadly as she snapped, "How dare you strike me! And how dare you accuse me of such things? Release me."

He struck her again, as she had suspected he would. This time her lip split against her teeth. Men of his and Leland's ilk almost relished defiance as an excuse to further their abuses. But she was beyond caring about physical damage. She was desperate to keep her spirit and self-respect intact. Narrowing her eyes and watching him steadily, she lifted her hand to wipe away the trickle of blood at the corner of her mouth. "Do you really think this is the way to win me over, Lord Barrington?"

"Damn you!" he cursed, thrusting her away as if disgusted with them both.

She stumbled back against the sideboard. "Leave, sir, and never return."

"You have no idea what you've done, Grace. What you've unleashed. I never thought you were stupid. How did Forbush put up with you all those years?" He took several backward steps toward the library door, and Grace knew he meant to lock it, not to leave. Her stomach clenched as she realized he was not finished with her. She would recover from whatever Lord Barrington did to her, but she would never recover if she lost her self-respect. The thin thread of self-control snapped and she ran to the fireplace to seize a poker, prepared to defend herself if necessary.

But Barrington's backward progress toward the door landed him solidly against Adam's chest. He must have followed them home within minutes of their departure from the hell.

She held her breath as Adam glanced between her, the poker clutched in her hand, Barrington, and then returned his gaze to her mouth. A muscle tightened along his jaw and one hand clamped over Barrington's shoulder.

"What the hell is going on here?" he asked, his other hand fisted at his side.

"Keep out of this, Hawthorne," Barrington said.

"Please, Mr. Hawthorne. Lord Barrington was just on his way out."

"The hell, you say," Adam snarled. "I heard you arguing from the foyer. What, precisely, are you accusing Grace of, Barrington?"

"None of your bloody business, you meddlesome pup!" He pushed past Adam, storming from the room. "Everything was fine until you showed up!"

When Adam turned to go after him, she called him back. "Please, Mr. Hawthorne, let him go. I could not bear any more discord tonight. He is gone. Let it rest at that."

The front door slammed and Adam turned toward her just as she dropped the poker. He reached out to her but she winced and shrank back, as if fearing his touch. Bloody goddamn hell! He should have gone after the son of a bitch! No matter. He knew exactly where to find Barrington whenever he wanted. The man would pay, sooner or later.

Her lip was swollen and the small trickle of blood at the corner of her mouth disturbed him more than he cared to admit. "Sit down," he told her gruffly. He went to the sideboard to pour her some brandy. It would sting like the devil, but it would clean the cut and stop the bleeding.

He took the glass to her and stood back while she drank. Her hand trembled as she returned the glass to him and a little shiver swept her as the alcohol hit the back of her throat. He knelt by her chair, removed his handkerchief from his vest pocket and dabbed at the blood.

"What did Barrington mean when he said that everything was fine until I showed up? Am I somehow responsible for…for *this*?" He dabbed again at her split lip.

"Coincidence." She sighed and shrugged. "You came to town the same day I asked Barrington to take me to some gambling hells. The two events are unrelated. Please do not blame yourself for any of this."

He struggled with this statement. He knew there was a connection, whether Grace knew it or not. "If I thought I was to blame in any way for this scene, I'd want to make it right."

She met his gaze and took a ragged breath. "My friendship with Lord Barrington has been a problem in the making for months now. Perhaps years, and I was just too blind to see it. I wanted to avoid unpleasantness, and instead—well, I've caused my own problems, Mr. Hawthorne."

"I thought we agreed on 'Adam.' At least within the confines of this house. And forgive me if I doubt you, Grace, but there is nothing you could say that would make that treatment acceptable."

Her eyes—those bottomless pools of emotion—grew luminous with tears that never quite escaped past the rim of dark lashes. "Thank you, Mr.—Adam. I—I needed to hear that."

She stood and pressed her index finger to the center of her forehead. "I am quite fatigued. I think I shall retire now. Please do not mention any of this to Dianthe. I am afraid she has more valor than is good for her, and she would likely confront Lord Barrington."

He stood and lifted her arm to display a livid bruise where Barrington had held her. The sight of that ugly stain on Grace's smooth, flawless flesh stirred his anger anew. "How will you explain *this* to Dianthe?"

"A week of wearing long sleeves and shawls, and there will be nothing to explain." She tilted her face upward to his, a plea in her eyes.

"He will do it again, you know."

"Yes, I know. And that is why our friendship is finished."

He touched her lip gently with the tip of his finger. "A cold cloth tonight should bring the swelling down." He trailed his finger across her cheek where Barrington's palm print was still visible. "I do not think there will be a bruise, but—"

"Rice powder," she sighed, her gaze dropping to the floor.

Ah, she'd done this before. Covering abuse was not new to her. And now he understood why Grace Ellen Forbush was an enigma. How often had he seen these signs in the ballrooms and palaces of Europe? Women—forced to hide a husband's abuse, a father's cruelty, a brother's brutality or a lover's spite—compelled to bury all traces of their own individuality and to disguise their true feelings for fear of ridicule or punishment. Grace had come to her tightly controlled character as a means of survival. But the real Grace was under there somewhere—perhaps the little girl with a dark pigtail— beneath the facade, and he was determined to find her. Who had subjected her to such treatment? Surely not his uncle? "Your brother—" he began.

Her head snapped up to look directly into his face. "He must not hear of this! Promise me, Adam!"

Stunned at the force of her reaction, he hastened to agree. "No, of course not."

He released her arm, knowing she was too damaged, too raw from this latest episode, to question further. He could not even hold her, comfort her. She would resent him for imposing on her vulnerability in the morning.

She walked slowly to the door, fatigue in every step. Her back to him, she paused with her hand on the knob but did not look back. "Thank you, Adam."

"For what?"

"For not making this more difficult than it needed to be."

"You are quite welcome, Grace," he whispered. He threw his jacket over a chair and went to sit by the dying fire.

Her voice caught as she said so faintly that he scarcely heard it, "I do not wish to speak of this again." Then the door closed quietly behind her.

Three days—three *nights*—in the same house with the lovely widow, and he was still no closer to discovering what he'd come for. He suspected a good many things—that Grace was hiding a secret, that there was more to her gambling than she wanted anyone to know, that, as evidenced by the now-abandoned poker, she had the courage to stand up to forces far stronger than she and that she had experienced abuse from the men in her life. Certainly from her priggish brother. Possibly his uncle?

He had a sinking feeling. Could that be the motive he'd been looking for? If Grace had suffered abuse at the hand of his uncle, or if his uncle had threatened to send her back to her brother, could she have ended that threat in the only way open to her? Did her willingness to use the poker hint at her willingness to use other means to rid herself of those she perceived as a threat?

Chapter Seven

On her way down to the library, Grace stopped to check her reflection in her mirror. Adam had been right. A cool damp cloth last night had kept the swelling of her lip to a minimum and, when Barrington's palm print had faded, there only remained the faintest bruise high on her left cheekbone. She applied a little rice powder and was satisfied with the result.

She straightened the long sleeves of her willow green gown as she hurried down the stairs. Within a week there would be no trace of Lord Barrington's loss of temper, including Barrington himself. When Mrs. Dewberry had brought her morning tea earlier, she had instructed her that, should Barrington come calling, to refuse him admittance. Only one thing remained to be done to counteract the possible effects of last night.

Taking a sheet of paper from the center drawer of her desk, Grace dipped her pen in the little inkwell and wrote.

Dear Leland,
I am in receipt of your recent letter and wish to thank you for your brotherly concern. My heart always warms when I realize how fond you are of me and that you always have my best interests at heart.

> *As to my recent gambling, allow me to reassure you that I have been most circumspect in my behavior, ever mindful of your reputation and standing in society.*
>
> *In regard to sheltering an unmarried man, dear brother, I would remind you that he is not just any man. Mr. Hawthorne could very well be the true legal owner of the Bloomsbury Square property. I am not yet ready to pack up and abandon the premises, thus I must wait for a court determination on the issue of inheritance. I fear that to deny him shelter would anger him and make him less amenable to settlement. I was confident you would not want me to risk any property unnecessarily.*
>
> *I pray your forbearance for yet another fortnight. Should the causes of your concern not be resolved by then, I shall inform you of it.*

Grace paused and tapped the end of her pen against her cheek as she thought. If she sounded the least bit disrespectful or defiant, he would arrive at her front door with a full contingent of servants to pack her up and cart her back to Devon. How, then, to phrase the last bit of business?

> *I have always been most appreciative of your sensitivity to my secret—although, why Basil had told him, she couldn't imagine—but I pray you will not use it against me. If that knowledge should become public, I fear it would cause you embarrassment and require me to take strong action to restore my reputation.*

Nothing was more important to Leland than his reputation. The wrath of God could be descending upon him, and as long as he appeared important and respectable, he would not care in the least. But would he be sensible enough to read between the lines and understand that, once her secret was known, he would have no further weapon to hold her hostage? That his authority as her brother might not end, but that any reason she might have to obey him would be gone? Pray so, else there was trouble ahead. She dipped her pen again.

> *Please give my best to Pricilla, along with my prayers*
> *for the restoration of her health.*
>   *I remain your devoted sister,*
>   *Grace*

Actually there was nothing wrong with Pricilla's health that a divorce would not cure, but Grace could not resist the subtle gibe. She blew on the ink to speed the drying, folded the parchment, addressed an envelope and placed it on the silver tray by the door for Mr. Dewberry to post later.

She had done everything she could to head off her brother and to mitigate the damage done by last night's scene at Belmonde's. She would have to go to that establishment again tonight, however, to put as good a face as possible on the fiasco. If she were seen whole and happy immediately after the fray, gossip would die a natural death. The ton, though still watching her carefully, would think it was all a tempest in a teapot. The rest was simply out of her hands.

Famished now that the unpleasant duties were done, she went to the morning room. Dianthe and Adam had already served themselves from the sideboard and were enjoying a lively discussion of Lord Elgin's marble artifacts. The scene was so comfortable and natural that she smiled to herself, wondering if this was what a normal family was like.

"Thievery!" Dianthe exclaimed. "Nothing less. Robbing the Greeks of their heritage. They should be returned at once."

"Preservation," Adam disagreed. "That future generations will have the benefit of learning and seeing firsthand the wonders and history of bygone ages."

"*British* generations," Dianthe exclaimed, waving her butter knife. "And how will that benefit the Greeks?"

"The Greeks had thousands of years to preserve their history. We have done a service to them and mankind."

"Peace!" Grace laughed at their congenial high-spirited disagreement. "It is too early in the day for such philosophy."

"Aunt Grace!" Dianthe exclaimed. "Adam told me you were very tired and would likely sleep late."

Grace poured herself a cup of tea and buttered a muffin before she dared to look at Adam. She suspected she could trust his discretion, but she prayed she would not see pity in his eyes. She could bear anything but pity. "I was exhausted, but I slept very soundly. Thank you for thinking of me, Mr.—Adam."

"No thanks necessary," he said, his voice steady and firm.

When she met his gaze, he gave her a smile of encouragement and a little nod of approval. Oh, dear. That was almost worse than pity. It was support, and she was not used to that. If she was not careful, she could end up needing him. She was already alarmed by the ease with which she'd grown accustomed to having him around. And how she looked forward to seeing his handsome face at her table.

"What tired you so, Aunt Grace? A grueling time at the tables?"

Grace applied a dollop of strawberry preserves to the spongy surface of the muffin. She would have to tell Dianthe something, and the sooner the better. She'd best just come out with it. "Lord Barrington and I quarreled, Dianthe. I regret to say that he will not be calling in the future."

Dianthe put her cup on the saucer and tilted her head to one side, studying Grace's face. Her clear blue eyes narrowed and she sat back in her chair. "You *regret* to say?"

"It is always difficult to end a long friendship, Dianthe, but sometimes necessary."

"Did he end it? Or you?"

"I believe it was mutual." Grace sighed. "I think he has had quite enough of me."

"I doubt that," Dianthe returned, "but what shall we do if he calls?"

"He will not."

"Hmm," Dianthe said, suspicion written on her face. She glanced at Adam. "Do you know something about this, Adam?"

"I? Oh, no." He laughed, raising his hands in protest. "You are not going to put me in the middle."

"I will explain later, Dianthe," Grace said.

Mrs. Dewberry hurried into the room carrying a kettle and with a parcel tucked under one arm. "This just came for you, Mrs. Forbush." She placed the parcel on the table and went to fill the teapot from her kettle.

Grace could not find a return address. The parcel was small, wrapped in brown paper and twine, and had evidently been delivered by messenger. She was suddenly afraid to open it.

Adam produced a wicked looking knife from somewhere under the table. She suspected he carried it strapped to his leg or in his boot, a habit shared by many military men. He sliced through the twine as if it were thread, and gave her a nod of encouragement.

The paper peeled away to reveal a dark blue velvet box and she realized what was afoot. She put it aside, intending to send it back unopened.

"You are such a tease, Aunt Grace." Dianthe smiled. "Open it, for heaven's sake. The curiosity will be the end of me."

Adam raised one eyebrow. "Can't have that, can we?"

Even Mrs. Dewberry looked on eagerly.

Reluctantly, Grace lifted the lid. Nestled in the blue velvet was a necklace of small diamonds with a large baroque pearl dangling at its center. The piece was stunning in its beauty and complexity. Beneath the necklace was an envelope with her name in a spidery script.

"Read the note, Aunt Grace. I warrant 'tis Lord Barrington wanting to change his mind."

Knowing it could be nothing good, she unfolded the paper and read silently.

Beloved Grace,

Please forgive me. I cannot say how deeply ashamed I am of my vile temper. The only thing I can offer in my defense is that when I saw you with those men, all of them competing for your attention, I was insanely jealous. I did not realize until that moment how my feelings for you had changed and how empty my life would be without you.

Honor me by accepting this paltry trinket as a token of my regret and sincere hope that you will accept my apology and allow me to call upon you again.

Your humble servant,

Lord Ronald Barrington

How could he think he could play upon her emotions so easily? She knew from bitter experience that once a barrier had been breeched, the second time was easier, and the third easier still. It was always like this—the argument, the abuse, the effusive apology afterward coupled with gifts, bribes and promises that it would never happen again. But it always did, sooner or later. No, if she did not want to replace Leland with Barrington, and if she wanted to live free of fear and intimidation, she must stand firm.

She ripped the note into shreds, dropped the pieces in the box, replaced the lid, and handed it to Mrs. Dewberry. "Please ask Mr. Dewberry to return this to Lord Barrington at once."

Mrs. Dewberry looked doubtful but took the box and hurried from the room.

"Thank heavens," Dianthe murmured.

Surprised, Grace asked, "Whatever do you mean?"

"I was always half afraid Lord Barrington might be mistreating you and that you were afraid to leave him. I could think of no other reason for you to remain with him."

Dear heaven! If Dianthe had seen, how many others might have thought the same? "Why would you suspect he was mistreating me?"

"He reminds me of Squire Samuels, back in Little Upton. The squire was always jovial and charming, and everyone in the village thought that he was ever so agreeable, but he often spoke condescendingly to his wife, and she always bore the strangest bruises. Of course, no one ever thinks a child notices such things, but it was as plain as the nose on your face what was going on."

"And you thought Barrington was…"

Dianthe smiled and leaned forward to pat her hand. "'Twas the way he would talk to you sometimes—so condescending and superior. I never saw any bruises, but thank heavens it never came to that, Aunt Grace. If I thought it had…well, I just don't know what I might have done. Or the ladies."

"The ladies?" Adam repeated.

"Aunt Grace's bluestocking society. The Wednesday League. They are all the best of friends." Dianthe smiled proudly. "They have made me a member."

Adam finished his coffee and gave Grace a nod as he stood. "I'm off to renew acquaintances, ladies. Please excuse me."

"Will you be home for dinner?" Dianthe asked.

Adam smiled. "I would not miss the meals for anything. I have not eaten so well in years." He turned when he reached the door, a thoughtful look on his face. "Do you ladies have any plans for the evening?"

"I agreed to accompany Miss Talbot to a musicale tonight. If I do not go, she will only have her brother, and you know what a dull lot they can be."

Laura Talbot? Ah, Dianthe was doing her part to keep Miss Talbot safe. Her brother could not harm her if she was to be seen in society, and with her wedding to Lord Geoffrey so close.

"Miss Talbot has a brother?" Adam asked. He smiled again, winking slyly at Dianthe. "Is he handsome, Di?"

She grimaced in horror. "Me and Mr. Talbot? What a ghastly thought!"

Adam laughed and turned to look at Grace. "And you, Grace? Are you going out this evening?"

She nodded. "Belmonde's." Now that she was well-known in several hells, she knew she would not be denied entry, but going alone would make her quite vulnerable. Perhaps she should take additional funds in case she was required to buy a subscription.

He regarded her for a long moment and Grace prepared herself for an argument. He would, no doubt, list all the excellent reasons why that would be a bad idea, not the least of which that it was Sunday. Men always thought they knew best but sometimes they could not see the subtle nuances of social protocol.

"Do you have an escort?" he asked.

"I…no."

"You do now. After dinner?"

Surprised, she nodded again, a soft warmth stealing through her. Oh, this was not a good sign.

Adam took Grace's cloak in the foyer of Belmonde's and handed it to a footman. By the way she was dressed, he judged her state of mind to be worse than he'd thought. She wore a light aqua confection with a scandalously low décolletage edged in transparent white lace. The sleeves were long and loose, covering her bruises. A braiding of aqua and white silk ribbons tied beneath her breasts trailed enticingly to the floor where a small puddle of fabric in back made a train. An aqua ribbon was woven through the coil of dark hair at her nape and a necklace of tiny pearls with an aqua stone in the center called attention to the lush curve of her breasts. Grace had dressed to enchant any man with blood running through his veins. And Adam had as much blood as the next man, though it had all just rushed to one part of his body.

They purchased counters before they strolled into the main salon. There were fewer people here tonight than last night, and the conversation hushed as their entry was noted—testimony to the fact that at least some of them had been discussing the events of the previous night. He felt Grace's step falter, but she quickly regained her composure. He glanced down at her and saw the little lift of her chin. Determination? Pride? Undoubtedly courage.

Adam realized just how right she'd been in her decision to return to Belmonde's tonight. Any rumors or speculation would be stilled by her appearance—hale, hardy and unbowed.

He leaned close to Grace's ear and whispered, "I am awed by your strategy, Mrs. Forbush. There isn't a man here who isn't impressed with your presence."

She smiled up at him, those dark, fathomless eyes swallowing him completely. "Thank you, Mr. Hawthorne. I had begun to doubt the wisdom of coming, but the sooner any gossip ends, the better I will like it. I think I should circulate."

He saw Freddie Carter in one corner of the main salon and acknowledged him with a nod. Had the man found something of interest and come looking for him? "I'd like to say hello to an old friend, but I'll catch up to you in a bit."

Grace looked relieved, her attention on the vingt-et-un table. "Take your time, Mr. Hawthorne. I will not be far."

Lord Geoffrey Morgan turned toward her from his place at the table as she approached. A slow smile lit his face as he moved aside slightly to make a place for her. "Ah, Mrs. Forbush! I am pleased to see you tonight. You have not abandoned your quest for excitement?"

She gave him her best carefree smile. "Not in the least, Lord Geoffrey. I fear I have become quite hopelessly addicted."

Lord Geoffrey took her hand and bowed gallantly. "I knew you would be back. I had money on it," he admitted.

"Indeed? My return tonight was made the subject of wagers? *La!* 'Twas never in doubt."

"I suspected as much. But now I owe you."

"How so?"

"Your appearance tonight has made me quite a sum, Mrs. Forbush." He pressed a dozen counters into her palm. "And here are your whist winnings from last night."

She glanced down at the counters, surprised. She had not suspected they had won so much. "I shall have to think of a way to make the most of this."

"What is your game tonight?"

"I haven't decided yet." She looked around the table, taking note of the players. She knew some of them by sight and others not at all. "Perhaps a hand or two of vingt-et-un and then a turn at the hazard table."

"Whist?" he suggested with a devilish gleam in his eyes.

"Hmm. Do you think we could find company as congenial as last night?"

He laughed. "Picquet, then?"

At last, a game for two where they could wager each other directly, without the intervention of the house or partners. "I have not yet learned all the rules. Will you teach me?"

"That, and anything else you may like to learn," he purred. "But first, vingt-et-un."

She glanced toward Adam. It was not difficult to pick him out of a crowd, even in these dimly lit rooms. Tall, dark, tanned and elegant, he caught every female eye. He moved with a casual confidence that must have come from his vast

experiences. Even in buckskins she had thought him one of
the most handsome men she'd ever seen, and he'd lost none
of that cachet going from buckskins to evening clothes. Her
heart bumped when she recalled how compelling his lips had
been, how thrilling his touch. He was conversing with a man
she didn't know, looking quite intense. From the look of them,
he'd be occupied for quite some time.

"Mrs. Forbush?"

She blinked and returned her attention to Lord Geoffrey.
She placed several counters on the table and nodded to the
dealer. "I am in," she said.

Adam studied Grace from across the room, scarcely hearing Freddie. He did not like the look on Morgan's face. The
man was hell-bent on seduction and Grace was far too vulnerable. Morgan, it seemed, was making his bid to be Grace's
next lover. Adam would have to put a stop to it, and soon.

"It's the oddest thing, Hawthorne. Every time I think I
have a hint of something unusual, it turns out to be nothing.
But there's even something odd about that. No one is so
squeaky clean as Mrs. Forbush. The closest I can come to any
scandal is the rumor that her husband's death was not completely natural."

"Are you certain?" Adam murmured, his attention still riveted to Grace.

"That there is something suspicious in the lack of gossip?
Or that her husband's death was not completely natural?"

"Either. Both."

"Did you hear me? Not a breath of scandal since her husband's death! No hint of anything shady. She cannot be paying hush money to everyone in London. *Is* she a saint,
Hawthorne? You've seen enough of her to know her character."

Yes. He had. And he still couldn't answer that question.
Grace Forbush was a woman in her prime. She was sensual

and seductive. She was vulnerable but strong, social but independent, open but secretive, worldly but oddly innocent. She was a paradox and uniquely herself. And he could not sleep at night just thinking of her lying in her bed down the hall from him. He'd stood outside her door every night, one hand on the knob, knowing that, one day very soon, he would open that door.

Carter nodded. "That you cannot answer is answer enough—she cannot be what she seems."

"What is said of her marriage?"

"That it was agreeable. That your uncle was fond of her but occasionally cross and prone to deep depressions and was heard to express concern that he could not keep her content."

Adam sighed. Could Grace's appetites have been more than his uncle could accommodate? Which appetites? The hell of it was that those reports could mean almost anything. He'd give a fortune for one straightforward answer to any of the questions. "What is said of Uncle Basil's death?"

Carter looked uncomfortable. "That the onset was sudden and the end was quick," he admitted. "From the time it was first reported to the end, perhaps a fortnight or less."

"And?"

"And that his wife was devastated. She had started to consult a round of doctors, determined to find one that could help him. Then he went very quickly. 'Tis likely the speed of his decline that spurred the rumors of foul play."

"Lord Barrington?"

"He was your uncle's friend of long-standing, and called frequently during his last days. Afterward, he…well, he helped your aunt with business matters. Rumor has it that 'twas then that he and Mrs. Forbush became acquainted. A year later, when she was out of mourning, they began keeping company. For a short period, her name was linked to several other powerful men, as well, but soon only Barrington was left."

So Barrington had hung around and outlasted the others? But what had Grace seen in him? Adam glanced at the tableau at the vingt-et-un table again. Morgan was laughing and Grace turned to him, a smile curving those luscious, full lips—lips he could still taste. His body betrayed him in the most basic way as he watched her lay her hand on Morgan's sleeve and say something that made the man laugh again.

Bloody hell! He needed the truth before it was too late to extricate himself from her life. "Did she kill my uncle?"

The man shook his head regretfully. "Impossible to know at this stage."

"Keep digging," Adam said.

Chapter Eight

Grace stretched and yawned luxuriously as the coach lurched into motion. Her cloak fell open to reveal a wide expanse of creamy flesh above the lace trim of her neckline. Adam couldn't keep his gaze from the way the aqua fabric of her gown tightened against her breasts, causing them to swell above the lace, and the way the chill night air firmed the little buds beneath the light fabric. Pray God, she didn't notice his fascination. Or the effect it was having on him.

He cleared his throat and repositioned himself against the leather squabs to ease the aching in his groin. "Did you enjoy yourself tonight, Grace?" he asked, seeking any diversion from his rising fantasies.

She turned to him and smiled. "I think we were quite successful in squelching the gossip. I did not even hear anyone speculate about why you should accompany me. I believe you are fitting in nicely. Yes, all told, a good night's work."

That comment surprised him. Had Grace been concerned about him? Or was she commenting on his new position as her escort? Before he could ask, she leaned toward him, took his hand and squeezed it. "Thank you, Adam. You have made what could have been a very uncomfortable evening into an enjoyable one. You cannot know how much I appreciate it."

Her touch raced through him like a shock of electricity. Could he believe her? Could he risk his unexpected feelings for her to cloud his judgment? But caution, as well as restraint, was damned hard to practice when he looked at Grace.

And, when the coach rounded a corner and Grace fell against him, his need surged upward, straining against the boundaries of his self-control. Those treacherous unprincipled needs. They had no conscience.

They had begun to run riot, from the most basic need to couple to the more complex need to find his place in society. He had sublimated those needs for the past four years to the needs of the tribe. His hunger for family had been delayed for tribal justice. He had denied his desire for home and belonging to find the savage murderers who had decimated the Indian village. And his longing for a meaningful future had been subjugated to the uncertainty that he would even have a future at the end of that bloody journey.

Finally back in England, he'd been all too ready to fill the void left by his uncle. Grace and Dianthe had become his family. Their smiles filled his empty soul, their lives twined inextricably through his. And this made him vulnerable to deception. He'd believe anything because he *wanted* to believe.

More than that. He *needed* to believe in Grace, to believe she could not be guilty of anything devious or underhanded. He needed to believe that a woman so beautiful in every way, a woman whose portrait had captured his imagination even before he'd met her, was not capable of what she'd been accused of in whispers and rumors. Of an act that would make Grace unredeemable.

He'd already begun to care for her more than he should. Those flashes of quickly hidden vulnerability she'd revealed hinted at the deep passion and buried hurts that lay beneath her cool exterior. He wanted to see and to feel that passion more than he'd ever wanted anything.

She turned and smiled up at him, and his lust rose again, full and demanding. He said the first thing that came to his mind. "I'd be happy to escort you whenever you'd like to go gambling."

She leaned toward him in confidentiality, her shoulder pressing against his. "You make a wonderful accomplice, Adam. Did you win or lose tonight?"

He gave her a veiled smile. "Won."

"Lord Geoffrey attempted to teach me piquet. I fear the rules are fairly complex. I shall have to buy a copy of *Hoyle's Rules* and study them. I lost." She laughed. "Heavily."

He regarded her somberly. Why would losing make her giddy? "You do not mind losing?"

"I would not want to lose all the time, but the game itself is so exhilarating that I do not mind."

"So you really are seeking excitement?" he asked, realizing for the first time that he had never believed that excuse.

Her smile faded and she turned introspective. "Oh, dear. I believe I am."

Did she even half realize how enchanting she was? Drawn to her, unable to resist the pull, he leaned toward her and lowered his lips to hers. Her lashes fell to veil her eyes and she surrendered with a little sigh, her soft full lips parting to receive him. He lost himself for a time, unaware of anything but the heat of her mouth, the taste of her lips, the shy way she melted into his arms. When he left her lips to savor the exposed column of her neck beneath her ear, she moaned in protest, turning her head to catch his earlobe gently between her teeth.

"Come back to me," she whispered, her breath a hot tickle in his ear.

Chill bumps rose on his arms. "Patience," he counseled. "I'll be there in a moment." He slid his hand upward to catch the coil of hair at the back of her head. His intention to unwind that tight chignon was forgotten when she moaned again, and he could do nothing but return to her lips. Her sighs inspired him. Her moans commanded him. She kissed like a virgin—innocent and hungry at the same time. The shy heat of her tongue touching his was almost experimental. Had she never kissed like this before? How had his uncle neglected such sweet instruction?

When she relinquished his mouth with a little sigh, he moved lower. She arched as he found the heated spot at the base of her throat. Her pulse beat against his lips in a wildly erratic rhythm. God! She had ignited like parched tinder. Her fingers tightened on his arms, biting into the fabric of his coat, and her breathing deepened. She was so responsive that he was driven to take her as far as she'd let him.

He slid her cloak off her shoulders to bare the creamy expanse of skin. Nibbling and kissing a path from her throat downward, he nudged her décolletage lower to free one breast. Her gasp was his reward as he closed his mouth over the firmed peak. She arched to him, cupping his head, tangling her slender fingers through his hair to hold him closer.

"Adam…" she moaned as he eased her down on the seat.

He'd been right. She was a woman made for love. With his other hand, he reached downward to sweep up her skirts. He was hard and aching for her, and she would know that. Aye, as a woman of experience, Grace would know full well what her responses were doing to him, and she would know that her encouragement was an invitation in itself. Pray she was not just caught up in a moment of passion. Pray she would feel this way tomorrow in the harsh light of day.

He skimmed his hand up one shapely leg, past her stockings and garter. When he reached bare skin, he moved his hand to the heat of her inner thigh.

She sucked in a deep gasp and shuddered. "Stop!" She fought for breath, a note of panic in her voice.

Reluctantly, confused and disoriented, he released her. Was she playing coy? How could she be so responsive one moment and panicked the next? "Easy, Grace," he said calmly. He smoothed her skirts down over her legs and edged away from her as she struggled to sit upright again.

She seemed embarrassed by her outburst. "I…we should be home soon," she explained in a breathless whisper, as if afraid Mr. Dewberry would hear her from his position outside in the driver's box.

"Of course," he said.

She busied herself putting her clothing to rights, tugging at her neckline and pulling the cloak back over her shoulders. When he moved to assist her, she shrank away from him, as if she were afraid he would hurt her in some way.

As he watched her, his anger rose. From what he'd learned of her so far, it was no wonder that she did not trust men. Whatever her previous lovers had done to her, *he* was paying the price. Or perhaps it was simply too soon after Lord Barrington for her to take another lover.

The coach pulled up at their door in Bloomsbury Square and Mr. Dewberry climbed down from the box to open the coach door. "'Ere we are, all safe an' sound," he proclaimed.

Grace took Dewberry's hand, stepped down and hurried into the house, leaving Adam and Mr. Dewberry standing at the curb.

"'Ard night, sir?" Mr. Dewberry asked.

Adam gave him a mirthless laugh. "You could say that." *Very hard, indeed, and still was.*

Late the next morning, John Ogilby, a balding, paunchy man of middle years, sat back in his chair at his office in Holburn and studied Adam through narrowed lids. "Are you accusing Mrs. Forbush of something, Mr. Hawthorne? Or me?"

"Not in the least," Adam appeased. He glanced around

the well-appointed office. Rich paneling and lush fabric told a story of wealthy clients and high fees. His uncle must have paid a pretty price to have Ogilby handle his affairs—a price Ogilby would be loathe to give up—and that could work to Adam's advantage. He smiled, deciding on his strategy. "In fact, I intend to continue my uncle's relationship with your firm once the settlements are finalized. I am only concerned that Mrs. Forbush may be living a little…recklessly. From all I've been told, her interest in gambling is a recent development."

Adam could see the wheels clicking in Ogilby's brain. "Hmm, yes, well, I see what you mean."

"I regret that my return has caused her undue stress, but there is nothing I can do about that. She has said that she instructed her factor to separate my estate from my uncle's, but that it would take a little time."

"Yes." Ogilby nodded. "I've been in contact with Mr. Evans, her factor. We are in the process of reconstructing the Forbush finances prior to the acquisition of your assets. We should be finished in another few weeks."

"That's just the point, sir. At the rate Mrs. Forbush is gambling, the assets may be gone by then." Adam squirmed with the gross exaggeration, but he needed to find a way to check Grace's descent into gambling ignominy until they'd had a chance to sort through their mess. And, in all honesty, perhaps this was a bit of petty revenge for the sleepless night she had just caused him. If she was forced to stay at home more, perhaps she'd see a little less of men like Lord Geoffrey Morgan and Lord Reginald Hunter. And more of him.

"Very well, sir. I see your point. I fear all we can do is freeze her assets until the settlements have been agreed upon and finalized in the courts."

"But for her living expenses, of course," Adam prompted.

"Of course."

The second part of his business was going to take more finesse. "I gather my uncle's will was current when he died?"

The solicitor glanced down at a sheaf of papers and rearranged some of the sheets. "Quite. He changed it after we had the news of your death."

Adam nodded and sat back in his chair, waiting.

"Ah, until that point, he'd left all to you, with the exception of an annuity and dower rights to his widow." Ogilby shifted his weight in his chair and shuffled a few more papers. "I do not know what you might wish to do about that, Mr. Hawthorne. If you'd like, we can petition the Chancellery court for a hearing on the validity of a will made in response to erroneous information. It is possible that they would reinstate the original will, and you would inherit the bulk. It is not an inconsiderable sum, sir—somewhere in the range of 250,000 pounds."

Actually, Adam did not care in the least how his uncle Basil had bequeathed his property. He wanted what was his returned to him, but the rest was of little concern. Ah, but freezing Grace's funds pending a court hearing would certainly slow her down at the vingt-et-un table.

What neither Grace nor Mr. Ogilby knew was that, as of noon today, Adam would be officially reinstated with the Diplomatic Corps, including four years of retroactive pay and the thanks of a grateful nation, whatever that meant. He'd asked Lord Craddock to keep this news quiet for a few weeks.

"I am afraid I am at my aunt's mercy at the moment, Mr. Ogilby. If I made a request of that nature, I believe the atmosphere at home would become quite uncomfortable."

Ogilby literally twitched, confirming Adam's suspicion that something was not quite right with the settlements. He let the silence stretch out, leaving Ogilby no choice but to make the offer.

"I, er, could file the petition in my own name as the solicitor of record. The request would not have to come from you directly, sir, nor from your…Mrs. Forbush."

Adam smiled. "Thank you, sir. I think that would be best. I am indebted to you."

Ogilby nodded but did not look happy. "I shall prepare the papers at once. I shall also inform Mrs. Forbush as soon as the court impounds her accounts. Since her situation is urgent, that could be as early as this afternoon."

Adam was not looking forward to her reaction to that news.

Grace read the letter from her solicitor for the third time. "I cannot believe this," she breathed.

Dianthe put her teacup aside and frowned with concern. "What is it, Aunt Grace? Another letter from Lord Barrington?"

"No. I almost wish it were. 'Twould be easier to deal with."

"Is it from Miss Talbot?"

Grace shook her head and passed the page to Dianthe. She stood and paced the breadth of the sitting room. How could things have gotten so out of hand? Could it be just a week ago that her life had been calm and completely within her control? Where had it all gone wrong? Laura Talbot? No, of course not. The Wednesday League had been involved in much more complicated and dangerous investigations than this one.

Behind her she heard a gasp and knew Dianthe had reached the part of the letter where her solicitor explained that her funds had been frozen. She shrugged. She had never been acquisitive or even cared about how much money she had in her accounts. She only needed enough to ensure her independence, and if the court decided in favor of the old will, she would still have an annuity and dower rights unless the truth were known—then complete disinheritance was a distinct possibility. And complete disinheritance meant poverty, and poverty meant a return to Leland's control. And Leland's control would surely destroy her. Destroy her as surely as if he refused to take her in. Either way, the future would be grim, indeed.

She stopped her pacing and turned to study Dianthe. The girl's head was bowed over the letter from Mr. Ogilby. Dianthe was almost heartbreakingly beautiful. Her pale blond hair fell to the middle of her back in silken shimmers and her clear blue eyes were so innocent and open that Grace feared for her. Women without artifice, beautiful women, did not fare well in London society. They were too easy prey for scoundrels. Everywhere they went, at least three men danced attendance on Dianthe, and Grace had been approached by several men who wanted to know whom they might address for permission to call. She had instructed them to ask Dianthe herself and, so far, none had come calling. For Dianthe's sake, if nothing else, Grace needed to keep herself focused and solvent. For Laura Talbot's sake, as well.

She would sooner become a kept mistress to one of the many men who'd suggested that in the past four years than be returned to Leland's control or leave Dianthe to her own devices. But then she'd have to bed them! She'd managed to avoid that so far, and hoped to continue her success.

Bed them? Adam Hawthorne's face rose to her mind, as it had looked last night in the coach. Heavy-lidded eyes boring into hers, stripping away her defenses and peeking beneath her carefully constructed lies! Oh, what she would give to stop living those lies! To stop pretending to be something she wasn't. To surrender herself to Adam's passion. She had never thought she would allow such intimacies again but, last night, she had nearly succumbed entirely. She was still oddly restless when she thought about it.

Adam! Ah, *that* was when her problems began. From the moment he'd arrived on her doorstep, her life had spun out of control. Everything had changed—from her ability to maintain her cool self-possession to calling into question decisions she'd made years ago.

Guilt washed through her as she sat in the overstuffed chair by the fireplace. No, she could never begrudge Adam his return home, nor could she blame him for her confusion. He had more right to be here than she. Heavens, she could not leave, but how could she get through the next several weeks until she'd cornered Lord Geoffrey and liberated Miss Talbot? She had to focus on that alone.

"Goodness, Aunt Grace," Dianthe said. "What are we going to do?"

"Nothing *can* be done. Mr. Ogilby said he would pay our daily expenses out of my funds until the court has made a decision. We will not be out of a home or starve. We shall simply have to budget our remaining resources and refrain from any unnecessary purchases."

"Your lovely new gown at Madame Marie's? Will you be able to pay for it?"

"I have reimbursed madame for the materials, but I will have to ask her to wait for the remainder. I shall insist she keep the gown until she is fully reimbursed, of course."

"And—" Dianthe paused, looking more concerned than Grace had ever seen her "—what of your gambling? How will that be accomplished without funds?"

"Oh, drat!" Grace stood and began pacing again. How could she ever persuade Geoffrey Morgan to wager with her if he knew she had no money? Grace was too savvy in the ways of London gossip to think this sort of news would be secret for long. Lord Geoffrey would hear of it within a day or two at the most. She must think of a way to counteract rumors or, at least, the effects. She turned back to Dianthe. "This news could not have come at a worse time! I shall have to find money somewhere."

"I confess I am worried about Miss Talbot," Dianthe said. She frowned and appeared to search for words. "I am deeply disturbed by the way her brother talks to her—as if she has no brains at all. At one point last evening, when Miss Talbot conversed with a young man of whom her brother did not approve, he squeezed her arm so tightly that she had bruises. Then, when someone asked her about them later, she lied about how she had come by them. It put me in mind of Squire Samuels again, and you know what that means."

Yes, indeed. Dianthe could have been describing Grace's relationship with Leland, and when she recalled the day before when she'd lied to Dianthe about the bruises she'd received at Barrington's hands, she could not still the shudder that ran through her. She wondered if Dianthe would have guessed the truth about Leland if she'd visited the Yorks more often. No, she could not abandon Laura Talbot. In fact, she would beg, borrow or steal whatever was necessary to save the girl from a loveless marriage and an abusive brother.

"Yes, Dianthe, I know," she said. "I shall do whatever is necessary to secure Miss Talbot's happy future."

Coming in through the kitchen door from the stables, Adam was passing the sitting room on his way to the stairs when he overheard Dianthe ask Grace in dismay what they were going to do. Grace had gotten the notice from Mr. Ogilby, then. An unexpected twinge of conscience made him uneasy. It was, after all, his fault that Grace couldn't pay her bills.

Things had certainly become twisted since he'd come to live at Bloomsbury Square. One moment Grace looked suspicious as hell and the next she was so innocently straightforward that he could not suspect her of anything devious or underhanded.

"I shall have to find money somewhere."

That statement stopped him dead in his tracks. Was Grace *that* desperate to gamble? He went back to the sitting room door and listened for a moment, but the conversation had turned to Laura Talbot.

"I shall do whatever is necessary to secure Miss Talbot's happy future."

What did this Miss Talbot have to do with any of this? How was Grace responsible for her? And what would that have to do with her gambling? And exactly how far *would* Grace go to secure Miss Talbot's future?

He shook his head, suddenly sick of all the secrets. Something very odd was afoot, and he'd damn well find out what it was.

Chapter Nine

Late afternoon sun streamed through the leaded glass panes of the library windows, illuminating the neatly stacked rows of books. Grace knew it had to be here somewhere. There could only be eight or nine hundred volumes or so in the entire collection. She moved the stepladder again and climbed to the highest shelf. She'd last seen it where Basil kept the books he felt were unsuitable for women, well out of her reach.

Human Physiology or some such obscure title. Or was it *Human Anatomy*? Perhaps it was with the biology or medical volumes. She needed the book because this was not a question she could ask a doctor. Or was it? Would a doctor feel the same need to protect her delicacy now that it was presumed she was an independent widow?

"Doing the high dusting?" a feminine voice asked.

Grace glanced over her shoulder. Charity MacGregor was standing in the doorway. She had forgotten she had asked Charity to come for tea today. Relief washed through her. Charity's uncle had been a doctor! Perhaps she would know.

"No, just looking for an elusive volume," she confessed as she backed down the ladder. She pulled Charity into the room and closed the door. "I am glad you're here, Charity. I'd like to have some rather frank words with you."

"Heavens. This sounds serious." Charity pulled her gloves off and removed her bonnet before taking a chair. "I hope nothing is wrong, Grace. Is it Morgan? Is he troubling you?"

"Yes. I mean, no. It is not Lord Geoffrey, it is…something else. I hoped you might be able to answer a few questions."

"Anything, Grace." She gestured at the teapot on the low table in the center of the group of chairs. "May I?"

"Please do." Grace sat across from Charity and glanced at the clock on her desk. She only had a few minutes before Dianthe would be down for tea and she did not want this to be a group discussion. The subject was not fit for Dianthe's ears.

She breathed deeply and launched forth. "I have recently had occasion…well, suffice it to say that the subject of virginity came up."

"We are certainly no virgins, Grace." Charity paused and a little blush stole up her cheeks. "And Drew makes certain of it often."

"Of course not." Grace smiled. "The question is more academic than personal. To wit, how would a man know, with any degree of certainty, whether his bride is a virgin or not?"

"And you are asking *me?*" Charity's mouth drew up in a smile and she looked as if she would laugh. "Wouldn't a man know the answer to that better than a woman?"

"Possibly. But I do not want to have this conversation with a man. I thought you might have overheard discussions, or had occasion to glance at medical texts. I know your uncle was a doctor, and thought…well, that you could…uh…" She shrugged.

Charity giggled and winked. "I knew sneaking into my uncle's study to look at those books would prove invaluable some day." She sat back in her chair and took a sip of tea. "Well, I cannot say with certainty. But neither could a man. I used to wonder about that myself. And I wondered how many virtuous women were shamed or shunned by their husbands because some childhood accident or simple deficiency deprived her of that little membrane."

Grace knew about the membrane, but, "Then you think men cannot positively know?"

"Absolutely not," she declared, "unless the barrier is obviously present and there is bleeding. An examination by a qualified physician could verify if the membrane was still there, but not what might have broken or removed it, if not. But then, of course, the membrane could be ruptured by the examination. And I gather the blood evidence can be anywhere from nonexistent, to a drop, to near hemorrhage."

"So you think not every virgin has a maidenhead?"

Charity shrugged. "I suppose. And conversely, I've heard that many not-so-innocent brides have been able to effectively deceive their grooms."

Grace nodded. "So if one could feign innocence, it stands to reason that one could also feign experience?"

"I suppose, but what would be the advantage to feigning experience?"

Grace's entire future hinged upon it, that's what—her right to inherit from Basil, most importantly. Surely, with all Basil's groping and desperate attempts to force himself into her, there would be no trace left of her maidenhead. In fact, she recalled one such incident when she had experienced some bleeding. At the time she had thought it was due to abrasion, but perhaps not. Yes, it was unlikely that there would be anything left that could prove absolutely that her marriage had been unconsummated.

Nearly weak with relief, she sat back in her chair and exhaled. "How odd that I have been unable to find anything that would answer that question," she mused.

Charity giggled. "Not so odd when you consider who writes those books. But what has you thinking about such things?"

"Just, uh, recent events."

"Oh! Say it is not Miss Talbot! If her brother ever found out that she was not a virgin, I cannot imagine what would happen. And Lord Geoffrey! Why he'd renounce her!"

"No, not Miss Talbot." Grace laughed, feeling at least twenty pounds lighter. "Purely academic."

Charity raised her eyebrows. "Who in the world are you having these interesting conversations with?"

The sound of footsteps on the stairway and a light voice humming carried to her from beyond the door. It would be Dianthe. Perfect timing.

Lord Barrington's clerk stood as Adam entered the outer office. He looked even more frightened than he had when Adam had arrived in buckskins, and Adam wondered if Barrington had left instructions to deny him an appointment. Well, he'd test that resolve right now.

"Barrington," he said, letting the single word speak for him.

"Not in, sir. If you will leave your name, I will send you an appointment date."

"I'll wait." Adam glanced at the straight-backed chair opposite the clerk's cramped desk.

"But, sir. Lord Barrington is not in."

"Check his office," he suggested.

The clerk flushed and glanced toward Barrington's private office. "I, um…"

Adam looked toward the clerk's desk again and read the miniscule name plaque. "Save it, Jameson. I know he's here. I don't care what he's in the middle of, or whom he is meeting with, I'll wait until he sees me."

"But—"

"I suggest, for both our sakes, that you let him know I'm waiting."

Adam saw the signs of surrender in the man's eyes.

Jameson edged toward Barrington's door. "If you'll take a seat, sir."

But he was not inclined to follow instructions. He crossed his arms and leaned one shoulder against the wall in an attitude of expectancy. The clerk slipped through Barrington's door and closed it quickly, as if afraid that Adam would force his way through. Not a bad idea, actually. But he was not quite that desperate yet.

A few moments later Jameson, flushed and pinched-looking, exited the office and nodded to Adam. "You may go in now, sir."

He found Barrington sitting behind his desk, a scowl fixed on his face. Was the man embarrassed by his boorish behavior two nights ago, or was he angry with Adam for some reason?

"What do you want, Hawthorne?" he asked.

"The name I asked you for, Lord Barrington. I am still waiting."

"Name?" Barrington dropped his pen on his blotter. "Ah, yes. The field commander at Fort Garry, was it not?"

"No. The military attaché," he corrected. He'd be willing to wager Barrington knew full well what name he wanted.

"Haven't come across those records, yet. I told you I'd send it along when I found it."

Barrington was lying. He knew precisely where to find that information. Adam was finished with diplomacy. "Since this task seems to be beyond your skills or capacity, I withdraw my request. I shall find the name on my own."

Barrington's jaw tightened and his eyes narrowed. Ah, it *was* personal. Having accomplished what he'd come for, Adam turned and headed for the door.

"Hawthorne?"

He turned, one hand on the knob. Naked contempt shown in Barrington's eyes.

"Keep out of Grace's business. You have no idea what you are trifling with."

A flash of Grace braced for attack with the poker clutched between her hands rose to taunt him and a primal anger surged upward. Releasing the knob, he crossed the room to Barrington's desk and leaned over it, his fists on the desk's surface. In a low, deadly tone, he said, "There is nothing trifling about what I am doing, Barrington. Leave Grace alone. If I hear that you've so much as touched the hem of her skirt again, I'll come looking for you, and it won't be good."

Barrington sneered. "You've been too long in the colonies."

Or not long enough, he thought, heading back for the door.

"Watch your back, or you'll be her next victim."

Adam threw the door open and the glass pane rattled in its frame. He was halfway down the stairs before the words sank in. What the hell did the man mean? How would he be Grace's next victim? Her next conquest? Too late for that warning!

Adam was waiting for Freddie Carter by the time he arrived at the Eagle Tavern. He tossed his whiskey down and pulled Freddie outside into the creeping darkness. The square was filled with peddlers hawking their merchandise, and coaches passed slowly, looking for fares.

Adam took the reins of his horse from the lad he'd paid to watch him. "I haven't much time, Carter. I have an engagement in scarce an hour."

"Urgent business?"

He smiled. "You could say that. But I needed to talk to you. Barrington is not going to give me the name I requested. I want you to put everything else aside and get me it for me."

Freddie cocked an eyebrow. "What can you give me to go on?"

"The man would be military, likely an officer, attached to the forces at Fort Garry in '16. He'd be in a position to receive military packets from the War Office and report back to them. His name should be on several lists. Look for a report of an attack on an Indian village southeast of Winnipeg in December of 1815 or January of '16. Who signed it? That's the name I want."

Freddie nodded, all trace of amusement gone. "I'll see what I can do. It is not always easy to gain access to War Office records, but I have some friends who owe me favors."

Adam clapped the man on the arm. "My thanks, Carter. And don't use my name in military circles. I'm afraid it won't open any doors for you. I've made an enemy of Barrington."

A short bark of laughter was Carter's only response.

"Day or night, the minute—the very *second*—you have that information, I want to know."

"I'll find you. And what of the investigation on Mrs. Forbush?"

"I'll take care of Mrs. Forbush," Adam said, turning to go.

"Take *good* care, Adam. It seems she has some very powerful friends. And a few enemies, too."

Adam turned back. "Is there something I should know about those enemies?"

"Nothing yet, just some rather odd coincidences. I'll get back to you after I've found the name of your military attaché."

Adam mounted his horse, making a mental note to ask Grace who might have a grudge against her.

Grace stood on the cobbles outside the Two Sevens, waiting for Mr. Dewberry to bring the coach around from its position on a side street. The avenues were still busy, but no longer crowded. Adam shifted restlessly beside her. She knew she'd surprised him when she'd asked to go to Belmonde's next. At a little past midnight, she suspected he wanted to go home. So did she. But she hadn't run into Lord Geoffrey tonight and she wanted to be certain he did not forget her, or her interest in gambling.

She glanced sideways at Adam and smiled. In the short

time he'd been back, he was civilizing nicely. The hollows beneath his cheekbones had filled in and now she knew those
little indents when he smiled were dimples indeed, not just
the result of a Spartan diet. When he'd taken up residence with
them, she had ordered heavier fare than she and Dianthe usually ate—more sauces, gravies and meats—and Adam had
taken to it like a babe to mother's milk. He was so solid and
strong standing beside her that she sighed with satisfaction
that she'd had even the tiniest part in the restoration of his
health.

He must have sensed her attention because he looked down
at her and returned her smile. "I must compliment you on your
energy at this hour, Grace. You look so delicate, but you have
the stamina of a lioness."

She laughed. "Have I worn you out? Would you rather
go home?"

He shook his head in denial, returning his gaze to a spot
across the street. "I've spent longer days in a saddle." He lowered his head slightly and narrowed his eyes.

Grace turned to see what had drawn his attention. A man,
dressed in a dark cloak, was crossing the street. His head was
tucked down, his hands were in his pockets and he was headed
straight for them. She had taken Adam's arm and now felt his
muscles tighten through the fabric of his jacket. He moved
slightly in front of her and took a firm grip on her upper arm.

Moving faster now, nearly at a run, the man began to withdraw his right hand from his pocket. She gasped as Adam spun
her behind him and lowered his head. Releasing her, he rushed
the man just as a pistol fired. A ball whizzed past her left
shoulder, leaving a hot rush of air in its wake. Her knees
weakened when she realized that, had Adam acted half a second later, she'd be dead!

She watched with her heart in her throat as Adam knocked
the man off his feet. They rolled across the cobbles amid the

late night traffic. She feared he'd be trampled by a horse or passing carriage. Then the attacker scrambled out of Adam's grip and staggered to his feet as Adam came up and prepared to lunge again. A horse and rider rounded the corner and, in the confusion, rode between them. The horse reared, causing Adam to jump back out of the way and allowing the attacker to disappear around the corner.

Cursing explicitly, Adam scooped the gun up at a run. "Grace, are you injured?" he shouted, returning a long evil-looking knife to his boot.

"No!" She could scarcely catch her breath and felt as if her knees would give out at any second.

He turned and looked in the direction their attacker had escaped, then spun around, checking in all directions. "A horse!" he shouted to no one in particular. "Damn it, a horse!"

Mr. Dewberry pulled around the corner in the coach and Adam intercepted him, reaching for the lead horse's harness. Was he going to cut the leather leads? But how would he release the traces?

With a shout of pure animal frustration, Adam dropped his arms and stepped away, allowing the coach to pass. He pocketed the gun and came to her as Mr. Dewberry drew up. "Thank God," he said.

Gripping both her arms, he held her so tightly that something of his urgency reached her. His breath came out in a low groan as he hurried her to the coach and practically lifted her in. "I want you off the street and out of sight before there's another attack on you," he explained.

"Me? But who would want to injure me?" A sharp stab of fear shot through her. Adam had to be mistaken.

Leaning his forehead against Grace's bedroom door an hour later, Adam's heart was still hammering—even after two stiff brandies. He could hear her moving about in her room, the swish of her gown as it slid to the floor, and he envisioned her gloriously naked. His body sprang to full readiness and he suppressed a groan. Was he doomed to a state of perpetual arousal?

When he'd come upstairs from the library, he should have kept walking down the darkened hall, his discarded vest and cravat in his hand, but he still had so many questions, so many concerns. At this moment he'd give half his fortune to find the assassin and thrash him within an inch of his life. Unfortunately that was not to be. Getting Grace home and out of harm's way had been more important.

And even though he felt as if he were invading her privacy now, they had to talk. The incident outside the Two Sevens, coupled with Freddie's and Barrington's warnings, had taken an ominous turn. Someone wanted Grace dead. But what could she possibly have done to provoke such an attack?

She'd been stunned to silence in the coach, but a tapestry of emotions had played across her face. Fear? Confusion? Doubt? Disbelief? Whatever she felt, she was obviously shaken to her core. God knows he was. And he kept coming back to one central question. Why the hell would anyone want to harm Grace? And could it have something to do with whatever secret she was keeping?

In the course of his duties in the Diplomatic Corps, he had encountered assassins at work and would recognize their tactics anywhere. The singular way the man had fixed on Grace convinced him that she had been his target. But why?

Through the wooden door, he heard a deep sigh and the sound of a poker stirring the embers of a fire. He imagined her illuminated by firelight and his stomach tightened with desire. *Who?* Who could ever want to hurt that sweetly vulnerable woman?

Lord Barrington came immediately to mind. As far as he knew, Barrington was the only enemy she had. But even Barrington, whose position put him in the way of assassins, could not be angry enough to want Grace dead. Being jilted might sting one's pride but was no cause for murder. And though he'd never been in love, Adam suspected one did not go from love to hate in the space of an instant. Barrington's anger in his office earlier had likely come from frustration and jealousy, not hatred. Certainly not the sort one needed to commit murder.

Putting a watch on Barrington would do little good. The man would not conduct his own dirty work, nor would he be seen meeting publicly with a hired assassin. Still, a reminder would not go amiss. Adam smiled grimly into the darkened hallway. Yes, he'd find Barrington in a private moment and remind him that, should anything happen to Grace, he'd better have his will in order.

An object clattered to the floor and Grace's muffled voice uttered something that sounded suspiciously like a curse. He smiled to himself, relieved to know that she was human, after all, and not a goddess above the touch of mere mortal men. Thus encouraged, he knocked.

"Come in," she called.

He pushed the door open and stood frozen, his every fantasy rewarded. Grace, her back to him, was dressed in a gossamer-white nightdress and bending to retrieve her brush from the floor. Luxurious dark masses of hair swirled around her. The soft light from the fireplace filtered through her nightdress, revealing her form in relief. Willow-thin, supple, elegant curves and delicate hues were all displayed with a subtlety that heightened her allure. His mouth went dry and he struggled to swallow.

"I thought I told you to go to bed, Mrs. Dewberry. Truly, I do not want warm milk." She straightened and pushed her hair back over her shoulder as she turned.

Before he realized what he was doing, he took several

steps toward her. Her eyes widened and her lush lips parted to say something, but the words did not come. Clearly she had not expected to find him in her room. She looked frightened and vulnerable. Dear Lord, could she see his hunger, his need? Did she understand how close he was to falling upon her like a demon possessed?

"Adam?" Grace's soft voice pulled him from his thoughts and broke the hypnotic hold of her beauty.

When he tried to answer, his voice had gone tight and hoarse. He cleared his throat and tried again. "I should have announced myself."

She nodded, sweeping her dressing gown from the end of her bed and slipping it over her shoulders. "I thought…that Mrs. Dewberry had come back."

"We need to talk, Grace."

She tied the robe at her waist. "I've been thinking, Adam. I—I am not at all convinced that man meant to attack me."

"You think it was random?" he asked in disbelief.

"Perhaps he was mistaken, or he could have… I think I was not his target. I cannot imagine what I could have done or who I could have wronged to make someone want me dead."

"Then…"

"I think the killer wanted you."

That thought had crossed Adam's mind and had been quickly dismissed. His duties with the Diplomatic Corps had put him in line of many tense, unpleasant situations. He'd forged truces, engineered deals, twisted more than a few arms and reasoned with the unreasonable. In the process he had probably made his fair share of enemies. But political assassinations were generally reserved for top-ranking officials and heads of state. And the more clandestine assassinations were aimed at secret agents who had infiltrated the enemy's inner defenses. Who would target a midlevel diplomat? And why? No, he wasn't at all convinced that he had been the assassin's target. There was only one person he knew who might want him dead… Grace. He hadn't been back long enough to make that kind of enemy.

Exasperated, he rubbed the whiskers along his cheek. A fluke, then? Wrong place, wrong time? Pray so, but he doubted it. The attack had all the hallmarks of a professional assassination. It had been quite deliberate.

He looked back at Grace, studying her for any betraying sign, any flicker of the truth. "The only person who might want me dead is you."

"I? But why would I want you dead?"

"To circumvent the court decision on the validity of my uncle's will? So you won't have to return my property?"

She looked stricken. "No, Adam. No. I would never… I couldn't."

She couldn't have pretended her surprise. She couldn't be such a consummate actress. She looked so innocent with her hair falling loose around her in glorious dark curls, but there was nothing innocent in the lush curve of her breasts or the hint of darker flesh at the peaks. He lusted for her to the point of total distraction.

Grace stood motionless. On some basic level there was a recognition, almost an acknowledgment between them, of what was growing and working its will with them. She knew what he wanted. She had seen it coming. She had even begun to prepare herself for it. She dreaded it almost as much as she wanted it.

Every part of her tingled in anticipation. Her breathing deepened and she leaned toward him. Everything she was or ever would be hung in the balance. Step forward and risk everything, or step back and live her safe constricting lie? Neither seemed acceptable. It was insane—she knew it was—but she could not stop it. Terrified of what loving Adam would do to her, she froze in place.

He made the decision, taking another step toward her. He was intently focused on her, as if trying to read her mind. He closed the distance between them with a low, hungry moan and pulled her into his arms with possessive strength. His left hand splayed across the small of her back, pressing her so close against him that she could feel the rise and fall of his breathing. The warmth of his palm seduced her, lulled her into complacency. She looked up at him and was caught by the deep hunger in his eyes. There was something tortured, almost reluctant, there. Slowly, as if against his will, he lowered his mouth to hers.

As soft and tentative as a bird taking flight, his lips touched hers. Not a kiss. Not yet. More of a promise. He nibbled her lower lip, speaking softly in praise of her mouth, using words like *rich* and *full* and *plump* and *sweet*. Then, when he finally kept his promise, her head swam with the sweetness of it— as surprising as their first kiss in the library and as overwhelming as the madness in the coach when he'd nearly ravished her.

His fingers twined through her hair as he buried his face in the strands and inhaled deeply. "Like silk to the touch and as fragrant as cherry blossoms," he murmured.

Grace wanted to protest and to deny that there was anything admirable in her hair, but her knees had grown weak and she had to cling to his shoulders so she wouldn't collapse. His muscles flexed and tensed as he bent over her to pull her closer, stirring her hunger for more. The heat of his skin seeped through his shirt and warmed her, infusing her with the certainty that there was better to come.

He kissed her again, fastening his mouth to hers greedily. His tongue demanded, his touch defined, his embrace consumed—she'd never been so wholly possessed by a man, and the sensation was exhilarating. She wanted more, though she couldn't have said what, precisely, it was that she wanted.

Her robe slipped from her shoulders and Adam cast it aside. He swept her up and carried her to the bed, looking as darkly intense as she'd ever seen him. She ran her finger along his jawline, feeling the heavy rasp of his whiskers. How unlike Basil he was—how unlike any man she'd ever known. He was polished and smooth, but his edges were hard and rough. The contrasts intrigued and excited her.

He placed her against the pillows and stood back to shed his shirt. Her heartbeat tripped as his bared chest came into view. His skin was the color of dark honey, tanned by the sun, and the corded muscles of his chest and arms told of strength and endurance beyond the ordinary. She'd seen engravings of the North American Indians in moccasins and breechcloths, and recalled how Adam had looked when she'd found him in her library. Who was the real Adam? Who did she *want* him to be?

God help her, she wanted him to be a man strong enough to take her and foolish enough to keep her.

Take her? Her gaze dropped to the bulge straining against the confining fabric of his trousers. Heavens! Not like Basil at all! Dare she take the risk that he'd be able to tell? She struggled upright and gathered the gaping neck of her nightgown in her fist, retreating to the safety of her lie. "No, Adam!" she gasped. "No…"

He stood looking down at her, his jaw clenching and his hands fisted at his sides. His eyes had gone so dark that they were almost black. Had she pushed him too far?

With an elegant dignity, he swept his shirt off the floor and stepped back from the bed. "I'm not made of stone, Grace. Next time you go this far, you'd damned well better be sure you want to finish it."

Chapter Ten

Adam propped his pillows against the headboard and crossed his arms behind his head, watching the sunrise stain the sky with violet blending to pink nearer the horizon, outside his open window. Another night had passed. Another night of lying awake down the hall from Grace—Ellie, he called her in his fantasies. Whimsical, light-hearted Ellie York from Devon. Ellie, with the long, dark hair falling freely in ringlets. She danced through his dreams and resided permanently in the back of his mind. He found no rest with her there, and impossible to banish her, so alive, so alluring. She had come to embody all that was desirable in womanhood. The disturbing things he was beginning to uncover especially intrigued him, lured him like a siren's call deeper into her life.

He kicked his sheets aside, reveling in the sensation of the cool breeze moving across his skin. He missed the closeness to the elements he'd experienced in the wilds. Everything had been so basic there, so pure. Things were what they seemed. No intrigue, no hidden motives, no polite games. Theirs had been a harsh existence, sometimes cruel, but they understood the necessity of recompense as a deterrent. He'd reminded himself of that every time they'd caught up with one of the men who'd slaughtered the village. And before each bloody execution, he asked the same questions. Who ordered the attack? Who'd led them? Each time the answer was unsatisfactory. Long Knife.

He unfolded his arms and glanced at the beaded wristband he wore. A pattern of red, green and white beads sewn to the leather strap told the story of a buffalo hunt. It was his talisman, his *raison d'être,* his constant reminder of his obligation. Each time he looked at it, memories haunted him, nauseated him and colored his world a deep bloodred—memories that came upon him at odd times, waking and sleeping, and caused a mind-shattering fury to take control. *Berserker,* the Norse called it. His blood brothers respected it. His enemies feared it. And he was deeply ashamed of it, but incapable of stopping until the blood debt had been paid.

He'd come close last night to forgetting the past and claiming a piece of happiness. But the gods had deemed him unworthy and snatched it back. Could hands stained with so much blood touch anything clean and pure without corrupting it forever? No, if he had any sense at all, he'd get as far away from Grace as possible, and with every bit of speed he could muster. No matter what she'd done, she deserved better than he could bring her. Until he found justice for Nokomis and laid her ghost to rest, the berserker part of him would always be waiting, ever vigilant, for the chance to assert itself. He was unpredictable and capable of things most men never dreamed of in their worst nightmares. His ruthlessness rose to haunt him when he dared to sleep.

As unsettling as those dreams were, they were still almost preferable to his waking and sleeping thoughts of Grace. She wanted him as much as he wanted her. He knew that as surely as he knew the sun outside his window was rising. The look on her face and her abandoned responses last night were evidence of that. But she fought her own desire as fiercely as he'd fought his. She would have at least a dozen reasons of her own why a liaison between them was a bad idea. She was his uncle's widow—may have been responsible for his death, she probably wished Adam had never returned from Canada, she had carved a place in society that had no room for him, she'd had powerful men—men of influence—as her lovers.

But, damn it, he *wanted* her, and the same lack of conscience that drove him to vengeance now drove him to her bed. He didn't care if it was wrong. He didn't care if he couldn't offer her a future. He only cared about burying himself inside her, feeling her heat and hearing her soft sighs as he claimed her. He'd have that much in payment for the long sleepless nights she'd caused him. She was no virginal maid, after all, but a woman in her prime, an experienced woman of the world. She had taken lovers before. Why not him?

Yes, he'd seduce Grace. He'd woo and win her. He'd see that she got, measure for measure, the pleasure she gave him, which, he warranted, was more than she'd ever gotten from Lord Barrington. And he'd do his damnedest to hide the monster he'd become from her.

Francis Renquist sat on the bench beside Grace and scattered the crumbs from his biscuit for the milling pigeons. He dusted his hands and sighed deeply. "I fear we may never get the goods on Lord Geoffrey, Mrs. Forbush. After all, if 'twere known how he cheats, he'd have been caught out by now."

Grace nodded her understanding. She glanced around the square at the nurses strolling with babies in the brisk morning air. It was too early for the ton to be out and about, so very little risk that she'd be seen with Mr. Renquist and remarked upon. "I've begun to wonder about that," she admitted. "I thought this was going to be easy, but it appears not."

"I've found plenty of men who swear Lord Geoffrey

cheated them. Several of them say his cunning wagers beg-gared them. But none know how."

"Did the various hells cooperate in investigating the complaints?"

"Aye. Decks were checked for marked cards and dice were examined for 'loads,' all to no avail. There was one in-cident where Morgan was searched to see if he employed any devices to retain cards up his sleeve. But nothing was found. I gather he's careful to lose enough at the various gambling establishments to satisfy them. The man's a slip-pery one."

Grace recalled Lord Geoffrey's easy charm and could see how he could get away with so much. But there had to be a missing piece of information. Why would a man like Lord Geoffrey, who had so much to lose, risk social censure and making formidable enemies in all of London's power circles? Surely there had to be a reason. With every major fortune he won, he made enemies—people who could wish him dead or who could ruin him socially. Were money and fortune enough to compensate Lord Geoffrey for that loss?

She turned back to Mr. Renquist. "Perhaps we have gone about this wrong, Mr. Renquist. See what you can find out about Lord Geoffrey's background and personal life."

"How will that help us find out how he cheats?"

"It won't, but it could tell us *why* he cheats. And under-standing that could help us determine how."

Mr. Renquist nodded. "Logical, Mrs. Forbush, and noth-ing else is yielding results. There's got to be a clue some-where." He stood and straightened the lapels of his brown jacket. "I'll have Marie get word to you when I have news."

Grace smiled distractedly as she stood, too.

"Uh, Mrs. Forbush? One other thing, if you please?"

She opened her reticule and removed ten pounds.

Renquist waved her hand away. "Not that, Mrs. Forbush.

Just a word to the wise." He shifted his weight and looked uncomfortable.

Her interest piqued, she said, "Go on, Mr. Renquist."

"Someone is investigating you."

That set her back. "Me? But why would anyone investigate me? My life is…" *Well, not an open book, but certainly easily accessible to anyone with a mind to ask.* "Who, Mr. Renquist?"

"Don't know. There's a runner asking questions about you, looking to stir up some dirt."

"Lord Geoffrey," she muttered. "Oh, I was afraid this would happen. He has heard that my funds are frozen and wants to find out how much I can lose. He will want to know if I am worth the trouble of cultivating as his next victim."

"Could be," Renquist agreed. "But could be something else. What would you like me to do about it?"

Something else? The thought of the gunman from last night flashed through her mind. But no, a runner would not be involved in something like that. "To do anything would arouse suspicions. Just let me know if you hear anything more."

"Aye, Mrs. Forbush." Renquist tipped his hat and turned down the path toward Hart Street.

Grace took a deep breath and strolled slowly down the path leading to her side of the square, her mind in a jumble. She would have to find some way to counteract Lord Geoffrey's concern. He must think she had the resources to support her betting, or he would ignore her as a prospect.

How very clever of the man to have hired an investigator— and she had little doubt it was Lord Geoffrey who was making inquiries. Barrington already knew everything possible for him to know. Leland would not bother—he'd simply appear on her doorstep and demand the information he wanted. And there was no one else who would care in the least—

Except, perhaps, Adam. Had that horrid, vicious rumor resurfaced that she'd had something to do with Basil's death? If he'd heard the rumors, it would be no small wonder that he would be suspicious of her. What must he think of her?

She sighed as she crossed the street to her house, thinking of the scene in her bedroom last night. Her heart pounded against her ribs and a giddy feeling rushed through her. She could still feel his arms around her, the heat of his touch and the reckless wanton way she had nearly surrendered. If he hated her or distrusted her, would he have been so intimate? How could he put those things aside to woo her so sweetly? That wouldn't make sense. One did not make love to the enemy.

Adam mounted his horse and turned back toward the city. Exiting the narrow lane onto Kent Street in Bermondsey, he urged the mount to a canter. It was late afternoon and he still had business in town before escorting Grace to yet more hells tonight. The task would be tedious but for Grace's company.

He glanced back at the row of small cottages with vegetable gardens in back, half expecting to see Mrs. Humphries shaking her fist at him. His uncle's former housekeeper had filled his head with more questions than answers. She'd berated him for abandoning his uncle to go to the "heathen wilds" and leaving poor Mr. Forbush to his wife's indifferent nursing. She'd even hinted that Grace had been glad to have his uncle gone, saying that "the missus" had been "entertaining" Lord Barrington even before his uncle was dead. When he'd asked Mrs. Humphries point-blank if she suspected a conspiracy, her answer had been a snort and tightening of her apron strings, as if to say that Adam was naive.

Clearly, Mrs. Humphries did not like Grace Forbush. From the time Grace had arrived as a new bride, Mrs. Humphries had said she had been excluded from areas that had formerly been her exclusive domain. She found Grace to be arrogant, too particular and to have ideas above her station. She had further hinted that the marriage had not been "All that a marriage should, if you see what I'm saying, Mr. Hawthorne, him being so much older and all."

All complaints aside, when Grace had provided a retirement for Bellows, she had provided a similar one for Mrs. Humphries. If Grace had disliked the woman, she hadn't let it taint her sense of fairness. The problem, as Adam saw it, stemmed from the fact that Mrs. Humphries had not wanted to retire. She said she'd been pushed out and was suspicious of the reason. "Wanted me out of the way, her and his lordship did," she'd said.

As Kent Street merged with White and Church streets, Adam glanced over his shoulder again, uneasy with the certainty that someone was following him. Traffic was heavy in all directions emptying into the intersection at St. George's Church. It was impossible to tell if anyone was watching. Damn. He really didn't have time for these games.

Turning his mount up Borough High Street toward London Bridge, he varied his horse's gait to see if anyone would match his speed. Still unable to identify man or beast, he crossed the bridge and turned left. He'd had far too much experience with tracking and being tracked to ignore his instincts. He had a tail, but he'd have to find a less congested street to determine who it was.

Attuned, now, to his surroundings and the sounds behind him, Adam turned another corner. He saw an inn sign and rode around to the back to leave his horse with the stable boy with instructions to keep his horse saddled and ready.

Quickly taking stock of the public room, Adam found a dark corner where he could watch the arrivals at both the front and rear entrances. He would have an advantage since his eyes would adjust to the dim interior before his tail. It did not take long. Within two minutes of Adam's arrival, a slightly built nondescript man edged through the door near the back stairway and glanced around, blinking rapidly to focus in the gloom. The man held a cocked pistol at his side.

Adam eased the knife from his boot and edged toward the man, keeping his back against the wall. Just as his tail turned toward him, Adam pressed his blade against his jugular and slipped his arm around his chest, not giving him a chance to raise his pistol.

Keeping his voice low to avoid attention, he spoke in the man's ear. "Turnabout, my good man."

A frightened whine was his only answer. With a grim smile, Adam pulled the man backward toward the rear door. In the small courtyard between the inn and the stables, he slammed the man against the stone wall, his knife still pressed to the terrified man's throat. "Drop it," he ordered.

The pistol fell to the ground with a dull thump.

"Your name?" Not that the man would tell the truth, but he had to start somewhere.

"Clark," the man squeaked. "Eddy Clark!"

"Talk," he ordered.

"Lemme go, gov'nor," his tail yelped. "I ain't done nothin'."

Because he hadn't had the chance. He pressed the edge of his blade a little closer, drawing a bead of blood. "Last chance," he snarled in the man's ear.

"Dunno!" the man squeaked. "I swear it, gov'nor! I was jus' told to follow an' see where you went."

That was not what Adam wanted to hear. He pressed the blade closer and the bead turned to a trickle. "Don't mistake me for a complete fool. You don't need to draw a pistol to follow me. Who hired you?"

"Dunno." The man's voice had become a wheeze. "I talked to a short, dark bloke who 'ad me pay. 'E said 'e'd meet me at Seven Dials tonight an' gi' me more if I 'ad news."

A short, dark bloke? That could have described the man who'd attacked last night. It could also describe fully a fourth

of London. Several possibilities passed through Adam's mind.
First, that there must be something he didn't know to cause
someone to resort to such drastic measures. Second, that either Barrington wanted him out of Grace's life, or wanted to
prevent him from finding the name of the military attaché at
Fort Garry. Third, that Grace had decided she didn't want to
share his uncle's fortune. No matter which was true, he had
a dangerous enemy and he'd best be on his guard.

Ah, but he was startled at the relief he felt when he realized that, if the attack on the street last night was connected
to this incident, he was the target, and not Grace. He, at least,
could deal with assassins like this little worm now dangling
from his knife.

The stranger squirmed and his whimpering became more
desperate. Adam realized he had increased the pressure of his
blade against the man's throat. He breathed deeply and eased
back a fraction of an inch. If he frightened the man more than
he was now, he'd never get answers.

"What time tonight?" he asked.

"I was to be there at eight. 'E'd come later, an' if 'e didn't
like the way things looked, 'e'd keep goin'."

Then there was no use in Adam going to Seven Dials tonight. The man who'd hired the tail would be watching for
problems. Seven Dials was always crowded at that time of
night. It would be impossible to pick someone out in the
crowd. And if Eddy Clark's employer knew Adam well
enough to want him dead, he'd certainly recognize Adam before Adam could recognize him. No, he'd have to send Freddie Carter to keep an eye on Clark.

"What am I going to do with you?" he said contemplatively
in the man's ear.

"Lemme go, sir," he gasped.

"Why should I do that?"

"I won't never follow you again. I swear it!"

"You were going to kill me. Why should I believe you?"

"Please, sir. I won't never do it again. It's the first time. I swear it."

The decision was more difficult than Adam would have liked. He'd become civilized faster than he'd thought possible. Two months ago he'd have slit the man's throat with barely a twinge of conscience. Killers killed again. And if Adam let this one walk free, it was probable that someone else would die—perhaps him. But, damn it, he needed Clark—he was the only connection Adam had to the man who'd hired him.

"Go to that appointment tonight," he snarled in the man's ear. "Tell him I'm on to him. Tell him to watch his back."

"Anything! Anything you say, gov'nor!"

"Because, if you don't, I'll hunt you down and finish the job."

Adam released the man with a little push. "Don't make me regret my generosity," he warned as the man dashed for the street. He'd have to come back, sooner or later, for his horse. By that time, Freddie Carter would be waiting. Adam would have a report within twenty-four hours.

Bloody goddamned hell! He'd been thinking like an Englishman. Acting like an Englishman. 'Twas time to put his English scruples aside before they got him killed. He spun on his heel and headed for the stables. 'Twas time to think like a "savage."

Chapter Eleven

Belmonde's. Again. Grace sighed as she moved from table to table looking for something to interest her. Only one and a half more weeks remained before Laura Talbot would be wed to Lord Geoffrey or happily entrenched at home—until the next time her brother played too deep and lost her in a wager. And why did Lord Geoffrey even want a wife? From what she'd been able to tell, he was rarely at home, if he had one.

She glanced toward the rouge-et-noir table where Lord Geoffrey was placing a bet. A pretty woman dressed in the most scandalous gown Grace had ever seen smiled and leaned toward Lord Geoffrey in a move that was certain to give him a glimpse of what little remained to his imagination. He grinned and raised his glass to the woman. In gratitude? He certainly did not act like a man about to marry. Of course, not many men won their brides in a game of chance. Perhaps Lord Geoffrey was a libertine as well as a cheat.

The woman, certainly of the demimonde, placed her index finger on one of Lord Geoffrey's counters and slid it toward her with a coquettishly charming smile. Lord Geoffrey merely nodded. Had they just struck a bargain? Ah, Lord Geoffrey, it seemed, was a man with varied tastes. Grace smiled. That would be a good thing for her to remember.

He looked up and caught her smile. He said something to his companion and she turned to give Grace an appraising sweep from head to toe. With a lift of her chin, she dropped Lord Geoffrey's counter down her cleavage and strolled away. Thus unencumbered, he left the table and came toward her.

"Mrs. Forbush. I am pleased to see you again. I missed you last night."

"How kind of you to think of me. Mr. Hawthorne and I went to The Two Sevens."

"I heard about the unfortunate incident," he said. "And how are you and your…uh, nephew?"

Grace smiled at his attempt at delicacy. "We are quite well, sir, though it was a near thing."

"Have the police found the villain?"

"We did not bother to report it, Lord Geoffrey."

He nodded. "Likely just some bold street thug who'd thought to relieve you and Mr. Hawthorne of any winnings."

Now why hadn't she or Adam thought of such an innocent possibility? Perhaps a guilty conscience had got in the way. She knew what she was hiding, but what about Adam? "Do street thugs often lurk near gaming hells?" she asked.

He offered her his arm and led her toward the room where the vingt-et-un tables were, knowing her preferences by now. "All manner of unsavory sorts lurk in and around gaming hells, Mrs. Forbush. Have you not noticed?"

She laughed at his self-mockery. "To the contrary, I have found the company to be unexpectedly charming."

"I had not until recently."

Was he flirting? Or merely being charming? Thinking it safer to change the subject, she asked, "Now that we are on the subject, Lord Geoffrey, perhaps you can answer a question. I have begun to wonder why these establishments are called 'hells'?"

"After Virgil's rather infamous observation, I believe. *Facilis descensus Averni.* The descent to hell is easy."

"Ah." She chuckled as they arrived at the side room. "Easy, indeed. All one must do is step through the door."

"Shall we?" he asked, sweeping one arm toward the open door.

It took Adam an hour and a half to separate himself from a small group of his old acquaintances and to move toward the shadows at the edge of the main salon where he could watch Grace. He leaned one shoulder against the wall and struck a casual pose. She appeared to be blissfully unaware that Morgan was circling her like a shark in bloody waters. Oh, Grace looked to be a tasty, tender morsel, but Adam knew from his own maddening experience that she was not a light-skirt or an easy mark. There was, in fact, nothing easy about Grace Forbush.

If it weren't for her marriage and subsequent long-standing relationship with Lord Barrington, he'd swear she was celibate. Never had he known a woman to have a more coveted reputation as a desirable lover with so little evidence to support it. And to all appearances, Morgan was determined to be her next lover. That thought alternately intrigued and infuriated him. How could a rake like Morgan think a woman like Grace would entertain an offer from him?

She and Morgan stood and strolled away from the vingt-et-un table and took a seat at a table across from one another. Morgan motioned a room attendant for a deck of cards. Were they going to play piquet? Adam did not much like that idea. The stakes could go higher in a private game than in a house game. Surely, Grace would not make any foolish wagers. Her lack of ready funds should see to that.

The heavy scent of musk roses wafted to him with the rustle of fabric. A soft swell pressed against his right arm and he looked down. The dark-eyed beauty who'd been with Morgan earlier had taken his arm and was pressing herself against him provocatively. She smiled up at him and batted her lashes.

"What's a handsome man like you doing here all alone?" she asked.

He'd almost forgotten about this part of English society. The shadowy demimonde—women who sold themselves for a lifetime or a single night. Beautiful women who had more to offer than the common street prostitute. Kept women. Professional mistresses. And this one was lovely, indeed, as dark and sultry as Grace, but lacking Grace's obvious depth, subtlety and refinement. Ah, but this one was offering herself to him. He grinned. What *was* he doing here alone? "Habit?"

"A nasty habit that should be broken," she purred.

He laughed. "And you're the one to help me?" He traced the line of her jaw with his finger. "Aye. You just might be, at that."

Her eyes half closed in a contrived bedroom look. "I could become your *new* habit."

"What's your name?"

"Elvina. But you may call me Ellie."

Adam swallowed hard. Ellie—but not the Ellie he wanted. He'd be willing to wager the name was a lie anyway. Women like Elvina did not give their real names unless they were under someone's protection. "Well, Ellie, as luck would have it, I'm here with a woman tonight."

"I don't see her," Elvina whispered. She pressed her breasts against his arm again as an enticement.

The low scoop of her neckline gaped a little with the move and afforded him a glimpse of her generous unbound breasts. Lush rosy tips were puckered with anticipation and Adam realized she was a woman ideally suited to her job. He didn't answer, nor did he point Grace out.

The girl shrugged. "I don't have to be a habit, Adam. I can be once, if you want, or sometimes."

He hadn't told her his name. This was getting interesting. "Now and then?" he asked.

"Here and now, if you like."

He laughed again. "Here and now might cause a bit of a sensation, Ellie."

"There's a room upstairs."

He lifted Elvina's chin with his finger and looked into her ancient eyes. She could only be twenty and two or so, about Dianthe's age, but the life she led was beginning to tell in the faint lines around her mouth and eyes. And, oh, the dull emptiness of those eyes! Though older in years, Grace was infinitely younger than this little package. "You tempt me, Ellie." He stalled, trying to think of an easy way to discover who had set her onto him. He really didn't want to use the hard way, but he would if pressed.

"Then come upstairs with me," she said. She wet her lips and parted them in an invitation. "I'll do anything."

Adam's blood surged and he groaned. Anything? That was challenging. Tempting. Intriguing. Unquestionably the best offer he'd had in years. Had it been Grace making that offer….

She moved in front of him, facing him and shielding her actions from the room. Before he realized what she was about, she slid her hand between his legs and cupped his genitals. He hadn't thought much could shock him, but he'd been wrong.

She scratched one fingernail beneath the weight of his scrotum and applied pressure to the base of his cock with her thumb. Her eyes were heavy-lidded again, and she expelled a soft sigh. "You're more than a handful, Adam. You'd measure up against the best. If you want it here and now, I can make that happen, and no one the wiser. Any way you want it. Wherever, whenever."

"Tempting, Ellie," he said. "But not a good idea. I think you should let loose of me before someone sees you."

"You cannot tell me you are not enjoying this," she accused with a knowing smile. "I can feel it. You do not want me to let loose."

To his shame, he didn't. Men, he thought with disdain, were such simple creatures, such easy prey for a savvy woman who was unafraid to use her sexuality. He glanced toward Grace's table and saw her lean toward Morgan and say something behind her fan that caused Morgan to laugh. A moment later she closed the fan with a snap and glanced around the room, as if searching for someone. When their eyes met, she smiled, and for a moment he lost himself, thinking it was Grace's hand…

Elvina emitted a soft moan. "There. See. You want it. You need it. Come upstairs and let me ease you."

"Let go, Elvina," he said in a low voice as everything suddenly came into focus. Morgan, the cagey bastard, had seen an opportunity to make his move! "Go back to Lord Geoffrey and tell him it didn't work. Grace will be going home with me."

In the unforgiving light of early afternoon, Grace stepped from her coach onto the pavement in front of the jewelry shop. Rundell and Bridges, she had been told, were discreet but well-known jewelers who had kept estates afloat by purchasing a family's jewelry at a fair enough price to pay gambling debts. She had contrived to lose heavily at piquet last night and, though Lord Geoffrey had offered to forgive her debt because she was a novice to the game, she had refused. She wanted him to be confident that she would always pay her debts or she would not be able to gull him into cheating her.

But Mr. Renquist's warning was clear in her mind. Morgan had hired someone to investigate her. And that investigator would know by now that her funds were frozen. It was imperative that she give the appearance of having access to great wealth and a willingness to risk it in order to gamble. Once Morgan knew the lengths to which she'd go to obtain funds for her gambling, he'd know he could "up" the stakes.

Gripping her little velvet-lined mahogany box, she lifted her chin proudly and walked into the elegant jewelry shop. At the sound of the shopkeeper's bell over the door, a clerk came from a back room and stood behind a counter.

"Is there something I can do for you?" he asked.

Grace put her box down and lifted the lid. The clerk's eyes widened and he reached out before he could stop himself. "Yes?" he asked.

She glanced around, relieved to find they were quite alone. She'd been right to come early in the day. "I need to have these things cleaned and the mountings examined."

A shadow flickered from the window and Grace glanced sideways to see if her hunch was correct. A man, there and then quickly gone, had paused to witness her opening the box. Better and better. She smiled to herself. Her plan was working perfectly.

The clerk selected her pearl and aquamarine necklace from the assortment and examined it under a jeweler's loupe. "Exquisite," he pronounced before returning it to the pile and lifting an elaborate diamond pendant that had been a wedding gift from Basil. "But the settings all seem to be adequate, Mrs...?"

"Forbush," she supplied. The shadow was back, just at the edge of the window. She did not look in that direction or betray in any other way that she knew she was being observed.

"I am Mr. Thomas," the jeweler said. "I will be happy to clean these pieces for you, Mrs. Forbush. Would you like to wait?"

"Oh, dear. I believe I have an appointment, and I am rather busy the next several days. Would you mind terribly if I left them here with you? Then you will have time to thoroughly check the mountings. You do have security, do you not?"

Mr. Thomas gave her a condescending smile. "But of

course, Mrs. Forbush. We will be pleased to accommodate your request."

"I shall be happy to pay you for your services now."

"As we shall have your jewelry as security, Mrs. Forbush, payment is not necessary until you collect your items."

"I insist. I have already included a ten pound note in the box."

Mr. Thomas looked beneath the pile of jewelry and nodded. "Entirely too much, Mrs. Forbush."

"I shall wait while you bring me the difference."

Mr. Thomas disappeared into the back room with her box and reappeared a moment later with a receipt and several bank notes. She prayed it would appear to any observer that she had just exchanged her jewelry for money. She reached out and claimed the notes before he could count them out and betray how little was in the stack, but she made a great show of folding the notes and stuffing them into her reticule.

As she turned to the door she noted that the shadow receded. She opened the door and called over her shoulder, "Thank you, Mr. Thomas. You've been very accommodating."

The weekly meeting of the Wednesday League was in progress by the time Grace arrived home. She had left Dianthe instructions to start without her if she hadn't returned. By the time she had shed her shawl and left her reticule on the table in the foyer, she was in time to hear Dianthe's summation.

"So Grace went to the jeweler's to make it appear as if she were pawning her jewelry. But we honestly don't know what we are going to do for funds when our current supply runs out. Mr. Ogilby said the courts could take as long as a *year* to decide!"

Grace sat amid a quick spate of gasps and exclamations. She held up her hands to quite the ladies before she spoke. "It is not quite as grim as all that," she said. "Our living expenses will be paid, but there will not be money for extras."

"Like gambling," Dianthe added.

"Ridiculous," Lady Sarah said.

"Absurd," Lady Annica agreed. "The courts should move faster than that. And why should anyone think your husband's will is invalid? He was of sound mind when he made it."

"Was he?" Grace asked. "I recall so little of those last days, but I have a recollection that he was somewhat muddled from the time we received the news of Mr. Hawthorne's death. He…he went so soon after that he might well have been impaired."

"Well, I think it is very mean-spirited of Mr. Hawthorne to contest the will after all this time," Charity huffed.

"Mr. Hawthorne is not contesting the will. Rather, Mr. Ogilby is seeking clarification regarding intent over actual wordage. And really, it is of little consequence except as it impacts our investigation."

"Yes," Annica said. "Dianthe has brought us up to date with that. Do not worry over the money. Sarah and I shall be happy to contribute to your gambling fund."

Grace sighed with relief that she would not have to ask for assistance. She poured herself a cup of tea and sat back in her chair. "Thank you. I shall try not to abuse your offer. I have thought that I could gamble with the jewelry I have held back, which will then have to be returned to me when Lord Geoffrey is exposed."

"But what if he's *not* exposed?" Dianthe asked. "What if he does not cheat, after all?"

Grace looked around the circle and smiled. "Then we have lost our money, and my jewelry, in a worthy cause."

Sarah nodded. "The pursuit of justice has never come cheap, but it is a price we have always been willing to pay."

"As long as that price is not your life," Annica said quietly.

The death of Constance Bennington still weighed heavily on the group. Years ago, when Lady Annica had been investigating a white slavery ring, Constance had been killed for her part in the inquiry, and she served as a reminder of what carelessness in their pursuit could cost. Geoffrey Morgan had been linked to that investigation by his affection for Constance.

"And that brings us to the other point, Grace," Sarah said, putting her teacup aside. "We heard about the incident outside the Two Sevens Monday night. You could have been killed."

"Heavens, no," she said. "Lord Geoffrey told me that footpads, ruffians and thugs lurk outside hells just waiting for the opportunity to relieve lucky gamblers of their winnings. I'm certain that's all it was. After all, Lord Geoffrey thinks we are getting on swimmingly. And I cannot think of anyone else who would want to hurt me."

"Dianthe told us about Lord Barrington," Charity said. "I would not have believed it possible, but now I wonder if he could be angry enough to—"

"Of course not," Grace laughed. "He was never that attached to me. I was convenient, as was he. And 'tis neither here nor there. Our…liaison is over, and that is all that need be said on the subject."

Adam paced the small upstairs room at the Eagle Tavern. Carter was late, and he was never late. Something peculiar must be afoot. He glanced out the window and anxiety twisted his gut. The sun had set and within quarter of an hour it would be fully dark. Unless he hurried, he'd barely have time to clean up and change before Grace would be ready for another night in the gaming hells of London's seedier side.

The door burst open and he spun to see Carter, his face pale, heading straight for the whiskey bottle on the table. "Thank God, you're here," Carter said, pouring himself a generous draught.

"You have news?"

His friend nearly choked on the whiskey. "You could say that."

"Trouble?"

"If you call murder and mayhem trouble."

Adam held his breath. Damn! He knew better than to let the would-be assassin go. "Who did the son of a bitch kill?" He poured himself a stiff glass of whiskey.

"No one. Eddy Clark was the victim."

Double damn! "What happened?"

Carter refilled his glass and took it to his chair by the fireplace. "I was at the inn when he came back for his horse. Just like you said, he went to Seven Dials. He stood in a conspicuous spot and waited. At a quarter past eight, a short man in a dark coat approached him, but the foot traffic was quite heavy. I moved to the side to get a better look at the man, but when my line of sight cleared, the man in the dark coat was gone and Clark was on the ground. A passing woman screamed and people scattered every which way. I ran to him—suspected what had happened. Sure enough, he'd been stuck."

"Did he say anything?"

"Didn't have a chance. Clark was dead by the time I got to him."

"Jugular?" Adam had seen men bleed out quickly from a slit throat, but rarely that fast. The assailant must have damn near severed Clark's head.

"That's the hell of it," Carter breathed. "It was the *femoral* artery. His killer must have held his knife under his coat and then stuck Clark without him even seeing it coming. The blade had to have been a stiletto. It sliced cleanly through the worsted of his trousers and severed the artery dead on. Clark didn't even have time to cry out before he lost consciousness from the blood loss. The killer just kept walking, and no one the wiser."

"Good God," Adam muttered.

"Professional." Carter nodded. "It has all the hallmarks of

someone who does this for a living. And has no conscience. Clark was doomed from the time he took the job to kill you. His employers never intended to let him live to brag about it."

"His employers didn't want to pay him?"

"I suspect it had nothing to do with money. I searched his pockets and he still had a wad of bank notes. I think they were eliminating the possibility of being traced. Dead men tell no tales, you know."

"They?" Adam asked. "Why do you think it is more than the man in the dark coat? I'd give you odds that he was the man who shot at us in front of the Two Sevens."

"*Think,* Hawthorne! Femoral artery, for Christ's sake! When have you last seen that done?"

Adam shook his head. He had thought of that, but it didn't make sense. "Political assassinations. Covert operations. It's not a tactic a common footpad would know, let alone use."

"Your man in the dark coat is a professional, Hawthorne. He didn't come after you himself because you'd recognize him before he could get close enough to kill you. If he were a sharpshooter, you'd likely be dead by now."

Adam couldn't argue that. In fact, he was feeling damn lucky to be alive. While he'd been at Belmonde's with Grace last night, Clark had been killed because Adam hadn't been. "Does this have anything to do with why you were late tonight?" he asked.

"I'll say it does." Carter snorted. "I was the one found bent over Clark's body. I've been hauled before magistrates and threatened with having my hands slapped to hanging. Everyone and his uncle, including the commissioner, has questioned me. None of them liked hearing that I hadn't the faintest notion who killed Clark or why. And they're all dead certain I know more than I'm saying—especially when they found out I am a runner."

"What *did* you say?"

"That it was coincidence. Wrong place, wrong time." He tipped his chair onto its back legs and let out a deep sigh. "That I saw Clark drop and a man running away and went to help. That I was searching his pockets to see who he was, not to rob him. Thank God, I wasn't carrying a stiletto or you'd be visiting me in Newgate. I sure as hell didn't tell them I was doing a favor for a friend."

"My thanks for that. Had I known this was going to be so dangerous, I wouldn't have asked you to help."

A slow grin spread over Carter's face. "Why? I haven't had so much fun in years."

Adam laughed. "Nevertheless, you're out. I won't have your death on my conscience. I don't even know what's going on, or what I've done to become someone's target. The only thing I can think of is that my search for the military attaché must have triggered something bigger."

"Ah, about that, Hawthorne." Carter brought his chair back to four legs, a serious look replacing his smile. "I've got that name."

Adam felt everything within him stilling, growing deadly cold. "Who?"

"A man by the name of George Taylor. He's a major, retired for the past two years."

"Where is he?"

"Cheapside. Bassinghall Street, White Bear Inn. Seems he's fallen on hard times. No rush. He's not going anywhere."

"Why do you say that?"

"The man's a drunk. Spends most of his days deep in his cups."

There was something appropriate about that, Adam mused. He'd feared he would find the man wealthy and retired in ease.

Carter passed him a folded piece of paper. "That's the address. I'm going with you."

"The hell you say!"

"Damn it, Hawthorne. I intend to keep you from murdering the man in a rage. I won't have you hang for some miserable sot who probably doesn't even remember who gave him the orders. Promise me you won't go until tomorrow. You need the time to cool off. Think about what you hope to accomplish, eh?"

Adam saw the sense in that. He'd never get answers if he killed Taylor. He nodded at Carter. "What time shall I call around for you?"

"Best if we go by noon. Any sooner, and he won't be awake. Much later, and he won't make sense."

Sighing deeply, Adam started for the door. "It's almost over. God, how I long to lay these ghosts to rest."

"It's just beginning," Carter contradicted. "Whatever forces are at work are formidable."

"What is that supposed to mean?"

"I'm pretty damned sure it wasn't Taylor who sent Clark to stop you. You've got another enemy—a powerful one—out there, my friend."

A cold anger roiled in Adam's gut and he heard the faint sound of Indian drums across the distance. That unseen enemy would be the man who ordered the attack, a man with whom he was now engaged in a clandestine war.

Chapter Twelve

By the time Adam had cleaned up, shaved and changed his clothes, Grace was waiting in the library. She stood with her back to him, gazing out the window at the square across the street. Her gown was an icy-violet fabric, almost fluid in the way it flowed over her form, and cut with long sleeves but deeply enough in back to reveal smooth ivory skin and the column of her spine. She'd done her hair in its usual chignon, and the contrast between the prim dark knot and the seductive expanse of skin was insanely erotic.

Contrasts. Grace was a study in contrasts. Could one ever truly know her—all the little twists and turns of mind, her longing for excitement, the cool composure that covered her seething sexuality? God, he'd like nothing better than to devote himself to that task.

She turned toward him and smiled at his expression. The deep V of the back of her gown was mirrored in the décolletage, where the curve of creamy breasts swelled at the opening. And there, a pale amethyst pendant dropped from a fine gold chain to nestle in that alluring valley.

"I do not know what to say, Adam," she murmured,

smoothing the fabric of her gown over her hips. "'Thank you' will have to suffice until I can repay you. How did you know?"

Ah, the gown he'd sent payment to La Meilleure Robe for. And worth every penny. He stepped into the room. "I overheard Dianthe speak of it. This past week has been difficult enough without you having to sacrifice your creature comforts."

"But how did you… I mean, where did you come by the funds? I thought you were waiting for reinstatement."

"Lord Craddock advanced me a sum to tide me over." He lied without the tiniest twinge of conscience.

"I shall pray the courts rule on Mr. Forbush's will soon. I do not like owing friends."

Friends? She thought of them as friends? They were about to be much more. "That does you credit, Grace, but is unnecessary. We are family, after all."

A satirical smile lifted the corners of her mouth. "Such an odd little family, are we not? You, Dianthe and I? Somehow it feels…"

"Incestuous?" he asked, praying that would not be the way she thought of them.

She shook her head. "Like a lie. I do not feel like you are…that is, my feelings for you are not that of…"

Unaware that he'd been holding his breath pending the outcome of her answer, he let it out in a long sigh. Thank God she did not think of him as a nephew, because his feelings for her were nothing like those for an aunt. "If that is how you feel, I shall be glad to allow you to repay me when your funds have been released."

"Thank you, Adam." As she passed him on her way to the door, she came up on her tiptoes and brushed a chaste kiss on his cheek. "You are a very thoughtful man."

Adam clenched his teeth. He wanted to seize her and take her on the library floor. How thoughtful was that? Well, if she wanted excitement, he'd give her excitement. "Grace?"

She turned back to him, her dark eyes wide with the question.

"I've changed my mind." He went to the small cupboard where his uncle had kept chess and backgammon boards, a deck of cards and dice. He removed the cards and turned back to her. "Let's bet for your dress."

She glanced at the cards and back at him. "You mean, to play a game?"

He nodded, noting her amusement.

"But what would you do with a gown, Adam?"

"Find someone to fit it."

She laughed. "If you wish." She came to the desk and looked at the cards. "High card?"

He shook his head. "Too easy." Too quick, actually. "Did you learn piquet last night?"

"The rudiments. But I am certainly not proficient yet."

He motioned toward the chairs before the fireplace with a low tea table between them. "Briscola, then. The rules are simple and it is easy to learn."

"Briscola?" Grace frowned. "I have not heard of that game. Are you certain you are not trying to gull me, Adam?"

He laughed. "I learned it when I was posted at our embassy in Italy." When she still looked doubtful, he made an offer he knew would entice her. "The first game will be for practice. We won't score until you feel perfectly comfortable."

"Very well," she said. She poured them a glass of wine from a carafe on the desk while he removed the jokers, eights, nines and tens from the deck before shuffling.

She sat at the table across from him and listened carefully as he explained the rules. "It's a simple enough game, Grace, if you just relax and enjoy it."

She smiled and shrugged. "It seems simple enough, but I am certain there are subtleties that come with experience."

"The same could be said of all games. Would you rather play another?"

"No, I am quite comfortable under your tutelage," she said with a slight heightening of color in her cheeks.

When had they stopped talking about briscola? Adam was fairly certain there was something else going on here. He dealt the hand, placed the remaining deck facedown between them, and turned up the top card. "Trump," he explained.

As he guided her through the play, he noted that she was quick to grasp the rules and, at the end, equally quick to master the counting of points. Adam won by a comfortable margin.

"I think you were being kind," she said as she shuffled. "But I like this game. May we have another practice game before we play for stakes?"

Adam nodded. "As many as you like. Practice makes perfect, you know."

"One more should do," she demurred.

As she dealt their hands, Adam sipped his wine. "And where is the fair Dianthe this evening?"

"She's gone with the Thayers to a preview of Vauxhall's opening. Hortense, Harriett and Dianthe are quite a draw together, and I expect they will not be home much before dawn."

He could well imagine Dianthe and her ethereal beauty paired with the Thayer twins and their redheaded hoydenish ways. The evening was bound to cause a headache for Mr. and Mrs. Thayer. Ah, but it was good fortune for him. He'd have a wealth of time to seduce Grace.

The next game went as quickly as the first, and with the same results, though not by as wide a margin.

"Well," Grace said with a deep breath, "shall we play for stakes now?"

"Yes. But not your gown yet. What else do you have that I might covet?"

She frowned thoughtfully, completely missing the thrust

of his question. He grinned as she said, "I haven't the foggiest notion. I have already put Mr. Forbush's personal items aside for you. Perhaps you would…of course! The portraits. They are of your family, after all."

A thoughtful wager. "Agreed. And what will you ask of me?"

That appeared to be even more perplexing. Did he have nothing she wanted? He couldn't blame her. He had precious little left in the world. He removed his gold signet ring with his initial engraved in onyx and placed it on the tea table.

"Oh, Adam, I couldn't take something so personal," she said.

"Why not? I am prepared to take your dress. Is that not personal? Besides, I don't intend to lose."

She didn't answer, but gave him an enigmatic smile. "Deal, sir."

Ah, she didn't believe he'd take her dress. A shocking miscalculation. He dealt the cards and turned the first one up. Hearts were trump. He could tell by the little furrows of concentration between her eyes that she was playing in earnest now. He paused long enough to pour her another glass of wine and to refresh his own. He decided to take his time and relish the slow inevitability of what was coming.

The game, he mused, was rather like a fox hunt. All the little twists and turns, the momentary escapes, were all the more exciting for knowing that the fox would eventually be run to ground. Ah, but this little fox would not be thrown to the pack. No, this little fox was all his.

He won again. The family portraits were his. Grace smiled and he had a brief twinge of uneasiness. He'd had the definite feeling that she'd wanted him to have them. Had she let him win? She waved one hand in dismissal.

"What now, sir? Are you ready to play for my dress?"

Adam shook his head. He left his ring on the table and reached out to run his finger the length of her necklace down to the amethyst nestled between her breasts. A little shiver passed through her and her eyelashes fluttered for a fraction of a second. No words passed between them, but Grace understood. She reached behind her to undo the clasp. When the necklace lay on the table beside the ring, she reached for the deck and began to shuffle.

"Diamonds," she pronounced as she turned the trump card up.

The play was intense but not as intense as Grace's concentration. Her face, the flicker of her eyes, the hint of a smile, all betrayed her, and he prayed to God that she was not so easy for Morgan to read. He would have to keep an eye on that. When he reached out to draw from the stock, his hand grazed hers and she grew still, as if she had frozen on the spot. He traced the soft underside of her wrist with his index finger, relishing her heat and the solid thump of her pulse as it pounded against his touch.

She swallowed hard and glanced up from their hands to meet his gaze. Her lips parted and she seemed about to speak, but she looked down again and slowly slid her hand away from his. He smiled. She was having the first stirrings of understanding. But why did he feel as if he were seducing an innocent? Did Grace make every man feel as if he were the first man?

She won. "Well done, Grace," he said as he gathered the cards and shuffled.

She slipped his ring on her thumb and held her hand out at arm's length to admire it. "Too big," she said with a hint of humor. "I think I shall have it melted down and remade into earrings." She glanced sideways at him, waiting for his reaction.

What a delicious little tease she was. He stood and removed his jacket and vest, leaving him in shirtsleeves and cravat. He removed the watch from his vest pocket. "My watch against your dress?"

She shook her head. "I still have my pendant."

"My watch against your pendant, then?"

Grace tapped the table with one finger. "I do not like to take so much from you, Adam."

"Let me worry about what I can afford to lose," he said in a low murmur. "And, as I've said before, I do not intend to lose."

The damn clock on her desk chimed the hour. He held his breath as she turned toward it, as if just now becoming aware of the passage of time. Would she insist they leave for the gaming hells of St. James Street?

She sighed as she turned back to him and tilted her head to one side. "D'you think they'll miss me at Belmonde's?"

"Undoubtedly."

"I've heard it said that absence makes the heart grow fonder."

He smiled. "Shall we test the theory?"

"I am thinking I shall have to open a gaming establishment of my own." She looked pensive. "'Mrs. Forbush's Club for Gentlemen' I shall call it."

"Careful," he said, "or some might think it is a different sort of establishment altogether."

She gave him a throaty chuckle. "You, Mr. Hawthorne, are quite naughty."

He refilled their glasses. "You have no idea, Mrs. Forbush," he agreed, toasting her as he sat. "To Mrs. Forbush's Club."

He shuffled and dealt the hand, declaring the trump suit, "Spades."

Grace fanned her cards and looked at him over the rim. The move was provocative, and he wondered if she'd done it on purpose. This, then, was a part of Grace's popularity with the gentlemen of the ton. A beautiful, sensual woman with a touch of coquettishness and a plethora of subtlety was every man's desire, and Adam was responding as any man would. As every man before him had.

The play took longer this time. Grace was more deliberate and Adam was more cautious. Where the play had been more in jest in the beginning, it had become earnest. They both knew there was more at stake than a pendant. And, in the end, Adam made certain Grace won. She smiled in delight as she pushed the cards into a single pile.

He stood and walked around behind her. Leaning close, he reached over her shoulder and retrieved the pendant. "Allow me?" he whispered in her ear.

She nodded.

He draped the pendant around her neck and fastened the clasp at her nape. The scent of jasmine wafted up to him from a spot behind her ear. He was growing so hard that movement was causing him pain, but he refused to rush this. Grace would have no reason to bolt this time. Starting at the clasp, he smoothed the chain against her skin on both sides, around and downward to the amethyst at the deep V of her neckline. He could feel her heart beating a rapid tattoo and he knew she had barely breathed.

His hands still resting on the slopes of her breasts, he hovered at her ear and whispered, "Breathe, Grace. I promise it will not hurt."

She took a deep, shuddering breath and he straightened, sliding his hands upward again until they cupped her shoulders.

"Now, Grace?" he asked. "The portraits against your gown?"

She nodded.

"My deal," he reminded, coming around her to sit again. He shuffled, never breaking his gaze from her. Her color rose and she became more flushed than he'd ever seen her. There was something unutterably intimate in their study, an acknowledgment of the fascination between them. Could she have sensed where this was going to end?

He did not look down until he turned up the trump card. "Hearts," he said, thinking how prophetic that was.

"Hearts," she acknowledged, looking down at the card. She picked her hand up and fanned the cards.

They played one hand and then another until the deck was gone and the game was over. Adam didn't have to count his points. He knew he'd won. The stakes had been high enough that he'd counted every card as it was played. He waited until Grace counted hers, then slid his pile across the table for her to count. He wanted her to know, without a doubt, that he'd won.

When she finished the count, she looked up at him, an unfathomable expression on her face. "Your gown, Mr. Hawthorne. I shall have it cleaned and pressed and delivered to your room tomorrow."

He shook his head. "You have my ring and watch, Mrs. Forbush. Debts are payable here and now. I want my gown."

A long moment passed while those words sank in, and then Grace's dark eyes widened. "Are you serious?"

He nodded once. "A debt's a debt." He almost felt sorry for her. But no, he would not go easy on her. She was finally going to pay for all those sleepless nights she had caused him—from the first time he'd seen her portrait to last night in his room upstairs, where even the cool, smooth sheets had abraded his skin, grown sensitive from arousal.

Standing, Grace moved away from the tea table and stopped before the fireplace in the center of the grouping of chairs. The heat of the fire warmed her back as she turned to face Adam. She'd undressed in front of a man before. But Basil had never looked at her the way Adam was looking at her now. She wanted to run. She wanted to deny the debt or to accuse him of cheating, but she knew he hadn't. He'd won. Fairly. And she'd give him value for his money.

He sat back in his chair and lifted his glass of wine, watching her intently. She realized he was savoring his moment of victory, and that this was what he'd wanted and not the dress itself. He'd planned this whole thing, but he could not know that she had much more at risk than the dress.

The memory of Lord Geoffrey telling her that the excitement of gambling was in the risk rose to her mind. And it must be true. Her excitement was rising alarmingly at this very moment. And some inner demon, some daringly wicked part of her she did not even know, urged her onward.

She lifted her hands to her bodice. The gown fastened with a hook and eye at the bottom of the V. She drew the moment out, allowing her hands to rest on her breasts, almost like a caress. Only when Adam twitched did she slip them downward to the clasp.

Once she'd freed the hook, she parted the fabric, revealing an edge of the satin trim of her chemise. She paused, waiting to see if he would stop her, but, of course, he didn't. The next hook opened easily, and the next. She shrugged one shoulder to free the fabric, then the other. The sleeves were loose enough to allow the fabric to slide down her arms and off. The rest of the gown went with it, gliding over her hips and puddling on the floor around her feet.

Adam finished his wine in a single gulp and sat forward in his chair.

She glanced down at herself, trying to see what Adam saw. Her shapeless white chemise, of a semitransparent lawn, came to just above her knees. Fine white silk stockings sheathed her legs, fastening to white ribbon garters beneath the chemise. Her slippers, of an icy violet satin to match her dress, looked out of place in the sea of white.

He stood slowly and the harsh rasp of his breathing reached her. He sounded as if he could not catch his breath, and she realized that she had done that to him. A sense of her own power made her giddy and reckless. He believed she was worldly and experienced. He would not know the truth about her. Was it possible? Could she fool him?

She tilted her head ever so slightly to one side, the gesture a question. If she were careful, would he ever have to know?

He came forward and circled her twice, an agonizingly slow process. Finally he stopped behind her, his breath hot on her neck. She expected him to reach over her again and to touch her breasts, but he didn't. Instead he pulled the violet snood off her chignon and removed the hairpins that secured the knot. Her hair tumbled down her back, as cool as silk against her fevered flesh. She shivered as he separated the strands between his fingers.

Only then did his hands come around her waist, pulling her back against his chest and then sweeping upward to cup her breasts. She gasped as his thumbs scraped across her hardened nipples and her head tilted back against him as pleasure coursed through her. She was suddenly two people, one screaming to run while she still could and the other crying out for more. Which? Which should she listen to?

"Ellie," he groaned in her ear. "Here you are, at last."

Ellie? Was that who she was? Unexpected tears filled her eyes as her past—always fuzzy, mostly painful—came into focus. Grace was her brother's creation, and Basil's and Barrington's, and every other man who'd tried to control her. Ellie was the free spirit her father had loved and cherished—and the woman that only Adam had seen still lurking beneath the surface. Ellie, wild and free and reckless. Ellie, the woman she had buried. She wept for all those wasted years, all those years of becoming someone she thought she needed to be to survive—of denying herself and of living a lie. Was it too late to reclaim a portion of it? Dear God, had she wasted her entire life?

The realization left her weak and trembling. She melted back against Adam's chest, slow tears coursing down her cheeks, and lifted her hands to cover his, still cherishing her breasts. They were damp with her teardrops.

"Are you all right?" he whispered.

"Yes," she moaned. "Yes."

"Are you frightened?"

She turned in his arms. "I am freed. I am redeemed." She looked up at him and rose on her toes to kiss him.

He looked dazed for one brief moment, then met her kiss with an open hunger and honesty that awed her.

"Yes," she murmured against the soft press of his lips, answering the question he had not yet asked.

He lifted her into his arms and stepped over the gown. Before she could think better of her decision, he had kicked the library door open and was halfway up the staircase. She was dizzy with anticipation when he did not stop at her door but continued down the hallway to his.

The experience was exhilarating, liberating. He left her in the center of his bed and went to lock his door. She pushed herself up against his pillows, brushing the long tendrils of hair back from her face. A crescent moon shone outside his open window and she smiled into the silver-dappled moonlight, welcoming the sacred darkness, so intimate, so safe.

Her slippers had been left on the library floor and Adam turned his attention to her stockings. Unfastening the garters, he lifted her leg to rest her heel on his shoulder, rolling the stockings down her leg, kissing each newly exposed expanse of skin. His smile and the deep intimacy of his touch made her feel luxurious and naughty at the same time. Doing likewise with the second leg, he then turned his attention to her chemise, unfastening the tapes at her shoulders and tugging from beneath her and over her head.

She had been naked with a man before, but Basil had never touched her the way Adam did. She had no time for modesty when he disposed of her smallclothes, leaving her clad only in the moon's glow and white garters, his gaze grazing over her skin like a caress. A faint rumble built in his throat and he bent to kiss her stomach. An immediate burning ignited there and she sighed deeply, tangling her fingers through his hair and holding him close.

He circled her navel with his tongue as he worked his cravat free, then discarded his shirt. By then she neither knew nor cared how or what he'd have to do to divest himself of the rest, but it was done quickly and he was back, reclining beside her.

He lifted strands of her hair and twined the lengths around his neck, as if he would bind her to him thus, and then turned his attention to her mouth. Long, lazy kisses gave way to deeper ones as his hands moved over her, defining, discovering, worshiping.

She grew frantic with longing. This was nothing like the endless, painful, humiliating, futile nights of failed attempts at consummation with Basil. This was sweet and urgent. It was beyond anything she ever could have imagined. She wanted more, and she wanted it now.

He dipped his head to nibble and kiss her breasts and at the same time he moved his hand between her legs. She gasped with the familiarity of such a thing, but when he drew her nipple into his mouth, she forgot everything else.

She whimpered when he found the vulnerable cleft shielded between her thighs, stroking, dipping, opening her. He moaned, and she realized she had curved down to him to tug at his earlobe with her teeth, making little mewling sounds each time his finger entered her. "Please…please…" she begged, keeping rhythm with his stroking.

"Not yet. There's more I want of you."

"No. Now," she demanded, feeling her courage slipping away.

"Ellie," he soothed. "Ellie…"

Yes. Tonight she was Ellie. Not Grace. Her courage returned and, stronger, more confident, she reached down and touched him, amazed by his size and power—such an impossible opposite to Basil. He winced, but grew larger and harder in her hand. Would it all go wrong as it always had with Basil? She couldn't wait. She couldn't risk it. "Now!" she demanded like an angry child.

He laughed. "Now, then," he said, positioning himself above her.

He probed at her vulnerable core, seeking entry. His thickness and length seemed impossible to accommodate and she knew there'd be pain. There'd always been pain. But she also knew she couldn't take another breath without him inside her. She arched to him as he drove downward, but his entry was shallow, blunted by her tense muscles. She made a concerted effort to relax and brought her knees up to cradle Adam's hips. He groaned and thrust again.

She held her breath, ready for the burning, aching discomfort. She wanted him deep inside her and he thrust again, surer, deeper. She caught her startled gasp before it escaped past her lips and arched her head back on the pillow as she lifted to him again, savoring the searing ache inside her. He filled her with himself, sliding downward. Slowly, slowly downward he pressed until they were fully joined. Chill bumps rose on her arms and she moaned with the mingled pleasure and pain.

"Ellie," he whispered into the silver moonlight, "are you with me?"

"Yes," she said, uncertain what he meant, but knowing everything would come all right now. She closed her eyes to fully appreciate the sensation. It was done. Irrevocably done. Gloriously, wonderfully done.

He began moving again, creating an exquisite friction by slowly rocking against her until she matched him, and only then taking longer, deeper strokes. When she opened her eyes again, she found him watching her. His hazel eyes were bright and his muscles strained and shook with his every move, as if he were contained under pressure, sparing her the full force of his passion. Was there a question in his eyes? Or exultation? As the pressure began to build within her, instinct led her to roll her hips upward to allow even deeper entry, and the foreign sensations began to soar out of control. Every part of her was tingling and chill bumps caused her to shiver with anticipation. She moaned with the intensity of building pleasure. She feared she might swoon with it.

Adam was smiling at her now, that irreverent little half smile of his that was somehow wicked and wise at the same time, a smile that said he knew what she was feeling, and knew that he had created those feelings. She smiled back and he laced his fingers through hers and held them against the pillows.

Slowly, still driving into her, he lowered his head and covered her mouth with his. His tongue moved over hers, mirroring the invasion where their bodies were joined. Her sighs fell into that rhythm and she tightened her muscles to rise to him.

He groaned and shuddered, coming into her with steadily building intensity, and she knew the end was near. Then, just when she could bear no more, heat and light burst through her, incinerating her in a mindless inferno, reducing her to ashes in an instant. Gasping, she closed her eyes and felt tears trickle down the sides of her face as the currents of pleasure dragged her deeper.

Adam released her hands and lifted himself away from her. He cupped her face and wiped her tears with the calloused pads of his thumbs as she gasped to catch her breath.

How utterly humiliating. Emotion was unladylike, Leland had drummed into her when she'd grieved openly at their father's death. Passion was unseemly, Basil had told her when she'd clumsily tried to help him consummate their union. And now, because of her tears, she was failing Adam, too. "I am...so sorry," she said. "I did not mean to cry."

"Sorry? Never be sorry for such a thing, Ellie. Sometimes it takes you that way. Not so very unusual. I am choosing to take it as the very highest compliment."

The tension drained from her and she gave him a breathless laugh. She opened her eyes again to find him looking down at her, concern etched on his handsome features. "It *is* a compliment, Adam. I…have never felt like that before."

"I gathered as much. And I wonder if I should take you further."

She sighed and stretched. "There cannot be anything further."

He bent to kiss the hollow of her throat before moving lower. She thought he would kiss her breasts again, and the anticipation began to build. But he did not stop there. Holding her hips steady, he trailed a path of kisses lower.

"Nothing further?" he mumbled against her belly. "Care to make a little wager on that, m'dear?"

Grace trembled as he traced his tongue around the dip of her navel. Her every reaction betrayed that she could not be as experienced as her reputation suggested. Though responsive beyond his wildest expectations, her surprise at the sensations he created in her told him that his uncle had been clumsy or unconcerned with her pleasure or comfort. And what lovers could she have had who had not taken the time to initiate her into the erotic arts?

He moved down, savoring the silken expanse of her lower belly. Her hips twitched and she caught her breath on a moan. How he loved discovering her, cherishing each new and exciting revelation. He held her hips to steady her. Her skin was warm and smelled of jasmine, as exotic and mysterious as Grace herself.

"Adam," she sighed, reaching her hand down to cup his head and catch his hair between her fingers.

She hadn't done this before. He was sure of it. Her reactions were too wild, too unschooled, to speak of experience.

But he would claim this right, this privilege. She wouldn't stop him. She wouldn't want to.

When he reached the crisp curls of her nether hair, she gasped. "No!" she said. Her plea was halfhearted and he knew it was born of ancient taboos, all the more beguiling for its forbidden nature. Grace might protest, but Ellie wouldn't.

He slid one hand from her hip to stroke lightly over the engorged little bundle of nerves that was his destination. She writhed with mingled pleasure and desperate need. Slowly, he moved his fingers downward and entered her passage. She was hot and tight, already on the edge of orgasm. Her muscles began to spasm over them and he withdrew regretfully. She was ready, but he wasn't prepared to let her go so easily.

"Oh!" She moaned. "Adam…please!"

"Soon," he promised. "Stay with me, Ellie."

He kissed his way lower until he was finally where he wanted to be. He gently ran his tongue over the seed of her passion. She tasted both sweet and salty, a blend enticing and uniquely female. His own desirè surged out of control when he felt her thighs trembling. Her pleasure became his pleasure. He could no more stop now than he could snatch the stars from the sky.

He gave exquisite attention to that heated place, savoring her responses, taking pride in her cries of delight. Only when her breathing grew shallow and ragged did he give her the release she sought. With insistent pressure and the soft pull of his tongue, he brought her to completion.

Before her tremors finished, he rose above her and sank into her, feeling her contract around him. Taking long, slow strokes, he felt her muscles pulling him inward, gripping him, greedy for the final stroke. A fine sheen of perspiration dewed her entire body. She was glorious. She was magnificent. She was wanton. And she was his.

He finished quickly, spilling his seed into her in a hot rush just as she reached another climax in rapid succession. Her head thrashed on the pillow and she repeated his name in a soft litany.

"Adam, Adam, Adam, Adam…"

He sank into her, finally at rest. No matter where life took him, no matter what came of tomorrow, he wanted to die hearing that sound.

Chapter Thirteen

Adam studied his face in the shaving mirror on the washstand in his room. Apart from shadows beneath his eyes, there was nothing to betray the fact that he'd spent a sleepless night. Even after he'd carried a deeply sated, sleeping Grace to her bedroom and deposited her between her sheets, he'd been unable to sleep. The question loomed large in his mind, and also his denial. It could not be so. But every time he dismissed it, it came back even more insistently. Still, despite his instincts, despite her reactions, there was absolutely no way that what he suspected could be true.

He wiped the remaining streaks of lather from his face and dropped his towel into the basin, glancing toward his bed. The vision of Grace, naked but for her amethyst pendant and the enticing white garters he'd left for their erotic counterpoint, rose up to entice him yet again. She'd been everything he'd hoped—deeply sensual, completely open and wholly abandoned. Yet she'd possessed a touch of innocence that was quite charming. If she made every lover feel as she'd made him feel last night, it was no wonder, then, that she'd gained such an envied reputation.

But how could he account for her tears? They'd surprised

him, charmed him with their sweetness, and they'd told him she was as deeply moved by the experience as he'd been. And there it was again. That damned question.

He couldn't put it off a moment longer. Though he dreaded the answer, he had to know. He took another step toward the bed before a knock on his door stopped him. "Yes?" he called.

"Mrs. Dewberry, sir. Come to bring your tray and fetch the dirty linens."

"Come in," he said. He took a fresh cravat from the bureau and draped it around his neck.

Mrs. Dewberry bustled in and placed a breakfast tray on the table by the window overlooking the park. "Eggs, sir, and ham," she announced.

"I dislike putting you to such trouble, Mrs. Dewberry. I was on my way down."

"Ach! No trouble at all. Everyone's rising late today. The missus hasn't stirred, and I know she's got an appointment before long. Miss Dianthe just came home as I was putting the kitchen in order for the day. She told me that she and the Thayer girls danced all night. Oh, to be young again, eh?"

She went to the washstand, wiped the basin and dropped the towel on the floor. She bent over to gather up his discarded clothing from last night, and he glanced toward the bed again. He'd better find out before Mrs. Dewberry made the bed. With no small amount of trepidation, he pulled the covers back. It took him a moment to accept what he saw. Just a trace, he decided, but enough to tell the tale.

"Mrs. Dewberry, I…uh, have a boil."

"Mr. Dewberry gets them all the time, sir, on his arse from coaching all day, bouncing on the driver's seat. Would you like me to lance it? You'll be more comfortable afterward, I vow."

"That won't be necessary, Mrs. Dewberry. I…ruptured it last night."

She came to stand beside him, staring down at the sheet. "Faugh! That's hardly nothing, sir. I've seen much worse, I can tell you that. Why, last year the mister had one that bled for days."

Struggling to find words, wondering what the hell was going on, Adam merely nodded. "I am fine now. I shall…try not to bloody your sheets again."

"Here," she said, tugging a corner of the sheet. "Let me wash these, too. Have to wash the ill humors out of them, else you'll get another."

Oh, he seriously doubted that. One was only a virgin once.

Harsh sunlight pierced the narrow gap in Grace's curtains. She stretched and yawned, feeling sinfully luxurious and strangely contented. Oh, but when she rolled over, the muscles of her inner thighs quivered in protest and the night came rushing back.

She sat bolt upright in bed and looked around. Thank God, she was in her own bed, though how she had gotten here she could only guess. And, heavens! She was stark naked but for her garters!

She jumped out of bed, snatched her dressing robe from the clothes press, and tied the sash around her waist. Her gown! Was it still on the library floor? She glanced at the clock on her nightstand and groaned. Noon! Mrs. Dewberry would have found it by now, along with her shoes and snood, and even the scattering of hairpins Adam had pulled from her hair. Oh! Her under garments were still in Adam's room!

She hurried to the adjoining dressing room to find her slippers and nearly collapsed with relief when she saw everything there, draped over the boudoir chair. Adam. Oh, bless him! She touched the fabric of the gown and sighed. He was not going to hold her to their wager. But would she ever be able to wear it again without thinking of last night? Not likely. But she would always feel beautiful when she did, because she would remember the way Adam looked at her.

She returned to the bedroom and pulled the draperies back to admit a flood of light before going to her dressing table to comb the tangles from her hair. There would be no time for a bath before she had to meet Mr. Renquist. She smiled at her reflection, congratulating herself that she looked quite the same. No betrayal of what had happened last night marred her features, no hint of her newly found sexuality showed in her eyes or face.

Color rose to her cheeks as she remembered how she had gloried in all of the things Adam had done to her last night. Where had he learned such delightfully wicked things? And where could she learn things that would please him?

Her door opened without a knock and Mrs. Dewberry peeked in. "Oh, you're up, Mrs. Forbush." She disappeared for a second and then reappeared with a tray. "Late night?"

Grace smiled and looked down at the amethyst pendant still around her neck. "Very late," she said.

"Aye. Everyone is late rising today. Miss Dianthe is still abed. She has a powerful snore for one so small." Mrs. Dewberry chuckled and poured a cup of tea from the pot on the tray, then brought it to Grace at her dressing table. "Mr. Hawthorne's gone, though. Left half an hour ago."

"Gone?" Grace had a sinking sensation in the pit of her stomach.

"Aye. Said he had an appointment with an old friend at noon, but if you ask me, I think he went to the doctor to have that boil lanced."

"Boil?" Grace frowned. She thought she could recall almost every inch of Adam's body, and she hadn't noticed a boil.

"Aye, Mrs. Forbush, but he said that he'd be back in time to take you gambling unless you'd rather stay in. Said he had something to talk to you about, Mrs. Forbush, something serious."

Serious? Oh, dear. He regretted last night. He was embarrassed. Or, worse, he was no longer attracted to her. Men found excitement in the chase, but perhaps he hadn't found the same excitement in the "catch." Perhaps she'd been a dreadful disappointment. Perhaps her lack of experience had made her dull and uninteresting as a lover. Or perhaps, even worse, he suspected her deceit. But wouldn't he have said something last night instead of continuing her initiation into those erotic arts?

"Aye, but he left the house whistling. Said if he didn't make it back for dinner, he'd meet you in the library later."

She breathed a sigh of relief. Well, she'd find out what was so important soon enough. She had her own errands to be about today.

Adam silently climbed the stairs to the second floor at the White Bear Inn on Bassinghall Street, Freddie Carter fast on his heels.

"Go easy, Hawthorne," Carter whispered. "By all accounts the man is a shadow of himself. The drinking—"

"Shut up," Adam growled. He had a tight enough rein on his anger without adding Carter's womanish cautions. He knew what he had to do. For Nokomis. For his pledge to his blood brother, Mishe-Mokwa.

At the top of the stairs, Adam slipped the knife from his boot and continued down the hallway to room four. Pressing his ear to the door, he listened for any sign of occupation. He heard the clink of a glass and then the sound of a bottle falling to the wood floor.

He eased the latch down and pushed the panel inward. Carter's breath behind him caught in a ragged sigh. The Bow Street runner really was afraid Adam would murder Major George Taylor in cold blood. Well, maybe he would, but not until he had some answers.

Taylor sat slumped over a small wooden table, his forehead

resting on the rough planks. Either he hadn't heard their entry, or he hadn't cared.

"George Taylor?" he asked, just to be certain he was not about to kill an innocent man.

An incomprehensible mumble was the only answer. Adam went forward and jerked the man's head back by his hair. "Taylor?" he asked again.

"Umph," the man replied, fighting to focus on Adam.

Adam took that as an affirmative. "Looks like noon wasn't soon enough," he said to Carter as he let go of the man's hair.

He planted his knife blade in the center of the table with a solid thump and took Taylor's glass out of his hand. "Sober up, Taylor. If I can't get answers from you, I have no reason to keep you alive."

"Who…who are you?" Taylor asked.

Adam leaned close to the man, just to be certain Taylor would recognize him. "My name is Adam Hawthorne. I met some of your friends in Canada. Of course, they're all dead now. You're the last, Taylor."

"Last," Taylor repeated.

"What a pathetic excuse for a Englishman," he told Carter over his shoulder. He turned back to Major Taylor. "Think back, Taylor. The winter of 1816. Fort Garry. A Chippewa tribe in winter camp southeast of Winnipeg."

Taylor moaned and his head rolled forward. "Didn't… know. Wasn't supposed to…happen that way."

"Explain yourself, Taylor. What *was* supposed to happen?"

"Wasn't supposed to be…a bloodletting. Just…" The man's head fell forward again. "Need a drink," he muttered.

Adam pulled the man's head back and held the whiskey glass in front of him. "Want a drink? Then answer my questions."

"You're…Hawthorne?"

Adam nodded, a grim feeling of satisfaction sweeping through him at the fear in the man's eyes.

"Knew you'd come," he said.

"It wasn't supposed to happen that way? Then how *was* it supposed to happen?"

"Just…eliminate the tribe. And you."

"Me?" Adam had toyed with that idea over the past four years, but couldn't come up with any motives. Who would want him dead—want it badly enough to slaughter an entire Native American tribe to accomplish it? Or was the tribe the target, and he was just a bonus?

"But you weren't there." Taylor looked bewildered by that fact, as if he'd been betrayed.

"Why?" he asked. "Why did you do it?"

"So I could come home," he slurred, his voice turning into a whine. "Jus' wanted to get out of that godforsaken wilderness. Said I could come home if I followed orders."

Adam pulled his knife out of the table and pressed it to Taylor's throat. "And for that you slaughtered an entire tribe? You skewered children?"

"Christ," Carter groaned, stepping back from the table as if giving Taylor over to Adam.

"It…it got out of hand." Taylor's gaze was fixed on the whiskey glass. "Madness. Insanity."

"Aye. Do you remember a little girl in beaded buckskins? So high?" He held his hand up to a point midway between his waist and his shoulders. "She always carried a doll made from a corn husk."

Taylor began to cry. He shook his head against the blade that Adam held steadily to his throat and drew blood. Taylor reached for the whiskey glass and Adam pinned his sleeve to the table with the knife.

"Not until you tell me who killed Nokomis. That was her name, you son of a bitch. The little girl who was disemboweled by an English sword."

Sobs racked Taylor, shaking his entire drunken frame. "Still... still see her," he gasped between sobs. "She haunts...me."

Blind rage seized Adam. Without quite realizing what he was doing, he pulled the knife from Taylor's sleeve and held it, tip first, to Taylor's throat again. His hand shook with the effort to hold it steady and not kill the man on the spot. From the corner of his eye, he caught a glimpse of Freddie, blanched and drawn, but silent. Adam knew he could kill this man with impunity and the temptation was overwhelming.

Slowly, he withdrew his hand and let Taylor slump forward on the table's surface.

Carter exhaled and took a step forward, clapping a hand over Adam's shoulder in a sign of support.

"The name," Adam rasped. "I want the name of the man who gave that order."

Taylor mumbled incomprehensibly, his head lolling on his crossed arms.

"Who gave the order, damn it?" he shouted.

"Came down from London," Taylor said, lifting his head and reaching out for the whiskey glass.

Adam let him have it this time. He retrieved the bottle from the floor and uncorked it. Wiping the neck on his sleeve, he took a long pull, praying for the moment when it would hit bottom and dispel some of the poison eating at his vitals.

Carter took a pull at the bottle next. He wiped his mouth on his sleeve and shook his head. "Good God. I thought you were actually going to do it, Hawthorne."

"I may yet," he said darkly, taking the bottle back. Why *had* he stopped? He'd lived for this moment for four years, and suddenly he had a conscience? Or was it Grace? Had her belief in him made him a better man?

All these years, and it had finally come down to this—a broken, pathetic man in a seedy room in London. A man who still hadn't given the answers Adam needed. Taylor was a pawn. But a pawn who'd killed Nokomis and led the men who had killed the others. Was Nokomis's ghost enough to punish Taylor? Was living with the memory of what he'd done a just recompense? The man was killing himself by inches. He didn't need Adam to finish the job. He'd do it himself, soon enough.

But not before Adam got that name. Taking a deep breath, he turned back to Major George Taylor and demanded, "London? Where in London? Whose seal?"

"War...Office," he slurred, and passed out cold.

Still not the answer he wanted. *A name, damn it, he wanted a name.* But he wouldn't get one from Taylor until the man sobered up.

On their way back down the stairs, he turned to Freddie Carter. "Put a man on Taylor day and night. No whiskey, no alcohol at all. Get some food in him. Then find me when the delirium has passed and he can answer some questions."

"Good heavens, Mr. Renquist! It is already June. Miss Talbot's wedding will be upon us in no time. The banns have been read twice, and will be again in another few days."

Francis Renquist shrugged and shook his head. "Be that as it may, Mrs. Forbush, I'm having the deuce of a time coming up with anything more than suspicions and accusations. 'Tis all a bunch of taradiddle and nothing solid, if you ask me."

Grace blinked and a creeping feeling of doom invaded her vitals. "You think Lord Geoffrey is innocent?"

"Didn't say that, Mrs. Forbush. I don't know. But I'm thinking we may not be able to prove anything unless you catch him in the act. Red-handed, as it were."

Grace had already begun to suspect as much. After all, if someone knew how Morgan was cheating, they'd have come forward by now.

She sighed and glanced around the bookshop. The aisles

were becoming crowded, patrons browsing as busily in the stacks as she had pretended to be until Mr. Renquist arrived. At least she had found a dark corner where they could not easily be overheard.

Her head buzzed with possibilities. She'd never thought Lord Geoffrey stupid or foolish, but she had not anticipated him being so clever. He had a certain sinister charm and, despite herself, she almost liked him. After all, he'd never been anything but courteous to her, though she'd seen flashes of his ruthlessness when dealing with others.

Then how was she to proceed? "Mr. Renquist, do you have any ideas or suggestions for me to follow? I am nearly desperate to make an inch of progress. Aside from Lord Geoffrey hiring a runner to follow me, I can find nothing against him."

A tall, fair-haired fellow edged a little nearer, reading the book spines on the shelves for titles of interest. Conversation impossible for the moment, Mr. Renquist pulled a heavy tome from the shelf and began paging through it.

Grace glanced down at the book in her hand, one she had selected at random when she'd entered the shop scarcely ten minutes ago. *A Woman's Guide to Marital Bliss.* Written by a man, of course, as was most propaganda on marriage. Curious, she opened the book to a page near the middle. A small illustration depicted a man sitting in a comfortable chair beside the fire with what Grace assumed to be a smile but which actually looked more like a smirk. A woman, ostensibly his wife, stood over his shoulder holding a tray bearing a glass of wine.

Was she to believe a woman found marital bliss through service to her husband? What utter nonsense! She was about to close the volume and replace it on the shelf when a single word caught her eye. *Intimacies.* She stopped and found the passage again and read. The author contended that a wife needed to do little beyond submit happily to her husband's "marital prerogatives" to ensure a harmonious union. If she could learn to bear such intimacies with good grace, so much the better.

Her heartbeat tripped as she recalled last night. She'd been married and had never learned to find any pleasure in the endless nights with Mr. Forbush. Yet she had managed to achieve something very close to contentment in the marriage. But in one brief encounter with Adam, she had found the most incredible pleasure with a man to whom she was *not* married. Had she managed such a relationship with Mr. Forbush, that would have been bliss, indeed.

She flipped back to the table of contents and read the chapter headings. The first half of the book seemed innocuous enough, concentrating on topics such as having his supper ready when he wanted, keeping a clean house and deferring to his superior judgment, but the last few chapters promised enlightenment. She found such subjects as learning how to determine your husband's disposition, discerning your husband's particular pleasures, how to create a mood of openness and relaxation, how to prevent him from looking for "succor" elsewhere and how to prevent "consequences" of such unions. If these things were true of husbands, they would almost certainly apply to lovers, as well. She decided to purchase this little treasure trove of information. It could prove very interesting reading indeed.

The intruder moved away and Mr. Renquist began speaking again, his voice low and furtive. "We can't be sure it was Morgan who hired the runner, Mrs. Forbush. I'm still looking into that."

"Thank you, Mr. Renquist. And were you able to glean any information regarding Lord Geoffrey's background?"

"That was a bit easier. The man is fairly well known and he has made no attempt to cover his past."

Graced looked around again, assuring herself that they

were private, and then nodded encouragement. "Is there anything he would wish to cover?"

Mr. Renquist shrugged. "You decide, Mrs. Forbush. He comes from a good family, comfortable, but not well off. The father was a baron from Yorkshire. He had only one sister. After school, he was commissioned in the Royal Navy, and from there he was transferred to some obscure government branch for service abroad. Still looking into that. But whilst he was in the navy, his mother died and his sister was wed off to an older gentleman of wealth but questionable reputation. She died of a fall two years later."

Renquist took a deep breath and shook his head. "It gets a little foggy from here on out. It was just before that when Lady Annica was involved in investigating the white slavery traffic and Miss Bennington was killed. Morgan disappeared after that. No one knows where he was or what he was doing. Rumors range from mending his broken heart to being on a secret mission for the crown. All we know for certain is that by the time he returned, his father had come to London on business and got caught up in the social whirl. Fell in with a fast crowd and found hells. They were all deep players, I understand. The elder Morgan depleted the family fortune to satisfy his gaming debts, then sold the mother's jewelry—"

"Heavens. But they must have had property?"

"Aye. But he lost that, too, and swore he was cheated. Challenged some young buck from Hampshire to a duel. Pistols at dawn, y'know. Morgan's father was killed."

How tragic, Grace thought. Lord Geoffrey had lost his entire family. But if he held gambling responsible, why did he now engage in it as an occupation? "Was Lord Geoffrey seeking revenge when he took up gambling?"

"That is what everyone thought at first. Now they say it's a family weakness. The difference is that Lord Geoffrey is skilled. If rumor is true, he's made a fabulous fortune at it."

He doesn't need the money, Grace thought, but he'd be anxious to hold on to it after his father's misfortune. So then the excitement *was* what brought him back to the tables night after night. And he must resort to cheating only if the stakes were high enough to put his fortune at risk.

"And what do the gossipmongers say about his cheating?"

"Most say yes, but it could be just devilish good luck."

Ah, but Grace had learned that gossip often had a core of truth. She glanced down at the book in her hand. The answer to her next question would determine her course. "Did you find any reason why a man like Lord Geoffrey Morgan would have to win a bride in a game of cards rather than court and woo one?"

"No speculation on that, Mrs. Forbush. He's had a mistress or two, but tired of them quickly. Recently he's only been seen with courtesans and the demimonde. I doubt many of the men whose money he takes would be willing to ask him home to dinner to meet their daughters. And I likewise doubt he has many invitations to balls and the like."

No reassurances there. She would have to continue her investigation. She thanked Mr. Renquist, arranged to meet with him at Marie's shop on Monday, and went to the counter to pay for her purchase.

The clerk looked down at her choice and raised his eyebrows. "Very forward-thinking of you, madam. Our usual purchaser is male."

She laughed, glad she was wearing gloves to hide the absence of a wedding ring. "I think it is always useful to know what our men are thinking that we should do to make them happy."

The clerk chortled, gave her the change, and wrapped her purchase in brown paper.

She stepped out onto the street and opened her parasol, her little book tucked under her arm. She would be home in time to take a long, leisurely bath before going out this evening and she would look into some more of the chapters then.

Mr. Dewberry, sitting in the box of her coach across the street, waved at her and hopped down to hold the door for her. Traffic was light and she stepped off the curb to cross the street.

From the corner of her eye, she noted a coach pulling away from its position a few yards down the street. She was half-way across the broad street when the driver cracked his whip over the horse's head and the coach picked up speed. He was going too fast to stop and he was headed straight for her!

Mr. Dewberry lunged at her in a flying tackle, driving them both to the ground and rolling away from the thundering coach. Grace heard a woman scream and men shouting. Someone lifted her to her feet and then helped Mr. Dewberry to his. She could not catch her breath as she looked after the coach, now disappearing around a corner.

Snippets of conversation stuck in her mind. "Lucky to be alive, miss." "Deuced drivers ought to watch where they're going."

And Mr. Dewberry. "You could've been killed, Mrs. Forbush!"

The crowd disbursed with the conclusion that it had all been an unfortunate accident. But Grace wasn't so certain. Was it too coincidental after the other night outside the Two Sevens? Could Adam have been right? Could she have been the target?

Chapter Fourteen

Grace sank into her bath with a contented sigh. The muscles in her stomach and thighs relaxed in the heated water, and the new bruise on her hip from Mr. Dewberry's rescue throbbed with a dull ache. But she couldn't dawdle long. She'd forgone dinner for this little luxury, so she intended to make the most of it. She pushed questions about the "accident" from her mind. If she thought about that for long, it would her drive her mad. Everyone had been so certain it was an accident that she felt foolish suspecting more. After all, who could possibly want her dead?

As she let the jasmine-scented water relax and soothe her, she opened her new book. Skipping ahead to the chapter on discerning your husband's particular pleasures, she read between the lines. The advice was general, of necessity. She managed to gather that she should take note of anything she did or said that elicited a desired reaction, then make use of those details at unexpected times to increase her husband's happiness. She put the little book aside and closed her eyes, thinking back to the night before.

She recalled standing in the library, unfastening the hooks of her gown. Adam had seemed quite distracted when she'd rested her hands on her breasts. And when she'd let her gown slip to the floor, his breathing had grown deeper. Thus, Adam must like seeing her undress. Perhaps the little delay had sharpened his desire for more. Or seeing her touch herself where his hands had so recently been had made him eager to touch her again. And he'd liked her garters enough to leave them on after all other traces of clothing were gone.

But how could she use that? She could scarcely start to undress every time she wanted to charm him. Oh, but perhaps there were more subtle ways to remind him of that incident. Ways that might even make her look more worldly and experienced. Yes, she would have to brazen out the incident last night as if it were a common occurrence.

After spending years practicing ways to distance men from her, to appear untouchable through her reputation and cool manner, Grace found that she wanted to pull Adam closer. Now that they were lovers…she would practice new skills.

She began by touching her earlobe, then sliding her hand slowly down her soap-slick skin until it touched her breast. Still sensitive from Adam's attentions last night, the aureole and nipple beaded into a hard little button. Yes, Adam had liked that, too. And so had she.

She picked up the book and turned the page and read that a husband is sometimes pleasantly diverted when his wife is playfully naughty. *Naughty!* Grace chuckled. What, precisely, would that entail? She'd never been naughty a single day in her life—until last night. But she was determined to learn.

Adam paced the library. He'd hurried home to join Grace and Dianthe for dinner, only to find that Dianthe had left early to go to a musicale at the Aubervilles' and Grace was supping in her room. He prayed he hadn't been too hard on her last night. Had he known…he could have spared her some of the discomfort, and he would not have used her so unrelentingly.

He'd taken a tray to his own room, bathed, shaved and changed for the evening out. Actually, he'd been relieved to avoid the dinner table. He didn't want his first encounter with Grace after their intimacies to be in the presence of others. He hoped she would talk to him about her past. Specifically, how the bloody hell she could still have been a virgin.

In pursuit of an answer to that question, after leaving Major Taylor in his stupor, he'd gone to his uncle's doctor's office, where he'd gleaned two very interesting tidbits. One, that Basil Forbush had been in excellent health for a man his age until the week before his death. And two, that he had not complained of inability to perform satisfactorily as a husband.

And yet Grace had unquestionably been virgin. Had she refused to receive her husband? Or had Basil been impotent and too embarrassed to confide in his doctor? Whatever the reason for her virginal state, Grace had clearly wanted to deceive him about it.

Should he confront her? Demand answers? Even if doing so would alert her that her deception had failed? But what if there was a more insidious reason for her deception? One that she couldn't risk him finding out about? One that might have to do with the death of his uncle?

When he'd asked the doctor if he suspected foul play in the death of his uncle, the doctor had shrugged. "I did at first, but some poisons are hard to trace and mimic the symptoms of other ailments. Your uncle was sixty and five. It is not unheard of for men of that age to fall ill to a malady from which they do not recover."

An inadequate visit in all respects. He'd hoped to find a simple, clear answer and he'd only grown more suspicious. Until he could be reasonably certain that Grace was not responsible for his uncle's death, he would have to be very careful—vigilant. It would be foolhardy to become her lover, and Adam was no fool.

The library door opened and Grace glided in, a soft blush staining her cheeks. She had dressed in a copper-colored gown of muslin trimmed in satin that made her skin glow and her dark eyes sparkle. The cut was unlike the one that she wore last night and he found himself trying to determine where the hooks were hidden.

She turned to close the doors, affording him a glimpse of the graceful curve of her neck and spine. Blood rushed to his groin.

"Good evening, Adam," she said as smoothly as if they'd last seen each other at afternoon tea.

"Grace," he acknowledged. She might want to ignore her virginity, but he wasn't about to let her ignore last night. He gave her a wolfish smile. "Did you sleep well?"

"Like the dead," she said as she passed him on her way to the sherry bottle. An exotic scent that was both floral and spicy, trailed in her wake, as did her little half smile. Very provocative. And there was a difference in the way she moved, as if she were more aware of her own body. She certainly knew how to give the impression of a woman of the world. He'd have to give her that.

She poured herself a sherry and walked back toward him, raising her glass as she came. When she was near enough, she touched the rim of her glass to his. "To Dr. Hawthorne's sleeping remedy."

He grinned in spite of himself. He was going to have to remind himself constantly to be on guard. Resisting Grace was not going to be easy.

Grace allowed Adam to take her cloak as she tried to hear snips of conversation. The crowd at Belmonde's was buzzing with excitement and she wondered what could cause such a stir.

She heard the names "Morgan" and "Lord Grayson" but she couldn't sort out the rest. A crowd was gathering near one of the private side rooms where patrons could wager each other.

She took a glass of champagne from the tray of a passing waiter and wandered in that direction. Adam had been stopped by an old friend and signaled that he'd be along momentarily.

She edged through the doorway and skimmed the perimeter of the room until she had a clear view of a table at which Lord Geoffrey and Lord Grayson were seated. The two men faced each other and the contrast between them was startling. Morgan appeared cool and hard-eyed. Grayson, on the other hand, was flushed and a fine sheen coated his face. He was staring intently at his cards and sitting forward in his chair. A single glance said that the man was playing for deep stakes, certainly more than he should have wagered.

Lord Geoffrey, on the other hand, was sitting back in his chair, looking relaxed and almost bored as he waited for a response from Lord Grayson. He folded his hand and lay it, facedown, on the table in front of him and glanced up at her. Although his expression did not change, Grace perceived a subtle difference in his bearing, a small spike of interest. Had his investigator reported that she had sold some jewelry? Had he marked her absence last night and wondered if she had been unable to come up with the funds to wager? She would have to reassure him once this little tableau was over.

Slowly, Lord Grayson pushed his remaining pile of counters across the green baize cloth to the center of the table. Grace couldn't tell what game they were playing, but the rest was evident. Grayson had just wagered everything he had left on his hand.

The crowd pressed forward to witness the conclusion and Grace's view was blocked. Drats! Whatever the wager, it was sufficiently large to tempt Lord Geoffrey to not leave it to chance. She'd watched as he folded his hand and placed it on the table, and she hadn't seen any signs of cheating or sleight of hand. But she could have missed something before she'd arrived, or after the crowd had blocked her view.

A collective gasp filled the room, followed by exclamations of disbelief and amazement. The crowd began to disburse until only a few men remained. Grace held her breath, waiting to see what would happen next.

Lord Grayson pushed back from the table and narrowed his eyes at Lord Geoffrey. "You cheated, damn you. How'd you do it?"

Still looking bored, Lord Geoffrey gathered the cards into a single pile and held them out to Lord Grayson. "Have them examined, Grayson. How many witnesses did we have? Did anyone cry foul? You cannot blame me for your folly."

"But I'm ruined!"

Lord Geoffrey offered the deck to the room monitor, who hurried off, ostensibly to check for marked cards or any other trick that might have given him the advantage. He turned back to Lord Grayson and shrugged. "You should have thought of that before you made the wager."

"You cannot mean to…"

"Hold you to your word? But of course I do. You'd have taken my wager in a trice."

"I have a family, damn it all. What about them?"

Grace thought of Mr. Talbot and wondered if he had made such a plea when he'd wagered his fortune and his sister away. But Lord Geoffrey's reply told how useless that would have been.

"It is their misfortune to have a fool for a husband and father."

Grayson's friends, gathered behind his chair, began to grumble at the insult. Lord Geoffrey pushed his chair back from the table and stood, apparently bored with the scene. Before he could turn away, Lord Grayson stood, too, and delivered a challenge.

Utter silence filled the room. Grayson must have concluded that his debt would be canceled if Lord Geoffrey were dead. To her shame, she realized that Laura Talbot, too, would be freed by such an eventuality.

A long moment passed as Lord Geoffrey studied Lord Grayson's face, as if trying to decide the degree of determination there.

He sighed. "Very well, Grayson. If you will have it no other way?"

"Call the wager void."

A dark smile curved Lord Geoffrey's mouth. "Not a chance."

"Name your second, sir."

Lord Geoffrey looked in her direction and, for a moment, she was absurdly afraid that he would name her.

"Hawthorne," he said.

She whirled to find that Adam had come up behind her. A sense of relief washed through her and she felt instantly calmer. He placed his hand on her back almost possessively. He looked reluctant and she sensed he would beg off.

"Come now, Hawthorne," Lord Geoffrey cajoled. "You needn't defend me, just attend the details, stand at my back and make certain my pistol's loaded."

"Very well," he conceded, but Grace could tell he was not comfortable with the duty.

Lord Grayson nodded to Adam and left the room, leaving his friends and Adam to follow.

Adam took Grace's hand and shot a quick glance at Lord Geoffrey. "I will be back as soon as we settle on the details, Grace. Meantime, stay here."

"Adam," she began, about to tell him that she could manage herself quite well, but the look in his eyes stopped her. She nodded.

The room was empty then, but for her and Lord Geoffrey. He sat again and gestured her to take Lord Grayson's vacated chair.

"I am astonished at your calm, Lord Geoffrey," she said.

"A man has just declared his intention to kill you. Are you not disturbed by that?"

"He's not the first, and I am willing to wager he will not be the last."

"Have you considered a change in occupations?"

He barely blinked, but turned the conversation abruptly, as if she'd said nothing. "How nice to see you again, Mrs. Forbush. When you did not appear last night, I feared you had grown weary of hells."

She sipped her champagne. "Not at all, Lord Geoffrey. I had pressing matters at home."

He smiled. "Yes, I gathered." He lifted his wineglass and toasted her. "You've cost me money this time, my dear."

"Another wager?" she asked.

He nodded.

"And you lost? How diverting. Would you mind telling me what the wager was?"

"Who you would take as your next lover now that Barrington is a thing of the past."

She was stunned. Although she had been aware of the rumors concerning her "discreet liaisons," she hadn't been aware it was a subject for wagers. Embarrassment warred with curiosity. Curiosity won. "But how has that cost you money, sir?"

"Hawthorne. I was betting on someone else."

Panic began to rise. Had it been so obvious? "What makes you think Mr. Hawthorne and I are lovers?"

A slow grin warmed his features. "I could tell the moment he entered the room. A man has a certain look when he has… known a woman. And the way he touched you. Proprietary, m'dear."

She struggled with that for a moment, wanting to deny it, but unable to resist his open honesty. "And who did you place your money on?"

"Me."

Grace coughed and put her champagne glass on the table to prevent it from spilling. She laughed. "You? But we scarcely know each other."

He tapped a hundred pound counter in front of him. "Allow me to speak frankly, Mrs. Forbush."

"Could I prevent you?"

"I have been sensing that you have something more than a casual interest in me. I am not certain what that might be, or why, but thought you might take up with disreputable men as long as you were taking up disreputable pursuits."

Oh, dear. She hadn't realized she'd been so obvious in her interest. At least he had not guessed why. "I think you are a very out-of-the ordinary man. I admire your composure in a crisis. I thought I could learn from you."

The room monitor came back and gave them a nod. Apparently the deck of cards had passed inspection. He took up his station at a discreet distance.

Lord Geoffrey turned back to her. "So you were looking for a tutor, not a lover?"

Grace looked down into her champagne. *Were* she and Adam lovers? He hadn't mentioned anything in the coach, nor had he done anything but hint at last night. Perhaps the encounter had meant less to him than it had to her. And it might be useful for Lord Geoffrey to think there was still a chance. "A single grain of sand does not constitute a mountain, Lord Geoffrey."

Now Lord Geoffrey laughed. "Was it an audition, Mrs. Forbush? Are you still casting for the role?"

She studied him over the rim of her glass. He was teasing. She was sure of it. Sure enough to call his bluff? Not quite. It was her turn to change the subject. "Do you know briscola?" she asked.

"Quite well," he said, signaling for a new deck of cards.

* * *

Leaving nothing to chance, Adam had Mr. Dewberry bring the coach around before fetching Grace from the tables. When he handed her into the coach, Mr. Dewberry started off at a slow pace, just as he'd instructed. He wondered why Grace hadn't told him about the attempt on her life this afternoon.

When Dewberry had let that little piece of information slip earlier, he'd been aghast. How could Grace forget to mention such a thing? Most women would take to their beds in vapors after nearly being run down by a coach. If not for Eddy Clark, he'd begin to think Grace had been the target all along. Unless…had his enemy sent him a warning by attacking Grace? Or was there some reason even Grace didn't know that someone would want her out of the way? Carter had warned that she had enemies.

Frowning, Grace turned to him and said, "What was that about, Adam—rushing me into the coach like that? Are you still concerned about that thief the other night?"

"I'd think you'd be a little more concerned, given the attempt on your life this afternoon."

"What attempt? Oh! Do you mean the coach that nearly ran me down? Heavens! That was my fault for stepping into the street without looking."

"Dewberry says it looked deliberate to him."

"Pish! He has become overprotective since the thief attacked us. I swear, 'tis coincidence. Now it will be years before anything happens again."

He hoped to hell it would be. The odds of someone wanting him and Grace dead at the same time were staggering. Still, there were rather too many accidents for coincidence. "Promise you will be more careful from now on. And promise you will take Dewberry with you everywhere."

She gave him a curious look. "Do you really think that is necessary?"

He gave her a grim nod. "At least for the next several weeks."

"Very well. But there is something else I am more concerned about."

"And what would that be?"

"Adam, please explain how the duel will be done."

"Are you worried for Lord Geoffrey?" he asked, annoyed by the little stab of jealousy that twisted inside him.

"No. Yes. Well, of course I would not want either Lord Geoffrey or Lord Grayson to come to harm."

Adam laughed. "Someone could die because of it. I'd call that trouble. I did, however, take steps to limit the possible consequences."

"How—"

"We are meeting at dawn near the Chapel House on the Isle of Dogs. We agreed upon pistols, and that a single shot would satisfy the requirements. With luck, both will go wide of the mark and that will be the end of it."

"They do not seem to be the sort of men to miss."

He shrugged. "There was little else I could do but have a surgeon standing by. Grayson's second wanted satisfaction to be a duel to the death, likely because it is Grayson's only chance to regain his fortune."

"Lord Geoffrey seemed implacable. I thought he would try to appease Lord Grayson. Or refuse the challenge."

Adam regarded her somberly through the gloom of the coach. Was she ignorant of the consequences of denying a challenge, or was she simply so concerned for Lord Geoffrey's safety that she did not care? "Have you voiced your concern to Lord Geoffrey?"

"When I broached the subject, he refused to speak about it. I only wonder what sort of man, well, makes the choices Lord Geoffrey has made."

He shrugged. "I can only say that I'd have made the same choice he made tonight. Had he forgiven the debt, it would have been tantamount to admitting he'd cheated and an invitation to other gamblers that he could be reneged on. Had he refused the challenge, he'd have been labeled a coward, and worse."

Grace looked up at him, a frown knitting fine lines between her brows. "What do you think, Adam? *Did* Lord Geoffrey cheat?"

He relaxed against the seat. She must not be all that fond of Morgan if she believed he might be capable of such behavior. "I was not there," he reminded her. "Anything is possible, and Morgan's reputation would not rule that out."

"Do you think they will both walk away from the duel in the morning?"

"I haven't the faintest notion. Grayson is a crack shot from what I hear, but Morgan has considerably more experience in dueling. Anyone's guess, I'd say. Who will you say your prayers for tonight?"

"For good sense to prevail," she breathed. "Adam, stop them."

He couldn't have heard her correctly. "Excuse me?" he asked.

"Stop the duel. The whole thing is ridiculous. The outcome will not prove if Lord Geoffrey was cheating or not. How will it set anything to rights?"

"It won't. But it *will* decide the matter and put an end to it. I will not interfere."

"Then I suppose I must," she said, looking up at him.

Adam grinned down at her. He might be determined to resist Grace's charms until he discovered what she was hiding, but he did not have to deny Grace *his* charms. That, in fact, would be the perfect ploy to keep her off balance. "Not if I have to tie you to your bed, Mrs. Forbush," he said.

Uncertainty flickered in those dark eyes. "You wouldn't."

"Wouldn't I? Is it so hard to believe that I would prevent you from coming between two men who are determined to kill one another?"

"I do not like anyone telling me what I may do," she warned in a low voice.

"Nevertheless."

Her mutinous expression almost made him laugh. He doubted she had used that particular expression since she was a child. He lifted her chin on his finger. "Come now, Ellie, be a good girl."

He bent to claim her lips and found them incredibly tantalizing. At first they were firm, as if she would protest or deny him. Then, ever so sweetly, they softened and molded to his with a sigh of surrender. He urged them open with a series of insistent kisses. She moaned as she gave him access to her interior.

Moving his hands beneath her cloak, he worked at the hooks at the front of her gown. When a full, ripe breast filled his hand, he nearly forgot his resolve to resist her. Taking a firm hold on his rising passion, he nudged her cloak away with his chin. When her took the rosy peak into his mouth, she gasped and her head fell back against the seat.

She took fire quickly, and Adam knew just where to touch, what to kiss, how to move, to incite her breathless responses. Her palm cupped his head, holding him closer as he swept his hand beneath her skirt and up the inside of her leg. Her drawers were no barrier to his determination. He stroked lightly upward until he found the already-swollen nub at the top of the lush folds shielding her sex. He moved his finger over it with a feathery light stroke and she shuddered, bringing one knee up in reaction. Resist....

He stroked downward, finding the sleek heat of her sweet, tight entrance. She was so responsive that he had to fight his instinct to take her then and there. Last night had whetted his appetite for more. But he couldn't risk letting his guard down. Couldn't risk her betrayal. Ah, but he could play her game. *Resist....*

Slowly, he increased the rhythm of his strokes, deepening

the pressure and penetration, until she was trembling and murmuring his name. He felt as if he were ready to explode and wanted nothing more than to bury himself inside her and move with the primordial rhythm until they both found ecstasy. *Resist....* He slowed his stroking, deliberately keeping her on edge and unfulfilled.

The coach lurched to a stop and Adam dragged himself from the passion-induced haze. He tugged her cloak together and threw the door open, hurrying to help her down before Dewberry saw her state of disarray. Murmuring something about fatigue over his shoulder, he ushered Grace into the house, leaving Dewberry to stare after them.

Grace clung to him as he led her up the stairs and down the hall to her door. She leaned into him as he turned the knob and pushed the door open. "Adam," she said, her hand fisting around his cravat as if she would drag him inside. Bloody hell! *Resist....*

He leaned down and gave her a bittersweet kiss before he straightened and stepped back. "I have an early morning, so I'll say good night, Grace." He gave her a gentle nudge inside and then closed the door before she could object. Hell—before *he* could object!

Damn it, resisting Grace was going to kill him.

Chapter Fifteen

"Heavens, Aunt Grace, what is wrong with you? I've asked the same question three times!"

Sitting with an open book in her lap, Grace realized she had not turned a page in fully quarter of an hour. She closed the book with a sharp slap and stood. "I am sorry, Dianthe. What did you say?"

"I asked what has you so preoccupied. It is Friday. Should you not be plotting your strategy for tonight? Did you not think to play deeper?"

"There may not even be a tonight, Di."

Dianthe, painting a miniature of a lily of the valley, wiped her paintbrush on a rag and frowned. "Of course there will be. I've never heard you so pessimistic. What has got into you?"

She glanced at the mantel clock. Eleven o'clock. She'd heard Adam leave at five. Shouldn't it be done by now? Had something gone wrong? She went to the window and looked for any trace of Adam's horse. Nothing.

A movement on the bench across the street caught her eye and she squinted to focus. A man who had appeared to be staring at the window stood and hurried away. But he didn't go far. Once concealed by shrubbery, he must have stopped, because he hadn't reappeared further along the path where the shrubbery thinned. Was that Lord Geoffrey's man, looking to find some dirt, as Mr. Renquist had warned? She simply couldn't care at the moment. Not until she knew what was keeping Adam.

She thought of him as she'd seen him last, at her bedroom door. She'd wanted him to come in. She'd wanted to do again what they'd done the night before. But he'd backed away from her, made an excuse about an early morning and closed her door in her face. Was he bored with her already? Did he no longer want her now that he'd sampled her?

A coach pulled into view. It was sleek, black, bore a mark Grace didn't recognize and, most disturbing of all, Adam's horse was trailing on a tether. When Lord Geoffrey hopped down, her heart dropped to the floor. Dear Lord, what had happened to Adam?

Lord Geoffrey turned and helped someone out of the coach, propping him with his shoulder as they turned and headed to the house. It was Adam! And his head was wrapped in thick white bandages!

Grace ran for the door and threw it open, taking up station on Adam's other side. "The library," she instructed, and indicated the direction with a nod of her head.

"What happened?" she demanded, and winced when she realized she sounded like an angry mother. Taking a deep breath, she softened her voice. "I thought it was *your* duel, Lord Geoffrey."

"It was, Mrs. Forbush. *That* part went well enough." He sat across from Adam. "I could use a brandy. Mr. Hawthorne, too. He's got the devil of a headache."

Adam lifted his hands to shift the bandages and winced. "It isn't as bad as it looks. I am the least of the casualties."

Grace turned and nodded to a wide-eyed Dianthe, who

then hurried to the carafe on the sideboard. "What has happened to you, Adam?"

"Didn't do it to myself," he said.

Dianthe brought the glasses and carafe on a tray and the men helped themselves. At a nudge from her niece, she remembered her manners. "Dianthe, may I present Lord Geoffrey Morgan. Lord Geoffrey, please meet my niece, Miss Lovejoy."

Lord Geoffrey bowed and gave Dianthe a slow smile of appreciation. "Miss Lovejoy."

She wiped her hands on her smock and bobbed a quick curtsy before offering her hand. "Lord Geoffrey, I am... pleased to make your acquaintance."

Oh, dear! She could tell by the hesitation in Dianthe's words that she had recognized their prey and was trying to think how she might help Grace. "Well, at least now I know why you have been distracted this morning, Aunt Grace."

Lord Geoffrey gave her a bemused look, then turned to Grace. "Were you worried, Mrs. Forbush?"

"It seems I had a right to be," she said. She turned back to Adam. "Are you well enough to tell me what happened, Adam?"

He sipped from his glass and sank back against the cushions, the tension draining from his posture. "Everything went as planned. One shot each. When Geoff—Lord Geoffrey turned at the count, he didn't raise his pistol. He waited until Lord Grayson aimed and fired. Grayson's hand was shaking so badly that his shot went wide."

"Is that—"

He shook his head. "When the smoke cleared, Lord Geoffrey took aim, adjusted his shot and hit Lord Grayson high in his left shoulder. A flesh wound, but it satisfied first blood."

Grace and Dianthe glanced up at Lord Geoffrey, who was downing his brandy. What extreme coolness the man possessed to allow Lord Grayson the first shot. In most duels the opponents fired simultaneously. And how deliberate he'd been in calculating the damage he could do.

"When Lord Geoffrey turned away to replace his pistol in the case, and while the surgeon was tending to Grayson, his second, Ralph Lucas, drew his own pistol and aimed at Lord Geoffrey's back. Seems they were determined to cancel the debt in any way necessary."

"And that's when Hawthorne lunged to knock me out of the way," Lord Geoffrey finished. "The ball grazed his temple. I owe him my life."

"I was your second. It was my duty," Adam mumbled.

"Being a second does not require you to throw yourself in front of a bullet," Lord Geoffrey disagreed. "Most would not even have seen it coming, let alone have taken the bullet."

Duty? Dear Lord! Adam had risked his own life to save Lord Geoffrey, who was a virtual stranger. That went rather beyond duty. "Thank heavens it was no worse," she breathed.

Lord Geoffrey laughed without the least trace of humor. "Oh, it got worse."

"How…"

"While Hawthorne and I were still getting to our feet, Lucas was reloading."

Dianthe's eyes grew round and she covered her mouth to stifle a gasp.

"It was the damnedest thing I've ever seen," Lord Geoffrey continued, shaking his head. "It's still a blur. Hawthorne pulled a knife from somewhere and threw it. Forty feet if it was an inch. Buried itself to the hilt in Lucas's chest. He's dead, of course."

Grace turned back to Adam. His jaw was set in a hard line, and she saw a haunted look enter the depths of his hazel eyes. She squeezed his hand. "It was self-defense. You are alive and that's all that matters," she whispered.

"Grayson swears he didn't know what Lucas planned, but

the other witnesses think otherwise. If he died, Grayson wanted to make certain his heirs would keep his fortune."

"Mr. L-Lucas is dead?" Dianthe asked in a thready voice, staring at Lord Geoffrey and Adam with a horrified expression.

Grace remembered that Mr. Lucas was one of the men who had paid court to Dianthe. He'd been a pleasant-looking man, tall, and with an excellent build. He'd had impeccable manners and bright blue eyes.

"Sorry, Dianthe," Adam sighed.

She hurried to the other side of his chair with tears shimmering in her eyes and took his hand. "No, cousin. Do not be sorry. I do not blame you. This is not your fault." She looked up at Lord Geoffrey and narrowed her eyes. "It is yours!" she said. "What business did you have to ask my cousin to be your second? You barely know each other! Are you so bereft of friends that you could not find anyone but a stranger to stand up with you? You are a devil disguised as a man!"

Grace gasped. "Dianthe!" Had the girl forgotten herself in her indignation on Adam's behalf? "You cannot blame—"

Lord Geoffrey's spine stiffened and his expression froze. "No, Mrs. Forbush. Your niece is quite right. I've imposed long enough." He placed his glass on the tray and stepped back, toward the door. "Thank you again, Hawthorne. I owe you my life, and I will not forget that." He bowed sharply from the waist. "Ladies, good day to you."

And he was gone. Adam gripped the arms of the chair and pushed himself to his feet. Dried blood stained the front of his shirt. "Please do not worry about me. I need to change and get to an appointment by two o'clock. Would it be an imposition if I used the coach today?"

"Of course not," Grace said. The last thing she wanted was for him to fall from his horse. "Are you well enough to go out?"

"Quite well," he reassured them as he went to the door.

Alone again, Grace sank into a chair and groaned. Her

stomach turned when she thought that Adam could have been seriously hurt—or worse. "Men! What possesses them?"

"I do not know," Dianthe breathed. "But now I have two reasons to want to see Lord Geoffrey Morgan brought low. He is a despicable man! Laura Talbot must not marry him!"

About to argue that Lord Geoffrey was not responsible for Ralph Lucas's perfidy, Grace sighed as the implications of this event would have on her investigation hit home. She buried her face in her hands and shook her head. "We may not be able to prevent the marriage now, Dianthe."

"Whatever do you mean, Aunt Grace? Nothing has changed."

"*Everything* has changed. Lord Geoffrey owes Adam his life. Do you really think he will cheat me now? No, he will consider it his duty to allow me to win because of my relationship to Adam. How will I trap him now?"

She stood and began pacing. "Oh! All the hard work, all the nights of cozening up to him, learning the games he likes to play, watching him at his work—all for nothing now!"

"You are assuming the man has a sense of honor," Dianthe snapped.

Did he? Grace thought back. When she was new on the gambling scene, he had allowed her numerous "practice" games before wagering for money. And when Ronald Barrington had bullied her, Lord Geoffrey had stood in her defense. Was that honor? Or outrage? And if the man was a cheat, would he have a sense of honor? Or would he be just as likely to cheat her now as before?

Dianthe narrowed her eyes. "Oh! It is almost like he planned this! The cad! But we cannot give up. We shall just have to think of another way."

My dear Miss Talbot,
I must speak with you at your earliest convenience.

Grace crumpled the paper and tossed it in the general direction of the fireplace. She did not want to alarm the girl. Pulling another sheet of paper from her desk drawer, she tried again.

My dear Miss Talbot,
   As time is growing short, I would like to meet with you to discuss alternate strategies should our original plan fail. Though I do not wish you to worry, recent events have put the outcome of our endeavor in doubt and I believe it would be prudent to be prepared.
   Please come to me Sunday after church services or notify me by return post of a convenient time and place to meet.
   Yours truly,
   Mrs. Forbush

She was still addressing the envelope when she heard an argument in the foyer just before the library door burst open to reveal a red-faced Ronald Barrington with a breathless Mrs. Dewberry fast behind.

Attempting to still her rapidly beating heart, Grace was careful not to show fear or dismay. She'd learned long ago under her brother's tutelage that weakness invited abuse. She stood, but remained behind the desk.

"Lord Barrington," she said. "Did you wish to see me?"

"You know I do! I'm finished leaving messages every day that you simply ignore."

Grace shifted her gaze to Mrs. Dewberry.

"I've been throwing them out, Mrs. Forbush," she admitted. "I knew you didn't want to see him."

"Thank you, Mrs. Dewberry, but I do not need you to censor my mail. Please do not do so in the future."

"Yes, Missus."

"You may leave us," she said, and waited until the door was

closed. "Sit down, my lord. I gather there is something you wished to say to me?"

"That infernal woman has been putting my mail in the dust bin? The gall! Though that does make me feel somewhat better. At least *you* have not been ignoring me."

He seemed calmer, too, Grace was relieved to note, but far too comfortable. Without asking, he went to the liquor bottle and poured himself a generous portion. When he turned to her, she shook her head and glanced toward the clock. Five o'clock. She prayed she could get rid of Barrington before Adam returned. The last thing he needed on a day like today was another altercation.

She sat and waited for Barrington to take the chair on the opposite side of the desk. "What was it you needed, Lord Barrington?" she asked in as pleasant a tone as she could manage.

"Why, to talk to you, of course. To explain. To make you understand that, had you not provoked me, I never would have—"

"Did I not tell you, my lord, that I forgive you and accept a part of the blame? But you do realize, do you not, that we cannot go back and undo the damage?"

"I do not see why we should, Grace. The memory of it should serve as a caution and prevent it from ever happening again. In a friendship as long-standing as ours, surely one small misunderstanding can be worked out."

Heavens! He was completely serious. If it were not for the fine sheen of perspiration on his forehead, she would believe he actually thought she would resume their friendship. She braced herself for unpleasantness. "As I said before, Lord Barrington, I hope we shall always be able to remain cordial. After so long, it would be a pity if we could not pass pleasantries when we find ourselves in the same place. But to pretend anything more would be a travesty. If I cannot trust you with my person, how could I pretend a friendship that I simply do not feel?"

"Because, Grace," he said, his voice dropping an octave, "if you do not, you will be in more trouble than you bargained for."

Her heart stilled and a feeling of deep foreboding grew in her. "Let us not mince words. Are you threatening me, Lord Barrington?"

"Take it as you will."

"What possible trouble could I be in?"

"I have heard whisperings about you and Hawthorne."

She shrugged. "There were whisperings about us, Barrington. And I did not hear your objections then."

"Are you saying that there is no truth to the talk about you and Hawthorne?"

She gritted her teeth before she could vilify him, and she knew the truth of her relationship with Adam would only outrage him. "I think I am finished with this conversation. You have no right to call me to account for anything I may or may not do. To pretend otherwise would suggest a relationship that does not exist." She stood and indicated the door with a sweep of her hand. "I am sorry if you feel you cannot put this ugliness behind us and go forward with a degree of civility."

Barrington, too, stood and finished his brandy in a single gulp. "Damn it, Grace. I came here to make amends and you will have none of it. Is it Hawthorne? Has he turned your head?"

Oh my, yes! Turned her head and more. But that was none of Barrington's business. She merely fastened him with a hard look.

"You are making a grave mistake, Grace. I am all that is standing between you and disaster. I would think you would embrace the opportunity to take me back."

That was the second threat he had made. She was struck by the sudden suspicion that Lord Barrington could be behind the rash of accidents that had befallen her and Adam. "What have you done, Barrington?"

"I? Nothing. But…no, I have said too much."

The excited tones of Mrs. Dewberry's muted voice carried from the foyer and Grace realized that Adam must have come home. She exhaled in relief and mere seconds later, Adam was standing in the doorway.

"Hello, Barrington," he said, and cast a searching glance at Grace. "Is there a problem?"

"No," Grace said. She sighed, the tension leaving her muscles. She hadn't realized she had been prepared for a fight until that moment. "Lord Barrington was just leaving."

Barrington flushed and glanced between the two of them. "I begin to think the rumors are true. If 'tis so, I would not give a farthing for either of you." He leaned toward Grace to put his empty glass on the desk and murmured in an undertone, "This conversation is not done, my dear."

"Would you care to explain that cryptic remark?" Adam stood back to free the way for Barrington's exit.

"You shall find out soon enough, pup."

Grace sank back into her chair, relieved to hear the front door slam. Adam came forward and took Barrington's vacated chair, facing her. "Is there anything I should know?"

"He has heard rumors about…us," she said. "I believe he may be jealous."

"What rumors?"

"That we are…that we have become…lovers."

A small smile played at the corners of Adam's mouth and Grace suspected he was not altogether displeased by this news. "And what did you tell him?"

"Nothing. I do not want him to know anything about what I do. And I certainly do not want him thinking he has the right to question me."

"Are you ashamed that we have—"

"No," she hastened to assure him. She really must remember to rid herself of virginal modesty. This blushing business was becoming tiresome. "Not in the least. But I do not like being the subject of gossip."

Seeking to change the subject, she asked, "Were you on time for your appointment?"

Adam grinned and nodded. "I was just checking in on an old friend."

"Is he ill?"

"I suppose you could call it that. He is going through a rough patch and not making much sense at the moment. I've been waiting several years to have a conversation with him, and I am growing impatient. Another day or two and he should be well enough."

"I shall pray that he recovers his health."

"Long enough to answer a few questions, at any rate," Adam said. At her quizzical look he changed the subject. "Are we gambling tonight?"

"I must, I'm afraid," she said. For the first time she noticed that the bandage swaddling his head was gone and only a small one, barely visible, remained. Still, the day must have been trying for him. He'd nearly been killed. "I shall go alone, Adam. I am well enough known that gaining entry will not be a problem."

He sat back in his chair and regarded her long and hard. "Why 'must' you gamble, Grace? If you are simply desperate for cash, I—"

"No," she interrupted. "I only meant that I wanted to gamble. The…the excitement, you see."

"Hmm. And a quiet game at home would not satisfy?"

Good heavens! That telltale heat was back in her cheeks again. Yes, such a game would satisfy. More than satisfy. But it would not trap Morgan and free Laura Talbot. Her throat had gone dry but she managed a shrug.

"Are you certain this has nothing to do with Geoffrey Morgan?"

"He was very kind directly after Barrington made a scene. I am certain he will be at Belmonde's tonight, just to face down his detractors. There will be people who will snub him, and I would like to be likewise supportive."

"I see," he said. "Then of course I shall escort you."

"But, Adam, your head. Are you certain you are ready—"

"What I am *not* ready for, Grace, is to send you into that den of iniquity alone. Shall we say eight o'clock?"

Adam at her side, Grace stepped into the main salon at Belmonde's. Since the challenge had been issued here last night, she was certain Morgan would return here tonight. The room looked as if it had been polarized. Opposing factions gathered at each side of the room, talking among themselves. The larger group appeared to be the friends of Lord Grayson, a much smaller group stood in conversation with Lord Geoffrey. A third group, apparently the neutral faction, stood near a buffet table. She recognized Lady Sarah's brothers, all four of them, in that group.

Always striving for balance, Grace would ordinarily have gravitated to the neutral group, but she felt an obligation to Lord Geoffrey for his previous support. She took a deep breath and headed for his group.

"Is this the first time you have taken an unpopular stand, Grace?" Adam asked.

Oh, if he only knew! "Publicly," she admitted.

Lord Geoffrey saw them coming and gave them a nod. When they arrived by his side, he took her hand and bowed over it. "Mrs. Forbush," he acknowledged, and then turned to Adam. "I'm glad to see your dashing good looks will not be affected, Hawthorne."

Adam laughed. He gestured to the room at large. "And I see that you know how to put a damper on the fun."

"Yes, I suppose you're right." He nodded toward the tables. "I believe the house would prefer that we were gambling."

The men surrounding Morgan clapped him on the back and moved away toward the tables and the bar. Lord Geoffrey took her arm and led her toward the hazard table, leaving Adam to follow them. She glanced over her shoulder to see him giving Lord Geoffrey a rueful smile and she gathered there was some kind of competition between them.

There was something uncomfortable in the atmosphere of Belmonde's, and Grace could not concentrate. After losing all her counters, Lord Geoffrey offered to loan her some of his, but she refused. The last thing she wanted was to be in his debt so soon, but when Adam made the same offer, she was tempted to take it.

Ah, but Lord Geoffrey's spy would have reported that she had pawned some of her jewelry. He would think he had her nearly at his mercy. She shrugged and sighed. "I do not like to borrow, Lord Geoffrey. I would rather risk only that which I can pay."

"A small private wager, then," he offered. He led them toward one of the private rooms. "A quick game of piquet?"

Was this how he drew his victims into his web? Grace realized that this was an opportunity to cozen Lord Geoffrey into believing she would play deep and keep her word. She smiled up at him. "I'm afraid all I have to offer are my ear bobs."

"I'll take them," he said.

She removed the gold filigree drops studded with jet that matched her black gown and placed them in Lord Geoffrey's palm in exchange for ten counters. It remained to be seen whether he would hold her to the wager if she lost. She did not want to lose her earrings, but it was more important to know if he would honor his debt to Adam by sparing her. The future of her plan depended upon that answer.

Lord Geoffrey took the deck and shuffled the cards.

Adam glowered at her as they sat. "Still looking for excitement, Mrs. Forbush?" he asked.

She wet her lips, suddenly dry with anxiety. Some little demon prodded her to taunt him for his rejection last night. "Wherever I can find it, Mr. Hawthorne."

The lines of his jaw were hard and she saw the muscles tighten. Adam was quietly furious! And that realization both frightened and excited her more than anything had in years. This was the man who'd given her indescribable pleasure, whose hands had been more gentle and persuasive than any she'd ever known, but he was also the same man who had fought with and against Indians, put himself in peril to rescue her and had killed a man this very morning. He could be capable of anything and she'd do well to remember that.

Either Lord Geoffrey had not heard the byplay, or he was ignoring it. He picked up his cards and waited for Grace and Adam to do likewise.

An insistent buzzing from the adjacent room grew louder as it moved toward them. Lord Geoffrey folded his hand and watched the door. Was he expecting trouble?

Lord Reginald Hunter, Sarah's brother, sauntered into the room and fastened them with a world-weary look. "Grayson has committed suicide."

Neither Adam nor Lord Geoffrey registered surprise and Grace realized they had been expecting something of the sort. Horror filled her. How could Lord Grayson have done such a thing? To leave his wife and children impoverished and unprotected was inconceivable. She shook her head in disbelief. "You are mistaken, Lord Reginald."

"I'm afraid not, Mrs. Forbush. Lady Grayson found him at his desk, a pistol by his side. She knew nothing of his wager or the duel. She is devastated."

"But why?"

"There were murmurings that he and Ralph Lucas had

conspired to kill Morgan if Grayson lost the duel. He was finished in society."

Grace turned to Lord Geoffrey. "But you would not have taken his last pence, would you?"

"I am famous for it," Lord Geoffrey admitted.

"But his wife and children! Surely you will not…you cannot put them out on the street."

"Come now, Mrs. Forbush. Do not be melodramatic. I would imagine she has family. A brother or cousins. It is doubtful she and the brats will be left to pick rags and garbage for their existence."

Horrified, Grace studied Lord Geoffrey's handsome face. Now, quite clearly, she understood his true nature. The man did not have blood running through his veins, but ice water, thin and chilling. His charm was only skin deep, simply a device to disarm his opponents. Still, she had to try to salvage something for Lady Grayson from this calamity. "Surely, as one with experience in the devastation of loss—"

She realized it had been a mistake to refer to his father's ruinous gambling and his sister's misfortunes as soon as the words escaped her lips. Lord Geoffrey's expression froze and he stiffened. His eyes took on a cold and forbidding hue.

"Do not presume to know what I am feeling or thinking, Mrs. Forbush. Grayson was a fool, and evidently a coward and a weakling, as well. Lady Grayson is better off without him. I am not the villain here. I did not twist Grayson's arm, nor did I force him to play deep. But I *will* collect his debt."

She would remember that. If Lord Geoffrey would collect debts, even from widows and orphans, she had no reason to believe he would spare her. She lifted her hand to her temple, where a stabbing pain had begun. "I am suddenly feeling unwell. Mr. Hawthorne, will you please take me home?"

Chapter Sixteen

Settling into her chair, Grace waited patiently for her factor to shuffle through some papers and reacquaint himself with her affairs. She had called on Mr. Evans without an appointment and he required a few moments to look through her ledgers. After the incident at Belmonde's last night, it was suddenly important to know just how much she could wager with Lord Geoffrey. Now that she knew the true nature of her enemy, she could not risk leaving anything to chance.

Mr. Evans cleared his throat and sat back in his chair. "Ah, yes, Mrs. Forbush. Your funds are unavailable still, are they not?"

"They are," she confirmed. "Do you have any idea how much longer it will take to make a determination?"

Mr. Evans closed the ledger and moved some papers around on his desk. "It has been but a week yet, madam."

"I am aware of that, but I was hoping it could be settled quickly."

He picked up his pen and tapped his cheek as he glanced out the window. "The courts move slowly. I would not hope for a resolution for several months."

Grace leaned forward, annoyed that Mr. Evans would not

meet her eyes. "What, precisely, is the court looking for, Mr. Evans?"

The man flushed and opened her ledger again, as if checking columns. "I…uh, there is some question regarding your right to inherit from your husband."

"My right? There was a will, Mr. Evans, that spelled it out completely."

"Yes, well—"

She nodded. "Yes, I know. The will was made in the belief that Mr. Hawthorne was dead. And, of course, I will want him to have everything that was his before the report of his death. With interest. And any of the family heirlooms, portraits and so forth."

"Generous, I am sure." Mr. Evans leaned back in his chair and studied the ceiling. "And we can hope Mr. Hawthorne will be as generous to you, should the decision not go in your favor."

"I don't understand. Why would the decision not go in my favor?"

"Should the courts decide to revert to the original will, which would be decidedly in Mr. Hawthorne's favor, your circumstances would be considerably reduced."

"I understand that. But I would still have my investments and the pension Mr. Forbush provided under the original terms."

The man now studied the toes of his shoes. "Perhaps not, Mrs. Forbush."

"And why, pray not?"

"Should the courts find…uh, fraud or duress…"

"Fraud?" Grace's mind spun. "Why would they find fraud? Or duress?"

"He died so soon after changing his will that…there might…"

Grace felt sick to her stomach. The old rumors were surfacing. Soon she would be under a cloud of suspicion. But what possible motive could she have? Apart from the endless nights and his occasional verbal abuse, Basil had been her rescuer, liberating her from Leland's control. She'd have done anything she could to keep him alive and well. She took a deep breath.

"Really, Mr. Evans, I do not see how anyone could prove such a claim. It is patently ridiculous."

"Well, uh…" Mr. Evans examined his fingernails.

A cold knot of dread grew in Grace's stomach. "What is it, Mr. Evans? What do you know that you haven't told me?"

"I'm sorry, Mrs. Forbush. It was such an innocent thing. And who would be hurt by it, I ask you? It seemed so logical when Lord Barrington proposed it, that we did not even stop to question it."

"What? Question what, sir?" Panic was rising, tightening her vocal cords, causing her voice to rise. She should have known better than to let Lord Barrington handle the details for her.

"Well, uh—" Mr. Evans met her eyes for just a second before shifting away to his office door as if he expected someone to burst through at any moment. "The will was not delivered to Mr. Ogilby until after your husband's death. It bore a date previous to that, of course, and the provisions were all logical in view of the fact that Mr. Hawthorne had been reported dead. Lord Barrington had signed as witness and swore to the accuracy of the date. Ordinarily, you see, given that Mr. Ogilby did not draw up the will, and that it was not delivered until after his death, there would have, um, been some question as to its authenticity."

Grace shook her head disbelievingly. "I knew nothing of this, Mr. Evans. Why was I not told?"

"Barrington and Mr. York both said you were too distraught to be troubled over it. Though it was highly irregular, Mr. Ogilby and I agreed to simply ignore the circumstances of the date and delivery. There was, after all, no other heir."

"Leland? My brother came to you?"

Mr. Evans nodded, looking painfully embarrassed.

She recalled that Leland had come to town for her husband's funeral, but he had not been around the house much, making excuses about business that needed his attention and people that he needed to see. She prayed the will was real, but she had a niggling doubt that it might not be. Had Leland and Lord Barrington, in an attempt to protect her, forged the will and presented it to Basil's solicitor as authentic?

Good heavens! If that was the case, they were all in trouble—Mr. Ogilby and Mr. Evans for skirting the law, Barrington and Leland for committing fraud, and even she would look suspicious. Though she hadn't known anything about it, who would believe her under the circumstances? After all, she had been the only one to benefit.

She took a deep, bracing breath before speaking. "If the courts do not accept the new will as legitimate, will they revert to the previous will?"

Mr. Evans frowned. "One could hope so, Mrs. Forbush. But if they decide to take up the matter of a possible forgery, there could be some...serious problems."

Yes, she supposed there could be. Mr. Ogilby and Mr. Evans could be brought up on criminal charges. Lord Barrington and Leland...oh! The consequences were too awful to contemplate. And she, as the beneficiary of a fraudulent will, could be named, as well.

Her stomach twisted with anxiety. Add this suspicion to the one that Basil's death had not been natural and she would be looking very suspicious, indeed.

And Lord Barrington! Had his last veiled threat been an allusion to this calamity? But how could he have her disinherited if it would also result in charges against him? No, she was safe against that quarter, at least.

"Thank you for your honesty, Mr. Evans." She stood and

fastened the man with a stern look that was meant to convey that he should have told her sooner. "Please keep me informed should there be anything further from the courts."

In an upstairs room in Haymarket, Adam cut a swath through the air with his foil before saluting Freddie Carter with the blade. Carter returned the salute and began circling. Adam had forgotten the degree of skill and concentration fencing required, though he was quickly regaining his proficiency. His years in the wilderness had not required grace or any particular adherence to rules of fair play. There his knife and sword had meant survival and the skills he'd needed were stealth, strength and ruthlessness. He'd learned to excel at those.

"Zounds!" Carter exclaimed as he defended against Adam's lunge. "I thought this was a friendly bout!"

Adam feinted to the left. "It is friendly. I don't intend to kill you."

"That's encouraging." Carter laughed as he lunged to put Adam on the defensive. "But I've got the feeling you are using me to vent some anger."

Adam parried, then followed with a riposte, concentrating on Carter's blade even as his thoughts slipped back to last night at Belmonde's. Grace's taunt at the gaming table that she would look for excitement wherever she could find it had eaten at him like acid. He'd be damned if he'd let her search for that kind of excitement anywhere else but at his door.

The only good thing to come out of last night was Grace's sudden disenchantment with Lord Geoffrey. He hoped that would be enough to keep her home more often. She'd been silent on the coach ride home and had gone directly to her room when they'd arrived. Was she angry with him for his rebuff of the night before?

The blunted point of Carter's foil made contact with Adam's arm and pulled him from his thoughts. He lunged, ducking under Carter's arm and making contact with his own blade.

"Damn! I thought I had you. What is it, Hawthorne? Taylor? He's keeping solid food down now. Another day or two and he'll be ready to answer your questions."

He nodded. "That is all I want, Carter. Just one answer, and I can put the past to rest."

"Why do I have the feeling that it's more than that? What is really eating you, Hawthorne?"

"Grace Forbush," he admitted.

Carter grinned. "Ah, the lovely widow. Yes, she'd be on my mind, too, for all the obvious reasons, and some not as obvious. Since we've contained Taylor, I've resumed my investigation. Did you know she's pawned a large quantity of her jewelry?"

Adam dropped his guard and straightened. "When?"

"A few days ago. She went to Rundell and Bridges, jewelers who are well-known for paying for quality pieces to gamblers in need of ready cash."

Then Grace's lust for excitement was worse than he'd thought. She'd been losing steadily, but it had not seemed to be in great amounts. When he'd requested the hearing on his uncle's will to stem the outward flow of cash, he hadn't anticipated this development. Grace was more determined than he'd thought. She still had a few pieces left, though. The image of her in her amethyst pendant and white garters rose to his mind. And the jet earrings she'd worn last night and left with Lord Geoffrey. Were those all that was left?

How could he contain her before she lost everything? And, by God, Lord Geoffrey was the wrong man to be gambling with. His unforgiving and remorseless attitude was proof of that. He would fleece Grace without a second thought and take whatever else she had in the bargain.

He removed his fencing gloves and tucked them under one

arm as he walked to the side of the room to make way for waiting fencers. "Is there anything else I should know?" he asked.

"Those rumors? The ones about your uncle? They are beginning to surface again in certain circles."

"What circles?"

"Legal circles."

"What is being said?"

"The inquiry into your uncle's will has turned up some irregularities. And that has given rise to hard questions."

Adam clenched his jaw and kept his face impassive. "What sort of irregularities?"

"The possibility of forgery. But I cannot think a woman of Mrs. Forbush's reputation could forge her husband's will and then murder him."

A woman of Mrs. Forbush's reputation? Who was in a better position than he to understand the complete myth of that reputation? Where was the multitude of lovers? How could she still have been virgin after all these years? What had become of the painfully correct and circumspect widow so admired by the ton? How many had she deceived, and for how long? And if she'd deceived them, then she could have deceived him.

Adam needed a drink. And some answers. Tonight.

Grace was more agitated than she could ever remember being. When Dianthe had departed for a few days in the country with the Thayers, she had waved goodbye with a sense of relief. A few days away was just the remedy for Dianthe's brooding on Mr. Lucas's death. And if the scandal regarding the will became public, at least Dianthe would be out of the way of the worst of it.

She paced the library, wondering what had become of Adam, and wondering if she should simply go to the hells without him. The clock had just struck nine, and he was not usually late. She went to stand at the side of the window and peek out at the darkened street and park. Was her watcher still there? Could she risk going anywhere alone if she was being followed?

She heard the library door open and spun around, feeling a guilty flush creep up her cheeks. Adam strolled in, an enigmatic smile on his face. He paused to look her up and down and then grinned. There was something faintly different about him tonight, as if he'd changed in some way.

"Adam! I had begun to think you did not want to accompany me tonight."

"Did you?" he asked. He went to the sideboard and poured himself a glass of sherry. "Why?"

She glanced at the clock again. "I...thought you would have been down sooner if you—"

"Well, I am here now. But you are right. I had a long afternoon, and would rather stay in."

She nodded, glancing at the window again. "Certainly." She went to the bellpull by the door and tugged. "I shall have Mr. Dewberry bring the coach around and I'll be off. I am sorry for relying upon you so heavily. I had no right. I'm certain there are things you'd rather be doing. Visiting friends and so forth." She began to feel awkward as Adam just watched her over the rim of his glass.

"I'll...just fetch my shawl," she said, going to the library door.

"Wait," Adam called. He hesitated until she turned to face him before he continued. "Let's make a personal wager, Mrs. Forbush. If I win, you will have to spend a quiet evening at home. If you should win, I will accompany you tonight."

A prickle of anticipation traveled up her spine and made her shiver. "What do you have in mind?"

"Mrs. Dewberry will answer the bell. I say she will cluck her tongue at some point while she is in the room. What do you say?"

Mrs. Dewberry only clucked her tongue when she was

perturbed. Grace glanced around the room. Everything was in place. The odds were heavily in her favor. "I say she won't."

"Done," Adam said, and leaned back against the sideboard to wait.

She stepped away from the door to allow Mrs. Dewberry's entrance. A moment later the woman bustled in and glanced at Adam, then at her. "Aye, Missus?"

"Will you please have Mr. Dewberry bring the coach around?"

"Aye, Missus."

Just as she was turning to leave, Adam dropped his glass. Mrs. Dewberry spun around and looked at the puddle of sherry and broken shards of glass on the wooden floor. Clucking her tongue, she hurried to the puddle, removed her apron, kneeled down and began cleaning the spill.

Without moving an inch, Adam met her gaze and smiled his wickedly amused smile.

Defeated, as Mrs. Dewberry stood with the glass shards wrapped in her soiled apron, Grace said, "Never mind, Mrs. Dewberry. I shan't be going out tonight after all."

"Are you sure, Missus?"

She nodded. "You and Mr. Dewberry may as well retire."

"Well, thank you, Missus. We'll make an early night of it then."

The door closed softly behind the housekeeper and Grace tilted her head to one side. "You cheated."

He grinned. "A simple accident."

She couldn't prove her charge, and wasn't certain she wanted to. She went back to her desk and asked, "A nightcap?"

"Nightcap?" he scoffed. "I was just getting started."

"Then perhaps I should retire," she said uncertainly.

"Not a chance." He brought the sherry bottle to her and poured more in her glass before taking another glass from the tray and sitting in one of the comfortable chairs in front of the fire. "Come join me, Mrs. Forbush. You've said you enjoy gambling, and I can think of dozens of wagers."

She should run while she still could. Every instinct told her so. But curiosity won. She took her glass to the chair facing his. The deck of cards still sat on the table, ready for a game. Adam nodded at the deck, indicating that she should deal.

"Briscola?" she asked.

He nodded.

"And the stakes?"

"If I win, I shall require you to fill my glass before it empties."

She smiled. "And if I should win, we shall go to the Two Sevens."

"What of Mr. Dewberry? He likely has his nightshirt on by now."

"Of course. Well, then, I shall require…" She frowned as she finished dealing and turned the trump card up. When Adam reached out to gather his cards, she saw a quick flash of the intriguing wristband he always wore. "I shall require you to tell me about your bracelet."

A muscle jumped along Adam's jaw and she thought he would refuse, but after a moment he nodded.

They played quickly and silently, with Adam winning handily. Grace fetched the sherry bottle from the desk while he dealt the next game.

"I still want to know about that bracelet. What stakes will you name?" she asked.

"Tell me about my uncle's last days. The last week should do."

A cold feeling settled in her stomach. "Adam—"

"No, Mrs. Forbush. I think I have a right to know what happened."

The thought occurred to her that he had not called her by her first name since coming down to the library. The formality seemed out of place for them now. But he was right. He had a right to know. "Very well. I shall do my best, but those days are a blur to me."

He opened his hand without comment and she began the play. Again, the game progressed silently and when the deck was spent and the points counted, she won. Keeping her bargain, she filled Adam's glass and sat back in her chair, waiting.

He took a sip of his sherry and looked as if he were composing himself. He cleared his throat and pulled his jacket sleeve up to expose the band before he began. "It was made as a gift for me by an Indian maid. Her name was Nokomis, Daughter of the Moon. She was the chief's daughter and though young, Nokomis was the most skilled at beading of all the maidens in the village. To receive a gift from her was a high honor."

"And you honor her still," Grace murmured. She almost wished she hadn't asked. Nokomis. Did Adam love her? Had they been intimate, as she and Adam had been? Ah, but he hadn't turned cold to her, as he had to Grace.

"I am trying, but it hasn't been easy."

Though the remark was cryptic, his expression was so dark that Grace feared to question him further. She gathered the cards and shuffled, trying to diffuse the tension. "Nokomis, Daughter of the Moon. It is lyrical, is it not? Was it difficult to learn the Indian language?"

"There are many Indian languages. Chippewa is complex, but not impossible. I learned to make myself understood well enough." His eyes darkened.

"Then that is our next wager. Teach me some Chippewa words. And what stakes will you ask?"

"My uncle's last days."

She nodded and the play began. The scoring was close, but Adam won by a narrow margin. He took the sherry bottle and poured more for her—a small recognition that this might be difficult for her.

"I was in a fog most of the time," she began. "I cannot recall much beyond the purging and delirium. When his illness first became apparent to me, I sent for the doctor. He asked how long Mr. Forbush had been ill, and I told him just a few days. But Lord Barrington said it had been going on for quite a while, and that Mr. Forbush had not wanted me to know. *Wanted to spare me,* I believe is the way Lord Barrington put it." She paused for a moment, struck by the number of times Barrington's name had come up in recent conversations. He and Basil had been friends and had met for a drink at their club every evening. She had always accepted his presence, but was there more to it than that? She cleared her throat and continued. "We looked to his diet but could find nothing to cause such symptoms." She paused to take a deep breath. Her voice had begun to rise and she deliberately slowed down before she resumed. "The doctor gave him soothing powders and an elixir that should have worked, but didn't."

She placed her glass on the table when she noticed that her hand was trembling. The horror of those days came back to her with painful clarity. "When it became apparent that the medicines were not working, I went to another doctor, then another. I—I cannot recall how many I consulted. They all agreed that he was probably afflicted with a cancer of the stomach. Such a malady can be present for a long time and then advance quickly, I was told, and…and that would explain so many other things."

"What?" Adam asked, leaning toward her.

"His inability to…that is, that he could not…" She couldn't tell him that! He was already looking at her as if she had grown another head.

Tears sprang to her eyes. "But he was in such agony that I could scarcely bear to watch. By the end…I was almost relieved, because it meant an end to his suffering. And then I felt so guilty to be relieved."

"You mentioned delirium?"

She nodded. "Mostly he rambled about his youth or about you. You were all he had, he said. The report of your death was blamed for his decline. I tried desperately hard, but I was never enough for—" She stopped, unwilling to discuss her relationship with his uncle.

"Anything else?" he asked.

"The funeral was large and well attended." She sighed, groping for anything that would give him reassurance or comfort. "Mr. Forbush disdained the social whirl, and so we hadn't been much in society. I hadn't realized he was so fondly regarded until so many of his friends called to pay their respects. Truly, Adam, I had no idea he had so many friends."

He picked up the deck of cards. "Do you still want to learn Indian words?"

She blinked her welling tears away and nodded.

"And I want you to do my bidding." He began dealing.

"I do not like that wager," she said. "It could mean anything."

"Do you not trust me?"

Had there been a challenge in his question? "Very well," she conceded, not wanting to look like a coward and wondering what his bidding might be.

And she promptly lost.

Adam sat back in his chair and took pity on her. Not enough to recant, of course, but enough to soften the blow. The stricken look on her face told more about her state of mind than anything else could have. *"Nenemoosha,"* he said.

She blinked. "What?"

"Nenemoosha. The Chippewa word for sweetheart."

"Nenemoosha," she repeated. Then slower, softer, *"Nenemoosha…"* in a wistful sigh.

He leaned toward her, unable to resist those words said so sweetly. "Say, *metea*."

"Metea?" she asked.

"Do not say it like a question," he instructed.

"Metea," she repeated.

He leaned the rest of the way across the little tea table and deposited a kiss on her lips. "Again?" he asked.

"Metea."

Again he kissed her, deeper, fuller.

When he sat back, she smiled. Ah, she understood that the word was an invitation. *"Metea, metea, metea,"* she said.

He stood and took her hand, pulling her to her feet. Tugging her into his arms, he took intense satisfaction in the feel of her against him. God forgive him, it did not matter if she was telling the truth. He wanted her. And that was all that mattered at this moment.

"You owe me, Mrs. Forbush," he said against her lips. "And I want payment."

"Your bet," she acknowledged. "Then what is your bidding?"

"Do unto me as you would want me to do unto you."

It took her barely more than a moment to understand that twist on the Golden Rule. Of all the possibilities she might have chosen, he was gratified when she kissed him, deeply and passionately, her tongue sliding across his. And he returned it, doing unto her…

She nibbled at his earlobe, her breath hot and moist in his ear, and he did the same to her. She moaned. He did not.

She pulled away from him, her eyelids heavy with desire. Taking his hand, she led him to the library door and up the stairs. She paused at her door, but he did not want to risk being interrupted by a nosy Mrs. Dewberry in the morning. He pulled her along the hallway to his door and kissed her again, waiting for her to make her wishes known. He'd have no questions this time. Tonight, Grace would indicate to him what she liked, what she wanted, in a way her words and modesty would have failed her.

She pushed his door open and stepped backward into the room, pulling him into the darkness after her. The moment the door closed, she pressed against him, her hands working at his cravat and shirt. He stood still, letting her undress him until she came to his waistband. By then he was so aroused that he was afraid the mere brush of her hand would bring him to climax. He'd had women in damned near every port, every capital of Europe, but he'd never had a woman who'd fired his blood like this woman before him now.

"My turn," he whispered, kicking his boots off and walking her backward toward his bed. He found the fasteners of her gown and had it gone in minutes. He lifted her chemise over her head and tossed it aside. When she stood with nothing left but her garters, stockings and slippers, she stopped him and began her slow, sweetly inept, disrobing of him again. He'd already undone his breeches and she peeled them down his hips, kneeling to tug them over his feet.

She looked up at him and her eyes glittered in the moonlight filtering through his window. Her hands slid up his thighs and she came up on her knees to reach her arms behind her neck. Her bare breasts raised and firmed with that movement, the pale flesh gleaming in the moonlight. He wanted to take a tempting tip in his mouth, to feel the tender aureole beading against his tongue and hear her moaning with pleasure. But he steeled himself to stillness, wondering what she would do next.

A moment later she shook her head and the dark spun silk of her chignon fell around her shoulders and down her back in a riotous tumble. Again he thought of Ellie, the lost child that Grace had been and was becoming again. How could she know the things that would drive him wild with lust? The things she was doing now?

Her hands moved back to his hips and fumbled with the closure of his smallclothes. Oh, God! She was going to—

The cloth dropped away and his shaft sprang free. She sat back on her heels with an astonished expression. He would have laughed had he not been afraid she would flee. He had no false modesty but, with her limited experience, he could not imagine what she was thinking.

He held his hand out to her to bring her to her feet, but she shook her head and slipped her hand across his thighs to take him in her hand. Her touch was like velvet and he moaned, reaching down to bury his fingers in the lengths of her hair. He prayed she would satisfy her curiosity quickly, before he fell on her like a demon-possessed beast.

She stoked the length of his shaft and sighed when the foreskin slid back to reveal the sensitive head, then ran the tip of her fingernail around the rim. A small translucent drop appeared at the end and she kissed it away. She tilted her head to one side and ran her tongue up the underside and he knew he was lost. She looked up and smiled, and he realized she was finally aware of the power she held over him.

She parted her lips, ready to take him in, but he knew he didn't possess the strength to hold himself in check. He would spend everything if he felt the caress of her tongue, the heat of her mouth. There would be time for this discovery later, but now he needed to bury himself inside her, to know that she was feeling the unbearable pleasure and deep satisfaction he was feeling—and experiencing it without the taint of virginal pain.

He took her hand and pulled her to her feet. His need soared to new heights when he kissed her deeply, felt her naked flesh against his and tasted himself on her tongue. When he tightened his arms around her and straightened, her feet came off the floor. She wrapped those slender legs around him and he walked with her pressed against him, their mouths joined, to the bed. He placed her against the pillows and came down on top of her.

She pulled her knees up to receive him but he wanted to be sure she was ready. Between her heated thighs, he moved downward, stopping to take one firmed nipple into his mouth. She bucked against him, exquisitely tender to his touch. When he moved to go lower, she grabbed a fistful of hair and pulled him up.

"No," she gasped. "You would not let me, so you cannot."

Yes, damn it. The Golden Rule. But he had to know. He ran a finger down her cleft to her passage and found it swollen with passion, wet and ready for him. He thought he would burst with his need and drew the moment out to regain an edge of his self-control. But when he rose to her, sliding against the length of her body, she pushed him sideways and rolled on top of him. *Why had he made that bloody infernal wager?* He wanted control, not to be at her mercy. But a bet was a bet, after all.

She straddled him, positioning herself above him. Leaning forward to brace her hands on either side of his head, her dark hair fell around them like the mantle of night itself. She hesitated.

"Adam?" she asked.

He helped her, guiding himself into her as she sank down on him, arching her throat as a shiver passed through her. Adam shivered, too, unable to comprehend how erotic she was. "Ellie," he whispered. "Ellie, Ellie…"

And finally they were fully joined. Her muscles closed around him, quivering with her hunger. She moved experimentally, almost clumsily, lifting, sinking, lifting, sinking. As breathtakingly beautiful as she was straining above him, he knew what she needed—what they both needed—even if she did not.

He rolled over her, taking the superior position. She raised her knees and lifted to him, welcoming him deep inside. When he withdrew nearly to the very end, she rose to him again, and he knew she was near. He increased his pace and she wrapped her legs around him, whimpering his name.

"Adam…Adam…Adam," she called into the night.

Her voice, her plea, pierced his heart and penetrated deep inside his soul. He answered with his body and finished with her in an explosion of kaleidoscopic movement, light and color. She was exquisitely beautiful in the throes of her passion, her eyes closed, her lips softly swollen from his kisses and parted in a sigh. She'd swooned in the grip of the *petit mort,* the little death, totally sated.

Unbidden, unwanted, words he'd never said before screamed through his mind as he gazed down on her. Illogically, impossibly, *I love you, Ellie,* he heard echoing in his head, and knew it was true. *I love you…*

How had he let that happen?

Chapter Seventeen

Grace ran her brush though the tangles of her hair and smiled at her reflection in the mirror. She was beginning to feel like a woman wise in the ways of passion. She could not doubt that Adam had found her desirable last night, nor could she doubt that she had managed to surprise him. He always seemed to know what she wanted without her asking, and she had likewise tried to anticipate his desires.

And, oh, the sweet sensations he evoked in her! Last night there had been no aching, no burning, only bliss. She had felt like a flower opening to the sun. The fullness of her passion was yet to unfold, but she did not want to miss a moment of it. She was suddenly more sympathetic to women who changed their views on marriage and passion once they had been indoctrinated. How satisfying and luxuriant it would be not to hurry back to one's own bed and waken alone.

Last night she had been the one to rouse first. Adam had not even stirred when she rested her weight on one elbow to study his face. The thick fan of his dark lashes had fallen across his cheeks like dark crescents and she'd longed to kiss him awake to see the deep whiskey sparkle of his eyes. Exhaustion had flushed his tanned cheeks and his dark hair curved around his face in damp wisps. The muscles of his chest and shoulders were strongly defined and one hand, large and calloused, rested possessively on her hip. Her heart had swelled inside her and she'd realized she had crossed some invisible line from sublime self-possession to dreaded dependency. Yes, it was true. She'd grown to need Adam in her life. She'd come to love him.

And he loved Nokomis.

That realization sobered her and she'd slipped quietly from beneath his hand, evoking no more than an incoherent muttering. Gathering her clothes, she'd dashed down the darkened hall for her own room, where she'd fallen into bed feeling a little lost without him.

How well he knew her! His wager, demanding that she do to him what she would want done to her was the perfect ploy, giving her responsibility for her own pleasure and permission to experiment with his. She glanced over her shoulder to the little book on her bedside table. Yes, that tome had given her courage in the belief that, in some things at least, men and women were not so very different. But affection made all the difference. She never could have done such things to Basil, nor—God forbid—to Barrington.

Mrs. Dewberry had told her that Adam had risen early and departed without a word. She wondered what business he had that kept him away from home so much. And then it occurred to her how little she actually knew about him. She wanted to know everything. Every little detail of his childhood, his rise in the Diplomatic Corps, the time he was missing in Canada and believed dead.

And why Nokomis, Daughter of the Moon, had been left behind. He had loved her, his softly spoken words had made that clear, but did he love her still? Grace's stomach clenched at the thought. Could he love Nokomis and love her, too?

Her clock chimed once, bringing her back to the present. She had risen too late for church and Laura Talbot would be here soon. She shook off her reflective thoughts and went to select a dress for the day, a soft pink muslin that mirrored her mood.

Feeling oddly at loose ends without Dianthe to anchor her day, Grace wandered down to the library. The sight of the deck of cards still on the tea table brought heat to her cheeks. She gathered them together and put them back in the cupboard. Would she and Adam play again? Oh, she hoped so—but not tonight! Time was growing short and nothing must be allowed to distract her now until she had settled matters for Miss Talbot. Tonight she would have to deal with Lord Geoffrey.

The front bell rang and she heard Mrs. Dewberry rushing to answer. A moment later the housekeeper ushered a flushed Miss Talbot in.

"Mrs. Dewberry, would you bring us tea, please?" she asked as she waved Miss Talbot to sit.

The moment the door closed, Miss Talbot blurted, "Do you have news, Mrs. Forbush? Have you found anything that can help me?"

Grace sat and took Miss Talbot's hand. "I am sorry, but I fear the news is not good. I asked you here to discuss alternatives."

"Alternatives? Does that mean you are giving up hope?"

Grace's heart fell at the sight of Miss Talbot's distress. "Never, Miss Talbot. But this is proving more difficult than we anticipated. I think we must be prepared for alternate solutions. I wanted to discuss the possibilities with you privately, as I would like you to speak frankly and honestly with me. You must be completely candid."

The girl nodded, pulling her white gloves off and making a visible effort to compose herself. "With the wedding just six days away, I have been overset. Sitting in church today, when the banns were read again, it occurred to me that it could really happen. I could actually be married that odious man."

"Not if the thought is truly abhorrent to you."

"But, how can that be? If you fail to prove Lord Geoffrey is a cheat, how shall I refuse the debt?"

"By simply refusing the debt. You cannot be forced into saying vows, Miss Talbot. This is 1820, for heaven's sake."

"I—I cannot refuse," she said, her eyes wide at Grace's ignorance.

"What would be the consequences of that?"

"I…my brother would be made to look a fool. His honor would be sullied forever."

Grace shrugged, wondering what honor there was in losing the family fortune and selling your sister into the bargain. "That is your brother's honor, Miss Talbot. I asked what the consequences would be to *you*."

Laura Talbot blinked her clear brown eyes. "Why, that my brother would punish me."

Then it was as Grace had feared. "Physically, you mean?"

"Yes." She began twisting a handkerchief in her lap, unable to meet Grace's eyes in her distress.

"Does he do you damage, dear? Or lock you in your room? Or deny you food and water?"

"I will not *have* a room if I refuse to marry Lord Geoffrey. The house, the land, the bank accounts—all belong to him now, and once he takes possession, he can evict us. I have heard he is a very hard man and would not hesitate to do so."

Yes, Grace believed that. She had just seen that side of him with worse consequences than looming poverty. Lord Grayson was dead, for heaven's sake! "You will not go hungry, or without a place to stay, Miss Talbot. I shall see to that. I shall have a room prepared for you here. Do you have younger siblings?"

She shook her head. "I am the youngest, Mrs. Forbush. My two brothers are older."

Sheltering a man who would abuse a woman was out of the question, and to do so would draw Leland's comments, as well. "They will get on well enough, Miss Talbot."

"They are counting on me to save the family honor. And my brother has suggested that, once I am wed to Lord Geoffrey, if I—" she paused and a deep blush stole over her cheeks "—if I behave in certain pleasing ways, I could have access to his wealth and use it to restore their fortunes."

Grace sighed. There was little she could do if Miss Talbot insisted upon taking responsibility for her brother's irresponsibility. She would have to try another tack.

"I have come to know Lord Geoffrey over the past week and a half. You are right about him being a hard man. And he does seem uncompromising. But marriage to such a man might actually liberate you from your brother's yoke. I do not think he would hurt you. Rather, I suspect you would be alone most nights." She thought of her own marriage to Mr. Forbush and said, "The worst you would suffer would be indifference."

"But I do not even *know* him!"

"He is really quite attractive," Grace said as persuasively as she could. "And I think he would not be unkind. I gather, by his success in gambling, that he could provide for you quite comfortably and—"

Laura Talbot looked at her, a horrified expression twisting her features. "But I do not *know* him! How can I submit to intimacies with a virtual stranger?"

The memory of being barely eighteen and standing before Mr. Forbush on their wedding night in a transparent nightgown rose to her mind. That night had been a nightmare of humiliation for her. She'd known so little of what a man and woman did together, but she knew she had failed him in some way. It had been years before she realized the failure was Basil's, not hers. Oh, but even that had been infinitely kinder than her brother!

"Consider it, Miss Talbot. In the best of circumstances, you would not have married for love, but for advantage. Lord Geoffrey could be an advantage in protecting you from your brother's cruelty and—"

"I cannot conceive that you would try to make me think such a thing would be acceptable! I have so come to depend upon you, Mrs. Forbush, and to rely upon your reassurances. *Everything within your power,* you told me. I cannot contemplate what losing that assurance would mean."

Yes, she had reassured the girl. But she had not anticipated the difficulty of proving the man a cheat. What if he wasn't? Or worse, what if he was but she could never prove it? How would she keep her promise then?

"There is a possibility that Lord Geoffrey is not a cheat, and that is an entirely different matter. If he is not, or we cannot prove he is, we cannot bring him down simply to negate your brother's debt. I was clear from the beginning that the Wednesday League obtains *justice.* Not revenge."

She stood and began pacing as Mrs. Dewberry brought the tea tray in and placed it on the table. When the library door closed again, she poured the girl a cup of tea and tried again. She thought back to the way Lord Geoffrey had stood in her defense when Lord Barrington had handled her so roughly and opted for bluntness. "Furthermore, I have reason to believe that Lord Geoffrey would be kinder than your brother."

Her eyes widened. "But I do not love him!"

A suspicion took root. "Miss Talbot, do you have…a suitor? Come clean now, or I cannot know how to help you."

The girl dropped her gaze to her teacup. "I feared you would not help if you knew I had not been completely truthful."

Truthful? There was that word again. "Do not be absurd," she said, trying to keep the annoyance from her voice. Oh, if she'd only known this in the beginning! "Run away with your young man, Miss Talbot. I shall give you the money for a dash to Gretna Green. Say your vows and have your husband protect you from the consequences."

The girl began weeping. She took a handkerchief from her sleeve and dabbed at her eyes and sniffed delicately. "I cannot, Mrs. Forbush. He…he is honorable and does not want to win me in such a manner. I had hoped there would be time to persuade my brother, but…"

"You may need to compromise, Miss Talbot."

"I—I still could not marry Lord Geoffrey. Dianthe has told me that she met him and thinks he is a dreadful man."

Oh, Dianthe! She had made Grace's job more difficult without even realizing what she'd done! But in the end, it did not matter. She would continue to help Miss Talbot because of Adam. She could not imagine marrying Mr. Forbush and submitting to his intimacies now that she'd known Adam's touch.

"Who is he, Miss Talbot? Give me his name and I shall make your circumstances known to him. He would not wish to lose you."

"No!" the girl gasped. "He would be angry if he thought I had been discussing our love with anyone else."

Defeated, Grace waved her hand in dismissal. "I shall do anything—everything—humanly possible, Miss Talbot."

Adam climbed the back stairs of the White Bear Inn. Today he would have his answers from Taylor whether the man was recovered or not. For better or worse, he would put an end to the blood feud that had given his life meaning for the past four years. And if he was still alive afterward, he would solve the enigma of Grace Ellen Forbush. Paragon? Liar? Murderess? None of that mattered now. He loved her, and he'd have to find a way to handle her past, whatever it was.

For the moment he knew all he needed to know—that she was vulnerable, kind, sensual and that the very thought of her could make his blood sing as never before. And, in a lifetime of loss and separations, she was the only thing he'd ever found that made him feel whole and think of a future.

The odor of boiling cabbage and meat carried to him from the kitchen below and the low hum of voices filtered from the courtyard in back. Ordinary. Normal. But an uneasy feeling swept through him as he reached the landing and walked silently down the empty corridor to Taylor's room.

Where was the guard? He raised his hand to knock and found the door was slightly ajar. He slowly pushed the panel open with his index finger. The creak of the hinges sent a chill up his back. Something was wrong.

The odor hit him first—whiskey, vomit, urine and something else. Something metallic and very familiar. He stood stock-still while his eyes adjusted to the dim light from the curtained window. An overturned chair, an unmade bed, a cold hearth, not even a lit candle by the nightstand. Adam took a step into the room and his boot crunched on broken glass.

The hair on the back of his neck stood on end as he realized what the metallic smell was. How could he have forgotten, even for a second? As he moved further into the room, a leg became visible from the opposite side of the table. And there was the source of the metallic smell. A pool of blood. And George Taylor, facedown. Bloody hell! He'd never get an answer from the man now!

He knelt beside Taylor's body and touched the man's shoulder. Cold. He tried to lift Taylor's hand to search for a pulse, but death rigor had settled in. He glanced around, his eyes accustomed to the dim light now. There was no sign of the guard, but from this side of the door he could see splintered wood around the doorjamb. What the hell had happened here?

Turning to the small trunk that would contain Taylor's possessions, Adam lifted the lid and began to sort through the items. Clothing, boots, discharge papers, letters of commendation—

"Christ's blood!" Freddie Carter stepped through the door and closed it firmly. "What have you done, Hawthorne?"

Adam glanced back at Taylor's body. "I didn't do this."

"Where's Shelton?"

"Who?"

"Shelton. The guard. Where is he?"

"Gone when I got here," Adam said. He knew how guilty he looked, and that he'd sworn to kill Taylor, but he wouldn't make any excuses. If his word did not suffice, then he'd pray that Carter did not try to stop him from leaving.

When Carter bent over the body, he turned back to the trunk. The letter of commendation was the only official document there and Adam folded the envelope and slipped it into his jacket. Carter, he knew, would want things left as they found them and all his personal effects turned over to his family. There would be an investigation. Taylor had not been a nameless drunk from the streets, he'd been from a good family and had served his country as an officer in the Royal Army.

"He's been dead several hours. I'd say sometime before dawn. That lets you out. It wouldn't take you hours to do a search of this hovel."

Dawn. When he'd been stirring, hard and aching, Grace's scent still clinging to his skin, the taste of her still on his tongue.

"Give me a hand here," Carter asked. "I want to turn him over and see what killed him."

Adam helped him roll the body over. He shivered at what he saw. He couldn't muster any grief for the man who'd killed Nokomis and the others, but he wouldn't have wished this sort of death on him. His eyes were wide and his mouth was open in a silent scream. Something had sliced through his shirt and there was a gaping hole in his chest. Sickened, Adam wondered if the man had been alive when his heart had been removed.

As if reading his thoughts, Carter pointed to Taylor's groin. "Femoral artery. Same as Clark. But why the heart?"

"It is an obscure Indian custom in extreme circumstances to take the heart."

"Indian custom?"

Adam nodded. "I am being set up to take the blame for this."

Carter sat back on his heels. "Method," he said, shaking his head. "Taylor died from blood loss before his heart was removed. It was the same assassin who killed Clark, and likely attacked you in front of the Two Sevens. I think it's a warning to you to leave this alone. *Stop asking questions or the same could happen to you.* You know the sort of thing."

Adam balked. "There's something wrong with that theory."

"Well, it doesn't matter now. It is over."

"Over?" Adam laughed. "It's far from over, Carter. Taylor may be dead, but the man who gave him the orders, the man who hired the assassin, is still alive. Until I find him—"

Carter groaned.

"Until I find him, this cannot be over." The attacks on Grace had probably been warnings, as well. If anything happened to her because of his investigation, he knew he'd never be sane again. "I am not safe, nor is anyone I love, until that person has been exposed."

"Go," Carter ordered, waving toward the door. "I'll take care of this. I don't want you anywhere close when the new police arrive."

"I'll find you later. There are some people I need to talk to. Some favors I'm calling in." Adam went to the door and paused. "Carter?" he asked over his shoulder. "You will let me know if you hear from Taylor's guard? Shelton, is it?"

"Aye. I'll let you know."

Grace assumed an air of sublime confidence as she allowed the footman at the Two Sevens to take her wrap. He looked as if he would question her about her lack of an escort, but she merely waved one gloved hand. "Mr. Hawthorne is with the coach. He shall be along in a moment." She could not risk being turned away because she wasn't with an escort.

The truth was, Adam had not come home since leaving this morning, a fact that that had her alternately concerned and annoyed. He could have sent word. He would likely not realize that she had waited past ten o'clock for him before deciding to come alone. There was no time to waste if Miss Talbot was to be redeemed.

She plucked a glass of champagne from a footman's tray and began a circuit of the main salon. If Lord Geoffrey was not here, as he had not been at Belmonde's, she would have the footman summon Mr. Dewberry and go on to 77 Jermyn Street. And she'd keep going until she found him. No time left for coyness or subtlety.

But luck was with her. Lord Geoffrey turned from conversation with a group of men. She thought it interesting that Lord Geoffrey could be friends with eminently respectable men such as Lord Reginald Hunter and his brothers, and still deemed unacceptable in polite society. Was it women who needed to fear him? Perhaps it was time she found out.

He saw her and gave her a polite nod. He was probably wondering if she was still upset with him over his indifference to Lady Grayson's plight. She smiled and nodded back, knowing that would reassure him. He excused himself from his companions and came toward her.

"Mrs. Forbush, how nice to see you."

"And you, Lord Geoffrey. I thought you were always at Belmonde's."

He shook his head. "Just of late. Where is your shadow?"

She wondered if Adam would find that amusing. "I really do not know. He did not accompany me."

His eyebrows went up. "Are you alone tonight?"

"Not at the moment," she said, smiling up at him. She took his arm as he led her toward a low banquette set just inside a curtained alcove.

The barest flicker of his eyes told her he had not missed the insinuation. "Are you…auditioning again, Mrs. Forbush?"

She gave a low, throaty laugh. "Are *you*, Lord Geoffrey?"

She sat on the velvet cushions and patted a place beside her. She was playing a dangerous game, but she took comfort from the fact that she was in a public place.

"I admit to a certain curiosity," he said, his gaze sweeping her from head to toe. "Have you and Hawthorne come at odds?"

Mindful that Lord Geoffrey had said that he owed Adam his life, Grace knew that he would not do anything that might anger Adam. "I had not thought so, but he simply did not turn up to escort me tonight. Perhaps he has tired of me."

"So you came out alone?"

He seemed bent on verifying that fact. Grace conceded the point. "Yes, Lord Geoffrey. I came out alone."

That seemed to answer some question and Lord Geoffrey half turned to face her. "I had thought you would not speak to me again, Mrs. Forbush. I collect you were quite upset with me for refusing to return Lord Grayson's fortune."

"You were within your rights. I would not presume to tell you how to conduct yourself or your affairs, Lord Geoffrey."

He reached into his vest pocket and removed her jet earrings. "I believe these are yours, Mrs. Forbush. We did not play the game."

She took them and dropped them in the reticule dangling from her wrist. "Thank you," she said. "I may yet need them for currency tonight."

"So you really intend to find a game tonight?"

"Of course."

"I do not think Hawthorne will like that."

"Mr. Hawthorne does not make my decisions," she said, letting an edge of her anger show.

Lord Geoffrey looked as if he'd been slapped. He signaled a footman and asked for a table and a deck of cards. Grace barely had time to wonder what was afoot before there was a small table placed between them and a deck of cards in the center. He held out his hand and Grace removed the earrings from her reticule and placed them on the table.

"There are other things to wager than your belongings, Mrs. Forbush," he said.

"I am a little short of the ready, Lord Geoffrey."

"Then shall we say 'favors'?"

A sense of foreboding invaded Grace's vitals. "Please define 'favors.'"

He gave her a suggestive grin. "Can you not guess?"

The silence stretched out at she studied him. He was not going to give an inch. Perhaps now was the time to ask the question that had been bothering her since meeting Lord Geoffrey. "I have heard that you are betrothed."

"Where did you hear that?"

"Gossip," she demurred. "I believe you won your bride in a game of cards with a man by the name of Talbot?"

"That is true. But that has nothing to do with this."

"You have not even said your vows, and you are already planning a liaison? That does not bode well for the marriage."

"The liaison will be over before the vows are said."

"Is it your intention to be a faithful husband?"

"That remains to be seen, Mrs. Forbush. How can I know what temptations I may face?"

"Why?"

He blinked. "Why, what?"

"Why did you agree to marry a girl barely out of the schoolroom and whom you had never met?"

His lips quirked in a derisive smile. "In case you hadn't noticed, Mrs. Forbush, marriage is a sham under the best of circumstances. A man buys a brood mare with more success than he weds a woman. At least with a mare, he knows what he's getting."

Grace could not recall hearing a more cynical opinion of marriage. "Then why marry at all, sir?"

"At a certain point, it is expected." He picked up the deck of cards and began shuffling. "Even rakes and reprobates have an urge to see their progeny inhabit the earth."

"But a *wife,* Lord Geoffrey? What on earth would you do with a wife?"

"The usual. Impregnate her."

He was trying to shock her, but she wouldn't rise to his bait. "And then?"

"Leave her to the raising of my heirs."

"And give her nothing in return?"

"Nothing?" he scoffed. "She will have the better end of the bargain, I warrant. Servants, gowns, a house, anything she wishes. And all she need do in return is to lie still and spread her legs on occasion and subsequently push out a brat."

She was glad to see, at least, that she'd been fairly accurate in what she'd told Miss Talbot. "What accounts for your poor opinion of marriage, sir?"

Lord Geoffrey gestured broadly to the room. "Would there be any need for hells and brothels if marriage was such bliss? They'd all be home, wouldn't they? Instead they are seeking excitement—something to spice their dull lives. And you, Mrs. Forbush? If marriage is so desirable, why have you not entered that state again?"

"Do not think to change the subject. I asked why you gambled for a bride."

"Because I win at gambling. Courting is a different matter. I do not meet the sort of women I would wish to marry in gaming hells. Decent women do not come here." He paused and grinned. "Present company excepted, of course."

"You should release Miss Talbot from the debt," she blurted, and was immediately mortified. Had she just ruined any chance to cozen Lord Geoffrey?

He just stared at her, the corners of his mouth twitching, as if he were trying to decide whether to laugh or to sneer.

"Thank you for your opinion, Mrs. Forbush. Picquet or briscola?"

"What…would it take to convince you to release Miss Talbot?" she asked softly.

"Replace her."

Grace stopped breathing. There it was—the price to redeem Miss Talbot was to damn herself. All she had to do was to marry Lord Geoffrey. Unthinkable. Slowly she gathered her wits. "Briscola," she whispered.

"And the stakes?"

"My earrings." Had he really expected her to say Miss Talbot?

He smiled as if he'd already won.

Chapter Eighteen

Where the hell was she? Adam glanced around the main salon of the Two Sevens, trying to bring his anger under control. When he'd arrived home and was told that Grace had gone out unescorted, he'd been infuriated. Whether she knew it or not, because of him, she could be in grave danger.

After he'd left Carter with Taylor's body, he'd gone in search of Reginald Hunter, then Auberville, for names. They had been loosely involved with the War Ministry and he hoped they would either have the answers he needed or would know where to look for them. It had taken him hours to run them down, and then both had denied any knowledge but had agreed to look into the matter. It had been an altogether unsatisfactory day.

Now frustration mingled with anger, edging him perilously close to unreasonableness. He'd been to Belmonde's, the Pigeon Hole, A Club House and 77 Jermyn Street all without luck. The Two Sevens was his last stop before heading to the Covent Garden hells. If he found her at the Blue Moon, he'd throttle her. Had she no care for her reputation? Her safety?

He stopped a footman and asked for a whiskey. He needed

something strong and raw to calm his ragged nerves. Grace was not at the rouge-et-noir, hazard or vingt-et-un tables in the grand salon, so he continued down a corridor to the smaller private rooms where more intense card games were in progress. Nodding to occasional acquaintances, he kept going, alternately cursing and praying he'd find her soon. Most disturbing of all, he'd been unable to find Geoffrey Morgan. Could they be together?

"Ah! Here you are, Hawthorne. When I saw Mrs. Forbush, I knew you could not be far behind."

Adam turned to find Ronald Barrington watching him. He nodded, giving nothing away. "Where did you see her?"

"Grand salon," Barrington said curtly. "In an alcove with Morgan. If I were you, I would not let her wager with that devil."

Adam nodded and turned to go, anxious to find Grace before she left or made some reckless wager.

"Are you lovers?"

He stopped. The hair on the back of his neck prickled. How dare Barrington ask that question? "Are you jealous, Barrington? Does it anger you that I might have had what you never did?"

"Did she tell you that?" Barrington snorted. "She lied. I did. Long and often. She did things to me that a whore wouldn't do. She can make your toes curl, can't she, Hawthorne?"

My God! Apart from the fact that he was a colossal liar, did he want to die? Adam stepped forward, seized Barrington by his cravat and twisted, constricting the man's windpipe. "Another word," he snarled in a low voice, "just *one,* and I'll be having your heart for breakfast. Do you understand?"

"Unhand me you insolent wretch," Barrington wheezed.

Adam released him with a little push that bounced him off the opposite wall. He waited for Barrington's challenge, but it didn't come. Just as well. Such a thing would cause talk and he didn't need any more enemies in the War Department. He wheeled around and headed back down the corridor to the grand salon. The footman approached him with his whiskey on a silver tray. He lifted the glass, tossed the god-sent liquid fire down and continued without missing a step.

In the grand salon, he noted one alcove with the curtain half drawn. He'd passed it when he'd come in, thinking it vacant. As he approached, the conversation carried to him.

"Now your earrings are mine, Mrs. Forbush. Anything else you'd care to wager?"

Adam did not like the hesitation before Grace's reply. "I shall have to take inventory of my assets. I shall let you know if I come up with anything I think you'd like."

Lord Geoffrey laughed. "Would you like some hints?"

Adam pushed the curtain aside and took in the intimate little scene. Grace was sitting, practically knee-to-knee with Morgan on a velvet banquette, a small table in front of them. The sight gave him an unpleasant feeling, on top of all the other unpleasant feelings he'd had today. Was her gambling so out of control that she would lose everything before stopping?

Morgan stood. "Hawthorne. Good to see you. Mrs. Forbush said you had tired of escorting her."

The day had been an exercise in aggravation, from Taylor's death to his confrontation with Barrington a moment ago. And it just kept getting worse. "Sorry to disappoint you, Morgan, but I managed to make it after all." Tense and angry, he glanced down at Grace. "Would you like some hints on what I'm thinking, Mrs. Forbush?"

The line of her jaw tightened but her lips curved up in a polite social smile. "I do not think that will be necessary, Mr. Hawthorne." She stood and inclined her head to Morgan. "Thank you for a pleasant evening, Lord Geoffrey. Perhaps I shall see you tomorrow."

She took his arm and looked sideways up at him as they walked toward the foyer. "What was that, Mr. Hawthorne? A flexing of muscles?"

"Do not tweak me while we are public, Mrs. Forbush, because it would take precious little for me to throw you over my shoulder and carry you out of here if necessary."

He retrieved her wrap and ushered her out the door. Rather than stand like targets on the street, he led her around the corner to where the private coaches waited. Mr. Dewberry saw them coming and disengaged himself from a group of coachmen and hurried to open the door.

"So y' caught up to us, did ye, Mr. Hawthorne? Where do we go next?"

"Bloomsbury Square," Adam said with a warning glance at Grace. He still didn't think of the place as home.

"Aye, sir." Dewberry handed Grace into the coach and then took his place in the driver's box as Adam swung up into the coach and closed the door.

When the coach lurched into motion and entered the stream of traffic on the thoroughfare, Adam broke the silence. "Are you mad, Grace? What were you thinking to come out alone?"

"I could not wait for you. Or chance that…that we would not go out again tonight."

"Are you so desperate to gamble that you would risk your life?"

"My life? Come now, sir. The consequences are hardly as calamitous as that."

"They are every bit of that. How many unexplained accidents have you had of late? How many close calls?"

Grace fell silent and stared into the darkness of the coach. "Are you saying that you think someone is trying to kill me?"

Adam ran his fingers though his hair in frustration. He was

now fairly certain that Grace's unexplained accidents had been meant as a warning to him. If anything happened to her, it would be because of his inquires into the attack in Canada. He could not stop the inquiry, but he would have to find some way to keep Grace safe. He doubted he could live with himself if anything happened to her.

He turned to look at her in the dim light afforded by the streetlamps they passed. He could not be with her every minute of the day to protect her. He had to make her understand the danger she was in. "The odds for so many accidents being coincidental are nearly astronomical."

She frowned and looked down at her lap. After a moment she asked, "What happened to you, Adam? I was worried when I did not hear from you."

"You were…" This was the first time he could recall anyone worrying about him. The knowledge filled him with guilt and warmth at the same time. "I am not used to someone worrying or waiting for me, Grace. I had business that took longer than I expected. If it happens again I will send you word."

"What business?"

He didn't want Grace to know he was bent on vengeance. If she knew about the blood already on his hands, she would cut him out of her life without so much as a blink of those sultry eyes. "Government matters that wouldn't interest you," he hedged, wincing at how patronizing he'd sounded. A quick glance at Grace told him she had not missed the slight.

"Wrapping up details from my assignment in Canada," he explained further. "It is…complicated. It should not take much longer."

She nodded, a little of the stiffness draining from her shoulders.

"As long as we are explaining ourselves, Grace, what is behind your gambling? I don't believe excitement is the sole reason. You are too disciplined a person to allow that to take over."

She turned away and gazed out the window at the passing streets. "I am growing bored with it. Perhaps I shall stop soon."

"When? When you've lost everything you have?"

"If that's what it takes," she murmured.

That comment was cryptic, even from Grace who was prone to puzzling remarks. "What do you mean?"

She turned back to him and smiled. "It should not take much longer."

By the time he realized she had given him back his own words, Mr. Dewberry was helping her down from the coach.

Dianthe appeared at the door, still in a coaching dress and bonnet. "Here you are!" she exclaimed. "I cannot wait to tell you of my adventures in St. Albans!"

He noted Grace's obvious relief and suppressed his own disappointment that there'd be no repeat of last night. They would have to finish their conversation tomorrow.

Grace exited Madame Marie's shop with her head down and her thoughts in a muddle. The meeting with Mr. Renquist had not gone as well as she would have liked. More questions tumbled through her mind than had been answered.

It would seem that Lord Geoffrey Morgan had not hired the runner who was making inquiries about Grace. And that runner was not the only one following her. What had she done to become the object of so much clandestine attention?

Mr. Renquist reported that a top runner by the name of Fredrick Carter had been making inquiries about her. Inquiries of a general nature—her reputation, her interests, her friends and family. Another, whose name was Langston, worked outside of Bow Street and was more interested in her comings and goings—who she saw, where she went, what she did. Langston was known to be a bit "heavy-handed," and there was speculation that he was not above doing an employer's dirty work. Mr. Renquist had been yet unable to ascertain who had employed them, but he was narrowing in on the information. But Grace was certain she knew one of those answers. Langston was a name she had heard Barrington use before.

A hand seized her arm and she whirled to face the person who had stopped her. She recognized him with a sinking feeling. "Barrington," she said. That confirmed one of the questions.

"Come for a ride with me, Grace. We need to talk without interruptions."

She glanced at the Barrington coach, following them at close quarters. Every instinct she possessed screamed that she should not put herself in Barrington's hands, or allow him to manipulate her into a position she could not defend. "No."

"I need to explain some things to you, Grace. I would not want anything…bad to happen to you."

A bluff was her best course. "I know you hired a runner to follow me, Lord Barrington. Why? What did you hope to gain?"

Barrington's complexion darkened considerably. "I don't know what you mean."

"Did you order the attacks, too?"

"Attacks? What are you… you've been attacked?"

"Several times."

"By God, I swear 'twasn't me! I don't want you hurt, Grace. That's why I'm here. To recall you to your senses before you make the biggest mistake of your life."

How like a man to think rejecting him is a colossal mistake. She pulled her arm away from him and straightened her sleeve. "I am not going anywhere with you, Lord Barrington. And you have one minute to convince me that you were not behind the attacks on me."

"I wouldn't do that, Grace. You know I'd never hurt you."

She raised her eyebrow and tilted her chin. "I have experience to the contrary."

"But not like that," he protested as she turned and started walking again. "I am trying to protect you—to keep you safe."

"Explain."

"It's Hawthorne. When he came back, it threw everything awry. We had to scramble."

"We?"

He seemed disconcerted that he'd said too much. "Never mind that, Grace." He seized her arm again and pulled her toward his coach.

"In two seconds I am going to begin screaming," she said in a low, deadly voice. "And I shall continue screaming until someone arrives to help me. Do you really want to be seen dragging a woman into your coach? Your coat of arms clearly tells witnesses who you are."

Whatever civility Barrington had pretended slipped away and his face twisted into a snarl. "I tried to help. You cannot say you were not warned. I'll remember this, Grace."

She did not begin to shake until his coach pulled away and disappeared around a corner. She had made a mistake by not having Mr. Dewberry drive her. She would count herself lucky today and be more careful in the future.

"There's a gentleman downstairs, Mrs. Forbush. I've put him in the parlor. He says he is your brother."

Grace dropped her towel, slipped into her dressing robe and pulled her wet hair over her shoulder. She could not have heard Mrs. Dewberry right. Leland never left Devon. This was likely another of Barrington's tricks. "What does he look like, Mrs. Dewberry?"

"A might like you, I suppose. Dark hair, fair skin, taller, though, and lanky-built."

That description sounded like Leland. Her heart began to

beat faster and she fought the impulse to run. They were adults. She was in her own house. He could do nothing to her. She took a deep breath and picked up her comb to work the tangles from the thick rope of hair. "Tell him I will be down presently."

"He said now, Missus."

Yes. That would be Leland. And then he would rail at her for not taking the time to comb her hair. She glanced at her clock. Six. Dianthe would be home from tea with the Thayers soon, and who knew when Adam might return. She wanted Leland gone by then. She could only imagine the sort of scene he would make if faced with her houseguests. She squeezed the excess moisture from her hair and dragged the comb through the lengths several times and secured it at her nape with a white ribbon. That would have to do until she could get rid of Leland.

They hurried down the stairs and Grace gave Mrs. Dewberry a reassuring smile and a little push toward the kitchen. She suspected the woman would eavesdrop, but that was to be expected. In the three years the Dewberry's had worked for her, this was Leland's first visit.

She took a deep breath, donned an unconcerned expression and opened the parlor door. Typically, Leland was not sitting, but pacing. He turned to look at her and his expression registered dismay.

Grace smiled and went to him. Rising on tiptoes, she brushed a dutiful kiss on his cheek and then retreated. "Leland. How nice to see you. Had I known you were coming, I'd have been prepared."

"Loose hair is a vanity, Grace," he said.

She twisted the hank into a knot but let it drop without hairpins to secure it. "Y-yes, I know, but I just got out of the bath and—"

"Do you often receive in your dressing gown?"

"I would have dressed but Mrs. Dewberry said you were urgent and—"

"That, at least, is a relief."

Grace took a deep breath and tried again. "How is Pricilla?"

"Lost another one," he said, resuming his pacing. "The woman cannot hold on to a babe to save her life."

She studied her brother in dismay. He'd always been insensitive, but he seemed to have gotten worse. He looked so like their father, but emotionally they were exact opposites.

"I am so sorry to hear that, Leland. How is her health?"

"The doctor says she is not likely to bring any fruit to bear. But I will have my heir."

Something snapped in Grace's mind. She was sick to death of catering to Leland's ill temper and selfishness. "Even if it kills her? Be reasonable, Leland."

"Reasonable?" He wheeled around to face her. "A fine word coming from you, Grace. What reasonable thing have you done in your entire life but marry the man I chose for you?"

She bit her tongue, telling herself that it was not because she was afraid, but because she wanted to be rid of him as quickly as possible. "Why did you come, Leland?"

"To recall you to your senses. I have heard that you have taken this Hawthorne person as your lover. Your behavior is beyond the pale. Have the Dewberry woman pack a bag for you. You are returning to Devon with me immediately. Allowing you to live alone has given you the illusion of independence, Grace. I never should have made that mistake. I shall have to remedy that now."

Grace could only stare at him. Surely he'd taken leave of his senses! She'd open her veins before she'd live under Leland's roof. And then, as if a cloud had lifted from her mind, she began to put all the troubling pieces together.

"It has been Barrington feeding you information, hasn't it? Every time something happened that he did not like, I received a letter from you. He has been spying on me. The two of you have been controlling me for years. Since…since Basil's death!"

"You have been allowed your freedom, Grace, providing you did not go too far afield. Now you will have to come home with me until you come to your senses."

"Why now?"

"You are completely out of hand." His voice was cold and unemotional. "Cavorting with that Hawthorne man, taking him as a lover and having him under your roof. Frolicking through every lowlife gaming hell in London in search of tawdry thrills. Risking everything on the turn of a card."

Grace knew she should retreat. Knew she should agree to anything Leland said to avoid the inevitable consequences. But she no longer cared. Cautious Grace was gone and defiant Ellie had taken her place. "Why do you care, Leland? The worst that could happen is that I would end up under *your* roof again, and yet that is what you are proposing now. You did not threaten to take me back when you thought Barrington was my lover. What earthly difference should it make to you who sleeps in my bed?"

Leland narrowed his eyes and delivered a sharp slap to her cheek then gave her a push. "Are you a whore now, Grace, willing to make yourself, and me, the subject of gossip? Did you really think I'd stand by and do nothing? Watch all my careful work go for naught?"

Her hip landed against a corner of the tea cart and she winced. Still, she backed away, angry enough at the moment to be grateful she did not have a gun within reach. All his careful work? The words clicked into place and Grace realized what had been eluding her. "You forged Basil's will, did you not?" she asked, still backing toward the door. "You and Barrington—to be certain I inherited?" Her mind reeled as old events took on new meaning. Even Barrington's veiled threats finally made sense. "That is fraud, Leland. I was supposed to marry Lord Barrington, was I not? And you would have shared Basil's wealth once I was no longer in control?"

Leland advanced on her, baring his teeth in an ugly snarl. "We will not be cheated, Grace."

Dianthe practically fell into Adam's arms as he came through the kitchen from the stables. Gasping, she landed against his chest and gathered his shirtfront in her fists. "Oh!" she gasped. "Thank heavens you're here! Come quickly, Adam!"

"What is it?"

"Leland is here. He's threatening to take Grace away!"

Grace's brother? When had he arrived in town?

"And he struck her!"

"Where are they?"

"The parlor! I just came home and heard them arguing. When I peeked in and saw him strike her, I came looking for help."

He headed for the parlor, waving Dianthe back. He did not want her in the way if there was a brawl. He heard Grace's voice raised in a denouncement and the sneering tones of a masculine voice. He threw the parlor door open and stepped in.

Both occupants turned to him. Grace, dressed in a soft pastel wrapper, her hair loosely bound in back, displayed obvious relief, while the man betrayed contempt.

"Hawthorne, I presume?" He sneered.

"Correct," Adam admitted. "And you are Leland York?"

"Get out, Hawthorne. This is between me and my harlot of a sister."

"Not on a cold day in hell, York."

Grace moved between them, backing up against Adam's chest as if prepared to protect him. He smiled down at the top of her head, charmed with the notion that she would risk herself for his safety.

"Get out, Leland. And do not come back," she said.

"You will need me someday, Grace, when your new lover has taken everything and left you a pauper."

"I will sell matchsticks on the street and sleep on the steps of St. Paul's first," she swore.

Leland York bared his teeth and took a step toward her.

Gently but firmly, Adam gripped Grace's shoulders and moved her aside. "You will go through me," he warned. His muscles tensed and his hands bunched into fists.

Leland made his move, a quick lunge with a roundhouse punch. But Adam did not fight according to any dandified London rules. He fought like an Indian. He ducked beneath Leland's swing and came up behind him. Seizing Leland's left wrist, he jerked it upward behind his back and slipped his other arm around the man's neck. Just because the man deserved it, he pulled the man's arm sharply upward until he heard a pop.

Leland howled in pain as Adam turned him around and walked him out of the parlor toward the front door. "You've broken my arm," he accused between sobs.

"Don't think so," Adam said, his voice filled with amusement. "I've dislocated your elbow. Have a doctor look at it. Painful, to be sure, but you'll be fine in a few weeks."

Dianthe, still waiting in the foyer, saw them coming and opened the door. Adam gave the man a push and Leland landed on his knees on the street.

"It takes a very singular kind of coward to prey on women. I do not like you, Leland. Do not come here again."

Dianthe closed the door and Adam turned back to Grace. "He struck you?"

She nodded. "It will not show, if that is what you are wondering. Leaving no marks is Leland's particular talent."

Adam felt sick to his stomach thinking of Grace at that man's mercy. No wonder she had buried Ellie deep beneath the surface. Men like Leland York would not find a free and joyful spirit of any significant value.

"Just the same, Grace, I think it would be best if you stayed home tonight. I doubt your brother is in any condition to lay in wait, but I do not want you risking your neck on it."

She sighed and shook her head. "I must, Adam. I really have no choice. Time is short and…I really must dress." She turned and hurried up the stairs.

"I have other plans, Grace. I cannot escort you."

"I understand," she called over her shoulder. "I shall be on my guard. And now that Leland has been stopped, I'll be fine."

Adam turned to Dianthe. "What the hell is she up to?"

"Oh, I…um, you'd have to ask her, Adam. I'm sure I wouldn't…that is…I think I'll go lie down. The afternoon has been quite taxing."

When Dianthe, too, disappeared up the stairs, Adam went to the library and poured himself a sherry. What the bloody hell was so important they couldn't trust him?

Chapter Nineteen

Sitting cross-legged on the floor in the darkest corner of the room, Adam knew he'd be almost impossible to see in the dim glow of the fireplace. He was absolutely still. Even his breathing was silent. He'd hunted enough men in Canada to know that he could remain in his current posture for hours. And he'd wait as long as he needed to wait.

He'd been with Freddie most of the night, chasing leads, following Barrington and Leland York. He was not particularly surprised when they'd met with a small group of disreputable-looking men in a seedy waterfront tavern. Could one of them have been the mysterious man in black who had attacked him and Grace, and who had been seen next to Eddy Clark before he'd collapsed on the street?

Adam stood and edged toward the door, ready to follow him outside, but the man quickly disappeared out the back. By the time Adam made his way to the stable yard in back, the man was already gone. The stable boy said that he'd exited down a side street away from the river. Adam had been furious, but he was calmer now. He'd find the man again. Yes, sooner or later, he'd find the man, and when he did…

The incident had revealed two certain clues. One he'd expected—that his accidents, and possibly Grace's, were connected to York and Barrington through that man in black. The other clue had actually surprised him—that his inquiries into the Canadian incident were also connected to Barrington and therefore, in some way, to Grace. Was she even aware that there was a connection between Barrington and her accidents?

His stomach burned as he considered the possibilities. Either Grace was in more danger than she could imagine, or she was only in danger as a result of her proximity to him.

Either way, he'd know tonight.

When Grace came home, the house was quiet but something felt strange. Not dangerous, but slightly odd. As she passed Dianthe's room, she opened the door and peeked in. A soft sigh broke the silence as Dianthe turned over. She, at least, was safe. She closed Dianthe's door and continued to her own. She hesitated and then went to Adam's door. She opened it just enough to verify that he hadn't returned from his "other plans." Wherever he was, she prayed he was safe.

Frustrated and tired, she dropped her reticule on her dressing table and kicked her slippers off. She sat and pulled the pins from her hair and combed the knot out with her fingers before applying her brush.

She'd gone from hell to hell tonight, and never managed to find Lord Geoffrey. Had he taken a night off? Was he ill? If he suddenly stopped coming to the hells, what chance would she have to free Laura Talbot? One thing was clear—because of the risk that Lord Geoffrey might become unavailable, she could not afford any more distractions. She must forge straight ahead until her task was complete. *And she must complete it at the first opportunity.*

She put her brush aside and stood again. Unfastening her gown, she let it fall to the floor. She was exhausted tonight, but she'd pick it up for Mrs. Dewberry tomorrow morning.

She lifted the hem of her chemise and unfastened her garters and rolled her stockings carefully down her legs to avoid snags, then removed her garters, too. That done, she pulled the chemise over her head and dropped it on top of her gown.

Naked, she went to her bureau to fetch a nightgown but before she donned it, she went back to the cheval looking glass beside her dressing table. Examining her arms, she was relieved to note that the bruises Barrington had inflicted were gone and the ones Leland had left were in places that would never be visible. She slipped her hand down to the bruise on her hip where she'd fallen against the tea cart—livid now, but soon to fade away, like Leland himself.

She closed her eyes, remembering the incident, and how Adam had challenged Leland on her behalf. No one had ever found the courage to come between Leland and what he wanted. She had no doubt that Leland would disappear for a time and then reappear as if nothing had happened. One way or another, he would eventually have his way. But not, she thought, with Adam.

Her heart bumped. When had she grown to love Adam? Had it happened the moment he'd turned to her in the library and said, absurdly, *Hello, Aunt Grace?* Or had it happened when, after Barrington's scene at Belmonde's, he'd quietly told her that she'd have an escort? She couldn't pinpoint the exact moment, but it had happened somewhere between their first hello and their last wager in the library.

Oh! Those wagers!

She shivered in the night air drifting through her window and tilted her head to one side to study the effects of thinking of him. Chill bumps covered her arms and her nipples had firmed and formed little peaks. She closed her eyes and touched them, then let her hands slip downward over her belly to the thatch of nether hair between her legs. "Adam…" She sighed, remembering.

No, she wouldn't have risked so much if she hadn't loved him, if she hadn't been willing to surrender everything to him. And now she could not draw breath without thinking of him, wondering where he was and if he was safe.

How odd that she had accepted that love would never come to her. Or the kind of soaring happiness her friends had managed to achieve. For her, happiness had been a fragile thing, ephemeral, elusive. Always, when she'd allowed herself to think she'd found it, took the tiniest taste of it, it disappeared in an instant, like mist in a morning meadow. So she'd settled for contentment, knowing to expect anything more was ridiculous—a prelude to pain. "Adam," she said again, savoring the feeling of belonging that came with it. Oh, how she prayed that this fragile happiness she felt in Adam's arms would not also turn to pain.

"Ellie," he said, his breath hot in her ear.

Her eyes flew open and there, behind her in the mirror, was Adam, dressed in his buckskins, his head tilted to one side to give attention to her earlobe. He cupped her shoulders, holding her motionless.

She watched him, took in the fierce hunger of his touch, the manner of his dress and the strength in his stance. "Where have you been?" she asked.

"Hunting."

His hands came around her waist and moved up to cup her breasts and she suddenly felt vulnerable and exposed. How had he surprised her so completely? She spun around in his arms and looked up into his face. "What…where?"

"The corner by your bed," he said against her lips.

She hadn't even looked in the shadows when she'd come in. "When?"

"I've been here an hour or more, waiting. And let me say, Ellie, you are well worth the wait."

"Oh!" She pulled away, burning with embarrassment, and

snatched her nightgown off the floor and struggled to drop it over her head.

"In fact," he continued, "it very nearly makes up for the fact that you've been lying to me."

"I do not know what you mean," she squeaked.

"We are going to get some things straight tonight. I've waited for you to tell me the truth, but it is apparent that you will not volunteer it. So, since your secrets appear to intersect mine, we need to talk."

"I don't know—"

"Of course you do," he said, lifting her chin on the edge of his hand.

Grace had the sinking feeling that she was not going to bluff her way out of this. Adam had that single-minded look on his face, and she knew he was right. It was long past time to tell him what he wanted to know. She sat on the edge of her bed. "Where…do you want me to start?"

Adam went to the fireplace and rested one arm on the mantel, evidently preferring distance to proximity. "Just start."

"I think everything is yours, Adam. Everything but, perhaps, a small annuity for me."

"Why?"

"Because, given what Mr. Evans and Mr. Ogilby have told me, I believe your uncle's will was a forgery."

A long moment passed and then Adam nodded. "What were you told?"

"That Lord Barrington and my brother brought the will to Mr. Ogilby directly after Basil's funeral. They told him Basil had signed it just days before his death. And they urged both men to accept it since there were no other heirs anyway."

Adam's eyebrows shot up and she noted that his muscles tensed. His expression did not change, but everything seemed different. As if he suddenly understood something that had been troubling him. "If there were no other heirs, why did they need a will?"

"I...don't know. To prevent lengthy court hearings?"

"When did you find this out?"

"I went to Mr. Evans's office on Saturday. He told me everything then."

"Did you suspect something before then?"

She looked down at her hands folded in her lap. Her answers were making her look suspicious and guilty of some sort of conspiracy, but she could not stop now. "Since your return," she said, "Lord Barrington started behaving oddly, and then there were his threats."

"What threats?"

Grace shivered at the ice in Adam's voice. "That I would regret sending him away, and some other veiled insinuations."

"Anything else?"

"I believe Lord Barrington and Leland are in league with one another. For the past several years, every time I tried to distance myself from Barrington, Leland would send a letter and threaten to fetch me back to Devon. I began to think that Leland was encouraging my relationship with Barrington, but I thought it was because he wanted an alliance with a peer. Now I think Barrington would warn Leland when I moved toward independence, and Leland would then make the threat he knew I could not resist."

"But you did this time, and that is why your brother turned up on your doorstep." Adam nodded. "How did you find the courage this time?"

You, she wanted to say. Where could she have found the courage without Adam's presence in her life? "Because I knew I was not alone," she murmured, knowing that was the truth.

The silence stretched out and Grace realized that he was waiting for more. But what more did she have to confess?

"I know, Grace," he said at last.

"What?" she asked.

"About you."

Was he referring to the rumors that she had killed his uncle?

"Did you think I wouldn't notice?"

She stopped breathing. No. Not that.

"You were a virgin, Grace. How did that happen? Were you actually married to my uncle? Or was that a lie, too? A lie you told to gain his inheritance?"

"No!" she gasped. "It wasn't like that, Adam. We were legally married, but…it was Basil. He…he couldn't. He tried, but he just couldn't. I tried to help, but—" She shrugged and fought the tears stinging her eyes.

"He couldn't," Adam finished for her.

Did he believe her? She could barely see his face in the dim light and shadows.

"And so, four years later, you surrender to me? With all the men who have tried, who have coveted the position as your lover, and you abandon your fate to the one man who could use it against you?"

The tears finally spilled over and trickled down her cheeks. She nodded, knowing it made no sense.

"Why?" he asked quietly.

"I do not know." She wept. "I am unraveling! My whole *life* is unraveling! I do not know me anymore. Nothing— *nothing*—is familiar and everything is completely beyond my control. I am doing things, thinking things, saying things that are beyond my ken. I—I feel as if I am disappearing and a stranger is inhabiting my body!"

"No stranger," Adam said, his voice softening. "'Tis Ellie. The real you. Ellie does not care what society will think or what people will say. One last question, my dear, and then we can go forward."

She sniffled and nodded, anxious for the question that would put this inquisition to rest and be done with the deceptions.

"For the last time, why are you gambling? I know it is not for the excitement. If you are addicted, Grace, I—"

She groaned and shook her head. This was the one question she could not answer without compromising Miss Talbot and the work of the Wednesday League. "I cannot tell you that. I don't understand what you want from me."

"What I want?" He gestured to her door. "I want to close that door, Grace, and forget the world outside. I want to be just you and me, with none of the secrets we've kept or the things we've done intruding. I want the blood to disappear from my hands and the hate from my heart. I want the hurt to fade from your eyes. I want it all to go away while I lie down with you and feel the rightness of the world and the perfect balance of the universe. You in my arms. There is nothing beyond that but the abyss. Make that happen, Grace. Tell me the truth."

She yearned to be in his arms, but how could she betray the Wednesday League and Laura Talbot? And how could Adam ever forget Nokomis? She shook her head, burying her face in her hands. "I cannot break that confidence. Do not ask me, Adam. It is because of you that I must go forward."

There was disbelief in his voice when he spoke. "You blame *me* for your gambling?"

"No." She shook her head. She could have left Laura Talbot to Lord Geoffrey's care in good conscience, until she'd learned that Laura was in love. After loving Adam, how could she consign Laura to a loveless marriage? "If I hadn't known you, I wouldn't have understood."

"Understood what?"

She could only shake her head.

"There are things afoot here. Things that could be a threat to your life. And mine. If you will not tell me what I need to know, I will continue to seek the answers on my own. And make no mistake, *Ellie,* I will not rest until I have those answers. Make a choice, my dear. Your secrets or me?"

If she betrayed the confidence of the Wednesday League and told him, he would go to Lord Geoffrey. But Lord Geoffrey would never give up the debt—it was not in his character. And once alerted to Grace's intention, he would never wager with her. She shook her head.

Adam stepped back, a look of profound regret darkening his hazel eyes. "You've made your choice. I hope you will be happy with it."

Lady Annica removed a wad of bank notes from her reticule and passed them to Grace. "Send to me if you need more, Grace. I am making a trip to the bank today and shall withdraw more should you need it."

Grace pushed the wad into her own reticule and glanced around at the other ladies of the Wednesday League, seated in a circle in Madame Marie's largest dressing room. Mr. Renquist stood in one corner, looking quite uncomfortable. He was the only man allowed at their meetings, but was rarely invited and his discomfort was clear.

Charity and Sarah both passed banknotes to Grace with nods of encouragement.

Grace took it all, praying that it would be enough. "Thank you. I shall repay you when my funds are unfrozen."

"Nonsense! You should not bear this cost alone, Grace," Lady Annica said. "Do not worry about repayment. Just find a way to stop this wedding."

"That's the problem, ladies," Mr. Renquist said, stepping forward. "Mrs. Forbush has not been able to catch him cheating, and I haven't been able to turn up anything that would help. That Morgan fellow is a slippery one. As time is growing quite short, I'd advise you to make alternate plans."

Grace shrugged. "I do not know if there are other options. Sunday afternoon, I talked with Miss Talbot. I presented her with several options should our plan fail, but she refused to consider them."

"What options?" Sarah asked.

"That she should simply refuse to honor her brother's debt. If she could not, or if he should become violent, she would have a place with me until such time as we could secure her future. She and Dianthe are already friends, so I thought that would ease the strain of unfamiliar territory."

"Well, I am not altogether sorry she refused," Dianthe said. "Miss Talbot is...rather weak. If I did not dislike him so much, I would almost pity Lord Geoffrey."

Dianthe's opinion validated her own but she wondered what Dianthe had based her view on. "Why do you say so?" she asked.

"When we went dancing last week, Miss Talbot shunned every man who asked her. I thought she was keeping herself for her upcoming marriage, but that was not the case at all. When a young man of effeminate manner arrived, Miss Talbot fawned over him as if he were the Prince Regent himself. I found it quite disturbing that she should make a spectacle of herself over a man who, at best, had only a passing interest in her."

"I was afraid of that," Grace said. "She confessed that she had set her affections on a particular beau. I offered to give them the wherewithal to make a dash for Gretna Greene, but she would have none of it. Her suitor was honorable, she told me, and just needed more time to win her brother's approval."

"Well," Dianthe sniffed, "if he is the same man that Laura fawned over, it will never happen. Not even an unfeeling rake like Laura's brother would approve that beau nasty!"

"Dianthe!" Grace was appalled at the girl's pronouncement.

Sarah and Annica covered their laughs with coughing and Mr. Renquist turned away, as if studying the painting of a landscape hanging on the wall.

"'Tis true. He was none too clean and had a manner about him that was almost obsequious." She shivered. "I vow that, had I let him take my hand, his palms would have been clammy."

"Some day you will fall in love, Dianthe, and it will not be at all what you expect," Sarah said.

Dianthe shrugged. "When I fall in love, *if* I fall in love, it will be with someone eminently suitable. But that is for the future. I am having far too much fun to end it with marriage."

Grace merely smiled. None of the women in the room had made a match that would have been termed "suitable," but all were quite content. "Then I do not regret urging Miss Talbot to consider marriage to Lord Geoffrey."

"What!" all the ladies said at once. Even Mr. Renquist raised his eyebrows.

"I thought of my own marriage. It was made for financial reasons to a man I'd met but once, and yet he and I were able to forge a…comfortable relationship. And Mr. Forbush was kinder than my brother. I enjoyed freedom, of a sort, and a standing in the community. It was not a bad arrangement, by and large. I thought Miss Talbot could benefit from a similar arrangement. Lord Geoffrey would not be much at home and—" She stopped, remembering Lord Geoffrey's unvarnished requirements of a wife from the night before. "Well, the subject is closed since she was not amenable to the suggestion."

"I should hope not!" Dianthe exclaimed.

"But where does this leave us?" Annica asked.

"With Miss Talbot holding me to my rash promise that I would do everything within my power to see that she would not have to marry Lord Geoffrey. The poor girl has very little common sense and no courage to defy her brother. Oh, if I could only take back my words! But I must go forward and I must conclude this quickly. Adam—Mr. Hawthorne is asking altogether too many questions about my gambling. Does anyone have an idea for an alternate solution?"

Silence fell as they regarded one another with puzzlement.

"We shall come by tomorrow afternoon and see if you have made any progress," Sarah offered. "Meantime, ladies, shall we all think of possible alternatives?"

"But why do you have to go out tonight, Aunt Grace? I'd feel much better if you would wait until Adam could escort you."

Grace secured the crystal-studded snood over her chignon and glanced at Dianthe in her mirror. "Dianthe, Adam is not likely to escort me to a hell ever again. We argued last night, and he…well, he is finished with escorting me anywhere."

"Why? He adores you. I see it in his eyes every time he looks at you."

Grace blinked away her threatening tears and took a deep breath. She assumed the woman-of-the-world role that had become so familiar in the last years. "Not any longer, Dianthe."

"What did you argue about?" Dianthe came to her and placed a comforting hand on her shoulder.

She sighed as she fastened her amethyst pendant around her neck—the last of her good jewelry. "So many things I hardly know where to begin. I have not lied to him, but I have withheld certain…information. The worst of it was when he asked me to make a choice between him and gambling. 'Twas then he walked away and said he hoped I'd be happy with my decision."

"Why does he care if you gamble?"

"He may think it is his money I've been gambling, depending upon the outcome of the court hearing, which, I might add, is not looking favorable for me at the moment."

"Why did you not choose him? There must be more than you are telling me," Dianthe guessed.

Grace shrugged, unwilling to go into the details of Adam's

late-night visit to her room or the fact that his love was still with an Indian maid named Nokomis. "We came to loggerheads over the gambling, though. I must forge ahead on this investigation, Dianthe, and as quickly as possible. Lord Geoffrey was nowhere to be found last night. What if he should disappear before the wedding? It is only days away. How would I find him out then? No. I must find him tonight and force an end to this, one way or the other. Whatever it takes, I shall do it."

"Surely not *whatever?*"

Grace stood and smoothed the icy violet gown that she'd last worn when she'd given herself to Adam. "Yes," she whispered. "Whatever. I just want this over with." She could not lose anything more important than she'd already lost. Adam's trust, because of her closely guarded secrets and lies, and probably his affection along with it. Adam, who would now think she was an unrepentant gambling addict.

Dianthe gave her a quick hug. "Do not worry, Aunt Grace. If we become destitute, we shall simply move into the little fortune-telling salon above Madame Marie's shop now that Afton is married and gone. I shall tell fortunes and you can… help Madame Marie."

Grace smiled. Dianthe's enthusiasm was contagious. "That would be an excellent solution. But let us hope it will not come to that."

"Will you be safe tonight, Aunt Grace?"

How could she define "safe"? Safe from outside danger? "Yes," she said. "Hells are well attended and, as long as I keep to the main salon, I shall be safe enough."

Safe from Geoffrey Morgan? That remained to be seen. But safe from herself? No. She had nothing more to lose now that she'd thrown her chance for happiness with Adam away. And nothing, it would seem, could protect her from her own unbending integrity once her word was given.

Chapter Twenty

Adam stared at the arsenic bottle in the distant glow of the lamplight. The sounds of the waterfront—raucous voices, drinking and fighting, whistles in the distance—all faded when he realized what this could mean. "Where did you find it?"

"In your stable," Freddie Carter said. "As you can see, there's only a small amount left."

"And my uncle's symptoms…" Adam trailed off, trying to comprehend the meaning.

"Are consistent with arsenic poisoning," Carter finished. "Of course, she may have acquired it for rats or other vermin, but the coincidence is enough to make one wonder, is it not?"

Adam slipped the arsenic bottle inside his leather tunic. Arsenic, a fraudulent will, an unconsummated marriage, a gambling addiction, a fear of being at her brother's mercy. To the authorities, each of these things alone would be motive for murder, but together? After their conversation last night, he'd left her to her own devices. Was she home? Was she safe? Would she be there if the authorities came for her?

"Hawthorne?" Carter asked. "Did you hear me?"

"I can't accept this," he said. Grace had already told him all this. All but the arsenic.

"Do you doubt me?" Carter asked, stark disbelief written on his face.

"Just your conclusion."

"For God's sake! It's enough to go to the police!"

Adam spun on him. "Say you haven't done that."

"Not yet. But I will in the morning."

"No...no." Was he a fool? He'd known her only two weeks. How could he be so sure? "Damn! If she just wasn't keeping secrets from me! If I knew what her motives were—"

"*She's* keeping secrets? *She* looks suspicious? Hawthorne, what about you? You're living in her house under false pretenses, you've been trying to make a case against her for murder, and who has greater motive to want to see her disinherited? And, if I know you, you've already seduced her. I'd say she has rather more cause for complaint than you. Objectively speaking, you have wronged the little pigeon vastly more than she has wronged you. Unless, of course, she used that arsenic."

Adam felt the bottle against his ribs. "Just say you won't go to the police," he repeated.

Carter backed away from him, his expression taking a dark turn. "I don't need your permission. If it's true, I have an obligation. We don't let murderers walk away from their crimes, Hawthorne, no matter who they're sleeping with. The man was your uncle!"

"You will go through me," he heard himself say for the second time in as many days.

"That would be a mistake."

"Yours." A deep feeling of relief spread through him. Until that moment he hadn't realized he would never accept that Grace was a murderess. Not Grace, and not Ellie.

"Damn," Carter muttered, and gestured to the door of the tavern they'd been watching.

The black-coated figure pulled his hat down to obscure his

face and turned his collar up. Glancing right, then left, he headed down a narrow lane in the direction of Covent Garden.

With a nod, Adam and Carter put their plan into action, Carter following their quarry, and Adam up another street and circling to intercept the man's path. He sprinted down the dark lane, his moccasins silent on the cobblestones. The London streets were easier to traverse than a wooded mountain or deep forest and by the time he rounded the corner and headed back, he was a full one hundred feet in front of their target.

The instant the man noticed Adam, he turned to head back down the lane, but Carter blocked his path. Another glance over his shoulder convinced him that his easiest route lay through Carter, and he charged the Bow Street runner.

Prepared this time, Carter raised his pistol, primed and ready to fire. The man skidded to a halt and tuned sideways, glancing one way and then the other. His muscles bunched and one knee flexed for a lunge but Adam launched himself before the man could act. They rolled across the cobblestones several times before slamming against the bricks of a building. Mindful of his opponent's skill with a stiletto, Adam drew his own knife as he stood.

Carter appeared and pressed the barrel of his pistol against the man's head. "Hands where I can see them," he ordered.

Slowly the man raised his hands in front of him, his gaze trained on Carter. Adam searched him, finding and removing the stiletto, a smaller dagger and a pistol. "Recognize me?" he asked.

"Aye," the man said in a thick Irish brogue. "You be the man with the devil's own luck. I don't miss."

"Outside the Two Sevens?"

"Aye."

"And Eddy Clark? Did you hire him and then kill him?"

"Ye're half right," the man laughed defiantly.

"You killed him," Adam guessed.

"Aye."

"And Major Taylor?"

"Him, too."

From the corner of his eye, Adam noticed that Carter's finger was tightening on the trigger. "What about Shelton? Taylor's guard."

"Aye, him, too. And ye're ladybird would be gone if I didn't have to make that look like an accident. I'm better at a straightforward killing than arranging accidents."

A snarl distorted Carter's features and his finger tightened on the trigger. Adam gave a quick shake of his head, warning him to ease off. He still had questions.

"Why Taylor's heart?"

"A lesson to him. And to ye. Ye were supposed to realize we were on to ye and back off. None too bright, are ye?"

"Where's Shelton?" Carter asked.

"In the Thames. He's halfway to the Channel by now."

Adam held his breath and took a tight rein on his fury. The man was a stone cold killer, but he was merely a hireling. "Who hired you?"

The assassin laughed. "Ye think I'm as addlepated as ye? I cross him and I'm dead."

"You're dead, anyway," Carter sneered. "You're not walking away tonight."

"I'm not hearin' any reason to help ye." The man laughed.

The sound turned to a gasp when Adam pressed the tip of his knife to the hollow of his throat. "You want a reason to tell us what we want to know? How's this—you can die fast and painless, or slow and in excruciating pain. The choice is yours. The last choice you'll ever make."

That sobered the assassin. He looked from Adam to Freddie Carter as if trying to measure their determination. "Don't know the name. I've done work for him before. Political or government types."

Adam believed him. Clandestine business in the upper circles was done without names or rank. And he knew who it was anyway—the only man who had the resources to find and hire a professional assassin and who would have reason to want him out of the way. Everything—from the arsenic and the attack on the Indian village to the attempts on Grace's life—fell into place. He'd known most of it since Grace had told him about the will and his uncle's last days. But it wasn't one man. It was two. That's what had confused him and kept him from guessing the truth sooner. That, and a clear motive.

He turned to Carter. "It's Barrington and York. Barrington ordered the attack on the Indian village to kill me, not the Indians, and when I turned up, he hired this man—" he nodded toward the assassin "—to finish the job."

Carter frowned. "Why?"

"That's where I got stumped. I knew Grace was somehow a part of this, but I couldn't believe she would murder anyone. Barrington wanted Grace to have clear, sole claim to my uncle's fortune. He and York must have planned to control the money through her, but she would not commit to Barrington, and their plan was stalled. When I returned, they needed to move fast before they lost it all. I had to be gotten rid of and Grace either had to marry Barrington or die. Because—"

"Because if you and she were both dead, York would inherit from Grace," Carter finished. "The son of a bitch tried to kill his own sister."

Adam backed away from the assassin, sheathed his hunting knife in his moccasin and rewound the leather strap tightly around his calf.

"Where are you going?" Carter asked.

"Hunting. Barrington's house, his office, his club, drawing rooms or state dinners. I'll find that son of a bitch and skin him alive before he can hurt anyone else. And I'll handle

York, too. I'll meet you later at the Eagle. Can you take care of him?" He tilted his head toward the assassin.

"Glad to."

Anxiety burned a hole in Grace's stomach. She'd been to Belmonde's, Fabrey's, Rupert House, Tremont Place, the Two Sevens and the Pigeon Hole, and could find no trace of Lord Geoffrey. That only left Thackery's and the Blue Moon in Covent Garden. What if Lord Geoffrey retired to the country for the remainder of the summer or until his wedding? What if the preparations for his wedding were keeping him so occupied that he had no time to gamble in the meantime? What if their last conversation had warned him what her intentions were?

The time had unfortunately come for her to lay all her cards on the table, as it were. One way or the other, she must bring the matter to a conclusion at the first opportunity since she might not get another chance.

She braced herself as she handed her cloak to a footman at Thackery's and kept walking deeper into the bowels of the infamous hell, not giving the host time to question her. If she appeared to have every right to enter, or to be meeting someone, perhaps she would not be challenged.

With the small fortune she'd collected from Annica, Sarah and Charity safely tucked in her reticule, though she hated to risk it, she was determined to secure Laura Talbot's future. If only she could find the man who held the current right to that future! She scanned the main salon and her heart sank. There was no trace of Lord Geoffrey. She filled a glass from a wine fountain on a long sideboard and made a circuit of the room, hoping she had missed him in the crush or to at least find someone she knew. Oh, for one of the Hunter brothers right now—anyone who could tell her where Lord Geoffrey might have gone.

Fighting despair, she climbed the red-carpeted stairs to a

mezzanine from which smaller rooms branched out. From that vantage, she looked down over the main salon again. Still no Morgan.

With fading hope, she glanced into the smaller rooms to see if Lord Geoffrey had found a private game. Only a few rooms were occupied, and none contained her prey. She would not go up the next flight of stairs. If rumors were true, that was where lovely courtesans waited for the patron's convenience and where illicit liaisons were conducted between members of the ton. It was, in fact, where one well-known lady of the ton was said to have granted her favors to satisfy a gambling debt she could not pay. Grace frowned, unable to imagine how the woman had gotten herself in such a compromising situation.

She finished her glass of wine and sighed, giving one last glance over the main salon. Only the Blue Moon remained, and that was too dreary to imagine. The crowd was considerably less congenial and much more cutthroat.

Just as she turned from her study, she caught sight of Lord Geoffrey. He had just entered the main salon and was taking the measure of the players. Almost instantly, as if he had felt her study, he looked up and saw her at the balcony above him. He nodded and disappeared beneath the balcony. She turned toward the staircase and waited, her heartbeat accelerating. Her plan was in action.

When he appeared at the head of the stairs, he smiled and came toward her. "I heard you were about tonight, Mrs. Forbush. And alone, at that."

He must have a very good grapevine, she thought. She returned his smile. "Alas, Mr. Hawthorne tires of the play."

"His loss," Lord Geoffrey said, offering his arm. "But you've said that before."

"This time I am certain of it," she said, taking his arm. His jacket was still cool from the night air as he led her back to the balustrade overlooking the main salon. Had he come looking for her? Or was it just coincidence that he appeared at Thackery's? The tables were turned, and now Grace suspected *she* might have been hunted. Had Lord Geoffrey decided to move in for the kill? That was what she wanted. Wasn't it?

"Have you come to gamble or just observe?"

"Gamble."

"You've found more than your jewelry to wager?"

"I have."

He grinned and gestured to the tables below. "What is your game?"

She tried for an indifferent shrug. "What are *you* playing, Lord Geoffrey?"

"I am at your disposal, Mrs. Forbush."

"Vingt-et-un?"

"Would you like to play me or the tables?"

How droll. He was giving her a chance to escape. But, of course, there was only one answer, and only one reason. Laura Talbot. "You, Lord Geoffrey," she said.

He led her to the first private room at the head of the stairs and summoned a monitor for a deck of cards and counters. She sat across from him and watched as he shuffled and dealt the first hand. Nothing, no fumble or hesitation, betrayed sleight of hand or trickery of any kind. She lost. And the second game, and the third. She had really expected to win a hand or two. Could it be that Lord Geoffrey had tired of toying with her and was now ready for the coup? At this rate, she'd have lost all her money within an hour.

She must have betrayed her consternation in some way, because Lord Geoffrey signaled the monitor over and handed him the deck. "If you please," he said, and gestured at a chair.

The man, now their croupier, sat and gave his attention to the cards. Was this yet another ploy to put her at ease? Lord Geoffrey kept up a stream of easy chatter, not taxing, not diverting, certainly nothing engineered to distract her to the point of being unable to play her cards and make decisions. He talked about his horse, a manor house he'd just bought in Wiltshire for his bride-to-be, his penchant for Scotch and his preference for gambling at Covent Garden hells.

"Anything can happen here," he said, a trace of amusement in his voice. "There are no limits and nothing is sacred."

Was he taunting her? Was he really so confident that she'd fall victim to his machinations? She smiled and kept her composure despite her pile of dwindling counters. She was aware that their game was drawing mild interest by the number of men who would wander into the room and watch for a time, then leave only to return with a friend.

Lord Geoffrey began to make slightly smaller wagers, as if drawing out his victory. Or prolonging her defeat. She could not decide which. With each win, Lord Geoffrey would look almost apologetic, as if he'd wanted to lose but just couldn't manage it.

Grace despaired that she'd ever determine how the man could be so infernally "lucky." It was beginning to look as if she had lost a disgraceful amount of money and expended considerable energy to no avail.

And, two hours after her arrival at Thackery's, with a hollow feeling of despair and a silent prayer, she pushed the last of her counters into the center of the table. She had a count of twenty. It was as good a hand as she'd had all night.

The croupier turned up Lord Geoffrey's last card. *"Vingt-et-un,"* he announced.

"I am awed by your skill," she said, pushing her chair back from the table and preparing to rise.

"Please, Mrs. Forbush," Lord Geoffrey entreated. "Sit down."

"You've won the last of my counters," she said, easing back onto her chair. "I have nothing left."

He smiled again, the smile that was somehow knowing and sinister. "You have other…assets."

Grace stared at him, trying to decide if he'd meant those words the way they'd sounded. When she did not speak, he took the initiative again.

"Your pendant, Mrs. Forbush. I'd say that was worth…oh, one hundred pounds."

That was generous. It had been recently valued at eighty. Laura Talbot's face haunted her. Everything within her power, she'd said. She nodded and Lord Geoffrey slid one hundred pounds in counters across the table to her as she unfastened the pendant and lay it on the table. He nodded at the croupier to deal another hand. Grace was aware that the crowd at her back was growing but she refused to turn around. If she acknowledged all those faces watching her, speculating on her, she feared she would lose her nerve.

And, in the end, she lost everything *but* her nerve. Again she pushed back from the table. Again, he called her back.

"Wait, Mrs. Forbush. I've won everything but what I wanted most."

The room, abuzz a moment ago, hushed. She felt a blush creep into her cheeks. Surely he would not shame her in front of a crowd. "What is that, Lord Geoffrey?"

"An answer."

She laughed. She had a slight satisfaction in that, at least. "An answer to what?"

"What you really want. I've watched you gamble, Mrs. Forbush. You are not addicted to the excitement. Nor are you caught up in the competition of winning. You gamble with a purpose, but I have been unable to determine what that purpose is, or what it has to do with me."

She arched an eyebrow at him, debating whether she should tell him now that she'd lost everything. She thought not. Leaving him with questions was the only satisfaction she had now.

As she moved to rise, he made her another offer. "One

more hand. If I win, you'll answer the question. If you win…"
He dangled her pendant from his left hand.

She eased back into her chair. "Very well, Lord Geoffrey."

And, again, he won.

He sat back in his chair and regarded her with greater satisfaction than she'd seen him display when winning her fortune. He raised his wineglass and toasted her. "I am ready, Mrs. Forbush. Enlighten me."

Conscious of the crowd at her back, and that this tableau would be grist for the gossip mill tomorrow, she chose her words carefully. "I thought you were a cheat, and that I could prove it if I could just tempt you into carelessness."

There were gasps behind her and she knew if she'd been a man she'd have been challenged for those words. But Lord Geoffrey merely smiled. "And what made you think I was a cheat?"

"Reports. After all, what could possibly account for your luck at cards?"

"Skill?"

"Lord Geoffrey, the cards could hardly arrange themselves for your convenience," she scoffed. "Common odds would have you losing occasionally rather than rarely."

"Then what of the old axiom about love? Lucky in cards, unlucky in love."

Grace would have laughed if she hadn't remembered Constance Bennington. Lord Geoffrey had been courting Constance at the time of her murder. Yes, he'd been unlucky in love.

"Why does it matter to you if I am a cheat, Mrs. Forbush? Do you think I cheated one of your friends?"

"No."

"Then what did you hope to gain?"

"Laura Talbot's freedom."

"Ah! So this is where Miss Talbot comes in. I wondered. Then these last few weeks have been an effort to expose me as a cheat so Miss Talbot would not have to marry me?"

"Yes," Grace admitted, almost relieved to be done with the deception. She stood and the silence behind her told her that the crowd was as stunned as Lord Geoffrey.

His expression did not change as he studied her. She'd have given her eyeteeth to know what he was thinking, but she never would have anticipated his next offer.

His gaze swept her from head to toe. "I told you last time we gambled, Mrs. Forbush, what I would require to release Miss Talbot from her brother's debt. Are you prepared to pay that price?"

She swallowed the lump in her throat, closer to losing her composure at that moment than ever before. Dear Lord! He was serious. He would take her in trade for Laura Talbot! But, in spite of her urgings to Miss Talbot, could she…marry a man she did not love? Of course. She'd married Basil.

Lord Geoffrey's requirements of a bride were not too taxing. In fact, if she recalled correctly, they required very little of her but that she "lie still and spread her legs on occasion and subsequently push out a brat."

She sank back into her chair, fighting her impending panic. "Would you forgive her brother's debt, as well?"

"What would that gain me?"

She was silent. It would gain him nothing. Exchanging Laura for her was an even trade. Both were female. Both would perform their required function. But forgiving the debt was no trade at all—nothing for him to gain, everything to lose.

She kept hearing her promise to Miss Talbot echo in her head, taunting her, prodding her on.

Her hesitation must have challenged him because it couldn't have been pity that led him to make the next offer. "I won't hold you to marriage, Mrs. Forbush. We shall cut for high card. If you win, I will grant Miss Talbot a choice in the matter, independent of her brother's debt. All I require is that she meet with me and talk to me before she makes that choice.

But if I win, you will go upstairs with me tonight and pay your debt. And Saturday I shall wed Miss Talbot as scheduled."

A single night with Lord Geoffrey in exchange for one last opportunity to redeem Laura Talbot? She looked down at the deck. A slim chance. Almost nonexistent. Better than none?

The years of Leland's torment rose to taunt her and urge her on. Nothing mattered now that Adam had turned his back on her—nothing but the chance to strike a blow against the inequity of women and the tyranny of men. And to uphold her promise to a woman too weak to stand on her own.

Could she actually do it? Could she not? Her reputation was already ruined. Adam was gone. She nodded.

When he'd been unable to find Barrington, Adam had gone to Leland York's hotel. After a brief chat, and getting the answers he'd been seeking, he'd put Leland on a late coach out of London with the promise to return only if Grace summoned him. Adam would take steps later to assure that Leland would never be a threat to Grace again. He'd made sure that Leland understood he owed his life to the fact that he was Grace's brother. Adam had all he needed to send Leland to prison for the rest of his life, or to have him hanged, and Leland knew it.

When a messenger intercepted him on the front steps of the house on Bloomsbury Square, he'd been surprised. Not that Grace had gone gambling without him, but that he'd been summoned. He'd be glad of the chance to straighten out their last quarrel. When Grace had chosen to keep her secrets rather than to honor his wishes, he'd been hurt and angry. He'd said things he hadn't meant and he'd left her with the impression that he was finished with her, hoping the thought would sober her and recall her to reason. And, as Carter had reminded him, he'd kept secrets, too, and had not placed his full trust in her. His mistake—one he wouldn't make again.

Now he drew more than a few curious stares in his buckskins, but he was beyond caring about polite social rules of dress and conduct. Thackery's did not appear to be the sort of establishment to adhere too strictly to such codes. He shouldered his way through the crowd in the upstairs room, uncertain what he'd find.

Grace was sitting with her back to the crowd, her amethyst pendant in the pile of counters in front of Lord Geoffrey. He was seated facing the crowd, his posture relaxed. He was tapping one counter on the tabletop, waiting for Grace to speak. Adam acknowledged him with a nod.

Grace's hand came up, and he knew she would be pressing that spot between her eyebrows. Then she nodded and an excited murmur ran through the crowd. One man hurried from the room, probably to spread the news of a new wager. But what was it?

Lord Geoffrey sat forward and glanced quickly at Adam with a shift of his eyes to the side. Adam began to edge around the crowd toward the side to come up on Lord Geoffrey's right. The room began to fill as men from the lower floor poured in.

The croupier shuffled the deck and pushed it into the center of the table, looking interested for the first time.

"You first, Mrs. Forbush," Lord Geoffrey said.

Was he the only one to notice how Grace's hand shook as she reached out toward the deck? He pressed closer to the side and finally reached a position where he could see her face. She looked feverish and terrified. What was the bet? He heard a whisper from behind.

"Her favors, that's what," a man was telling his companion. "High card. If she wins, Morgan's fiancée can beg off. If he wins, she goes upstairs with him."

No longer concerned with subtlety, Adam shouldered men out of his way in an effort to get to Morgan's side. At last he knew the reason for Grace's gambling. But what the hell was Morgan thinking? One thing was certain—Grace really was unraveling!

Her fingers slid the depth of the deck, then up again, as if searching for the exact place to cut. Her shoulders rose with a deep breath and she parted the cards midway down and turned the cut up. The knave of hearts. She sat back with a sigh. It was a good card.

She wasn't safe yet. There were still thirteen cards that could beat hers. Adam finally broke free of crowd and came up behind Lord Geoffrey's chair. Grace looked up at him and her flushed complexion went instantly pale. Her dark eyes glittered and her teeth worried her lower lip as she held his gaze.

Lord Geoffrey reached out and made a careless cut of the cards. He tilted the cut so that only he and Adam could see the card he had exposed. The ace of spades. He replaced the cards facedown on top of the deck and smiled.

"Your win, Mrs. Forbush."

Exclamations and gasps went up from the gathered crowd. Money changed hands and backs were slapped as the room emptied. Adam understood. Lord Geoffrey Morgan had just repaid his debt. At that moment, he almost liked the man.

Grace stood unsteadily, gripping the back of her chair for support. "I shall have Miss Talbot arrange an appointment with you at her earliest convenience, Lord Geoffrey."

Chapter Twenty-One

"Miss Talbot was the reason for your gambling," Adam said as he handed Grace into the coach.

Grace nodded. "She did not deserve to be her brother's pawn."

"As you were Leland's?"

"Yes," she said.

He had suspected that Laura Talbot had had something to do with her gambling, but she had brought herself within inches of total ruin. There had to be more. "You lost half your fortune, your reputation and nearly any claim to virtue. How could you have risked so much?"

"Because I..." She took a deep breath and started again. "Because love is worth any risk."

The slight catch in her voice told him she wasn't talking about Miss Talbot. He reached out and touched her cheek. "Miss Talbot is in love?"

The color rose in her cheeks. "Deeply, she says."

"Are you done now, or is there more?" he asked gently.

She tried to smile but looked more as though she would cry. She turned her face and kissed his palm. "I am done."

"Good," he said, backing away, closing the coach door. If he stayed a minute more he wouldn't be able to send her away. "I want you safe at home. I have one last detail to attend and then I will come to you. There are some matters we need to discuss." He was going to marry this woman and he'd do whatever it took to win her consent.

"Adam, I do not want there to be rancor between us. I wish—"

Rancor? Then she really did not suspect how he felt? He warmed as he thought of the many ways he would tell her when he had finished this last task. "Please, Grace. I have reason to believe that you are in imminent danger. Can you just do as I ask?" He waited until she nodded, then asked the question that nearly threatened his sanity, afraid of the answer. "Would you have honored your wager with Morgan?"

She frowned. "I thought I could until I saw you standing there. But now I know I could not. Thank heavens, an angel was watching over me."

The devil, more likely. He laughed with profound relief as he closed the coach door. With a call to Mr. Dewberry, the coach lurched forward and entered the late-night traffic.

The moment the coach disappeared around a corner, he headed for the Eagle Tavern. Now that he knew Grace would be safe, he could finish his long odyssey.

The house was silent when Grace arrived, and she knew Mrs. Dewberry would be in the coach house waiting for her husband. A candle burned on the foyer table, flickering faintly in the glass globe protecting the flame.

Leaving her reticule on the table, she climbed the stairs to her room, feeling emotionally drained but wonderfully light and free. Though she hadn't been able to prove Lord Geoffrey was a cheat, she had achieved her main objective. Miss Talbot would now have an honorable choice as to her fate. Grace hoped she'd choose wisely. The privilege had cost her and the Wednesday League dearly.

And tonight, she'd finally go to Adam with no secrets and nothing held back. He knew everything. He'd seen beneath the veneer. After all the barren years between, Adam instinctively recognized the girl she had been beneath the woman she had become. She'd been so careful to hide it, fearing Leland, fearing that part of her was wicked, that no one, certainly no man, had discovered that part of her. Adam had seen the worst of her in her willfulness and her rash wagers. Tonight she'd show him the best.

She disrobed, leaving her clothes in a pile on her dressing room floor, and poured tepid water into her washbowl. She lathered and rinsed every part of her with her jasmine scented soap, knowing how much Adam liked the scent. She would seduce him tonight in a way he'd never forget. And *she* would forget, at least for tonight, that he loved someone else.

She slipped into her light dressing gown, removed the pins from her hair and shook it out. The dark lengths fell around her hips, curling gently at the ends. She would not braid it or tie it back tonight. And tomorrow she would cut it to her shoulders. No more prim little chignon. No more tightly controlled facade to give the impression of calm elegance. She was Ellie again. And she'd be Ellie as long as Adam wanted her.

She lit candles for the bedside tables and brought a wine carafe and glasses up from the library. She wouldn't worry about falling asleep tonight or leaving Adam to hurry back to her own bed. She'd lock her door and hold out the world. Tonight she'd finish what she'd begun before Adam had stopped her with a promise for the future. The things she intended to do to him! It would seem she had no shame at all. She hadn't known that about herself.

She smiled as she untied the sash of her dressing gown and let it drop to the floor, then went to her bureau and rummaged through the bottom drawer. The white silk nightgown she'd been given as a wedding gift was still wrapped in tissue.

She'd never worn it for Basil, afraid he would call her bold or brazen. But Adam would like it.

She dropped the nightgown over her head and gloried in the cool fabric sliding over her skin as it settled around her. Adam's sense of touch was acute, as he'd demonstrated on more than one occasion, and he would appreciate the sensuous feel.

She went to the cheval mirror and looked at herself. Heavens! She looked younger than she had in years, and the nightgown was just the right touch to make her look both naughty and nearly virginal. The hint of darker tones at her breasts and the juncture of her legs would tempt Adam and make him smile the boyish smile that made dimples appear in his cheeks.

She heard the click of her door latch and turned with a rush of anticipation. Adam. Adam was home at last.

Shock froze her smile in place.

"How did you get in?" she asked.

"I followed Dianthe," Barrington told her. "Your faithful servants are in the coach house, tucked up for the night."

"Where is she? Did you harm her?"

"Don't think to call her, Grace. She won't come. She's in the library, tied up and gagged."

"If she is injured—"

"She is fine. But she won't be any help to you, my dear."

Her relief was short-lived when she realized what Barrington must be planning. "Adam should be home any minute, and he will not be pleased to find you here." She swept her dressing gown up from the floor and struggled to pull it around her, hating that Barrington had seen her thus.

Barrington grinned. "You're quite enticing, Grace. Too bad I don't have more time at the moment. But your Adam won't find me here. He won't find you, either. That's not in my plans."

Chills ran down her spine. "If you think I'll go anywhere with you, you are mistaken."

"Not mistaken in the least, my dear," he said in his most jovial tone. If not for the circumstances, Grace would have thought him in a drawing room or parlor. "I am well aware that you will not willingly go anywhere with me. That's where the plan went wrong, you see. We should have been married a year or more ago but you are a stubborn wench. Your brother warned me, but we thought we could pull it off together. I knew I couldn't push you too hard or you'd send me away. *Patience,* I told Leland. *I am winning her slowly.* But then Hawthorne turned up alive and everything went wrong."

"What did you think you could pull off?" she asked, edging toward the fireplace.

"Wrapping up the Forbush inheritance, m'dear. Once we got the news that Hawthorne had been killed in the Indian attack I ordered, we put the rest of our plan to work. First, Basil had to go, then I'd marry you, the fortune would become mine and I'd pay your brother his share."

She shook her head. "There wasn't enough money to warrant such a plot. How desperate were you and Leland for money?"

"You don't know the half of what Basil put away. He was a canny investor and knew how to hide it from the taxman. If he hadn't bragged about it to me, we'd never have known." He started for her, his smile growing larger.

She had to keep him talking. If she could keep him distracted, perhaps she could reach the poker by the fireplace. "What investments? I've never seen anything like that in my factor's reports."

"Aye, but now that the courts are on to it, they'll find out. York and I won't see a farthing of it now. Too bad it all went wrong."

"What went wrong?" she asked, inching nearer to the fireplace.

"Hawthorne was too slippery. My best assassin couldn't

kill him. Then Leland's amateurish attempts on you went awry. I had to have my man clean up after him."

Her accidents had been Leland's attempts to kill her? The horror of it made her mind spin. Her own brother? And Barrington had tried to kill Adam? Kill both of them? "Why?" she asked. "If I were dead, how could I marry you? How would you ever inherit then?"

"I wouldn't. But Leland would."

Grace felt sick to her stomach. There was no fondness between them, but they sprang from the same womb, shared a father and mother.

Lord Barrington grinned. "He was the one who suggested it. It's the money, you see. There's so damned much of it. Enough to set us up anywhere in the world, be rulers of our own kingdoms. Too much to let you gamble it away, or marry Hawthorne, especially when the best part of my plan was to have you at my side. Especially after Leland told me that Basil confessed he'd been unable to consummate your marriage. Then Hawthorne comes to town and moves in on my territory. He's had you, hasn't he?" His eyes took on a mad look. "The money slipped through my fingers, but you haven't. I'll have that much satisfaction, at least."

"What satisfaction?" She was nearly to the poker, but Barrington was closing the distance between them.

"You. I've wasted four years on you, Grace. You owe me. You're going to be my bait. And then you're going to be my doxie. Get your cloak. The heavy one. Don't want you catching your death." He laughed again, as if he'd made some sort of joke.

She frowned, her blood chilling at the implication of that word. "Bait for what, m'lord?"

"Hawthorne. He'll come after you, and I'll be ready for him."

"Where are you taking me?"

"East India Docks. I've booked passage for Australia, set

to sail at dawn. I've left clues here and there. He'll show up. And when he does, I'll kill him."

Just a few more steps…she had to keep him talking. "Then what? Do you intend to kill me, too?"

"Haven't decided. Imagine, Grace. If you show me how agreeable you can be, I might let you live. You'd have to be very agreeable, though. I've always suspected you had the makings of a proper slut. Or would you rather be my servant in Australia, eh? Yes, picking up after me, seeing to my needs, scrubbing my floors. Yes, just might do that. Fitting, don't you think, after the years I spent dancing attendance on you, cozening you, trying to make you love me? But you'll need to persuade me. I'm not remembering your rejection too kindly. You'll have to convince me."

Grace caught her breath on a gasp. This Lord Barrington was a stranger to her. He lunged and dragged her away from the fireplace.

"Twit. Did you think you could get away with that twice? That's no way to cozen me. Fetch your cloak and let's be away."

He pushed her roughly in the direction of her dressing room, following her so that she could not shut him out or find something she could use as a weapon. When she hesitated, he pulled a winter cloak from a peg on the wall and dragged her from her room. Half stumbling, half dragged down the stairs, she began calling to Dianthe.

"Di! Tell Adam not to come! Tell him it's—"

Barrington's fist caught her a glancing blow on her cheek but it was enough to stun her. Her ears rang and her knees buckled. He dragged her through the front door and out to his waiting coach.

Adam stared at the man next to Carter. "Renquist? How are you involved in all this?"

The man looked impatient. "Carter and I have been investigating the same men. But when he started following Mrs. Forbush, he drew my attention. She is the one who hired me."

"You work for Grace?" Adam asked, just to be clear.

"Indirectly, yes. I don't know what sort of dirt you're looking to dig up on Mrs. Forbush or her friends, but it will not go down well with a good many people. Most especially, me."

Adam held his temper in check. "Then what are you doing here now?"

"I came to talk to Carter. We are in the same…fraternity. I wanted to warn him away from defaming Mrs. Forbush or her friends. And, since we were both following the same man, I thought it would be of interest to him that Lord Barrington booked passage to Australia this afternoon." Renquist paused and glanced out the window. "The *Blue Gull* is cleared to sail from the East India Docks within the hour."

Adam puzzled this development. York was back in Devon and would not present a danger to Grace any longer. Barrington would be gone to Australia in another hour or two. Suddenly his deep need for vengeance seemed less important than going home to Grace. Ah, but there was still Nokomis. Sweet little Nokomis, Daughter of the Moon.

"Useful information," he told Renquist. "We'll follow it from here."

Renquist shifted his weight from one foot to the other. "He bought passage for two."

The second passage would not be for Leland York. Ice crept slowly through Adam's blood. He glanced from Renquist to Carter and back again. "Grace," he said, the hair on the back of his neck prickling. His heart began to pound. "I sent her home with Dewberry but I haven't been able to find Barrington all night."

"*Jesu,*" Renquist breathed.

"Where is the assassin?"

"He…uh, had an accident," Carter told him.

"What kind?"

"The kind you don't recover from."

That, at least, was one thing he didn't have to worry about. Already on his way to the door, he called over his shoulder, "Renquist, go to Bloomsbury Square. Stay with Grace until I return. If she is not there, send the police to the *Blue Gull*. Carter, where's your horse?"

"Just left him in the stable."

Adam took the stairs three at a time and raced for the stables. He caught the stable boy just as he was leading the stallion to his stall. With nothing but a bridle, Adam swung himself up onto the steed's bare back. He looped the reins through his left hand from long habit, leaving his right hand free to wield a knife or war club. He was ready for battle. Carter's voice carried to him as he wheeled the horse for the street.

"I won't be far behind!"

While she was still stunned, Barrington had tied Grace's hands behind her back, concealed beneath her cloak. The moment his coach left them at the ship, he dragged her to the gangway and held her in a painfully cruel grip, standing behind her.

She fought her encroaching panic. Barrington was going to use her as a shield when Adam came, and then shoot him, certain Adam would not risk hurting Grace to get at him. Pray Dianthe had heard her screams. Pray she would tell Adam it was a trap.

Grace shivered in the cold, damp night and peered to see through the rising mist. Her cloak strings had come loose and the front flapped open and closed in the breeze off the river. Her silk nightgown afforded her little protection from the damp and cold. "Adam will not come, Lord Barrington."

"He'll come," the man snarled in her ear.

"He is angry with me. He sent me home without him."

"And that is why you were preparing for him?" He laughed, his breath rising in a moist cloud around them. "The only thing I feared was that I wouldn't get you away before he came back."

"What if the ship sails before he arrives?"

"His misfortune. I'll just leave your body for him. An eloquent message, do you not think? A little memento of my regard. He will pay—one way or the other—I don't care which. It would be a pity, though, since I had such interesting plans for you."

"He...he'll hunt you down. Even in Australia. He'll find you and make you sorry."

"He'll never find me. I've already established another identity. You learn how to manage these things when you work with covert operations, m'dear."

Shuddering with the cold seeping upward from her bare feet, Grace began to lose hope. She closed her eyes to pray but she was too panicked to say the words. She said the only thing she could put into words. "Don't come. Don't come. Please, don't come." Over and over. Her tears were hot as they rolled down her cool cheeks. "Please...I'd rather be dead than live without him."

She felt the barrel of Lord Barrington's pistol, concealed in the folds of her loosening cloak, grind into her ribs. "Too bad you never felt that way about me, m'dear. We wouldn't be here now. I'd have been good to you. I'd have kept you safe from Leland."

The lapping of water against the side of the ship was the only sound to break the silence and Grace jumped when she heard the voice of the captain from the deck above them.

"Come aboard, Mr. Short. Your friend is not coming to see you off, and it's time for us to be away." Silent seamen began to unfasten the ropes from the moorings and cast them up to the deck to be coiled.

"Just a minute longer, please," Barrington called back. "I'll come aboard when you raise the gangway."

The captain disappeared from the rail and Barrington leaned closer to her ear, whispering, "Say goodbye, Grace." The pressure of the barrel increased.

The thundering of hooves reached her even before she felt the vibration of the planks beneath her feet. A terrible blood-curdling war cry sliced the heavy air as Adam appeared through the mist, riding as if all the demons of hell were at his heels.

Barrington froze, as unprepared for this tactic as she had been. Elated, terrified, desperate, she tried to spin away from him. "No, Adam!" she screamed.

He was coming at such breakneck speed that she feared he would not be able to stop. She saw him reach for something in his moccasin, then he threw one leg over the stallion's haunches and dismounted at a run before the horse had come to a halt.

"Adam, he has a pistol!"

Barrington struggled to free his hand from the folds of her cloak and pushed her forward, out of his way. She fell to her knees and then forward on her elbows. Adam leaped over her, colliding with bone-jarring force into Barrington's chest. The man went down backward, tangled in the folds of Grace's cloak. She expected to hear the pistol discharge, but no sound came.

When she sat up and turned, Adam, straddling Barrington, was grasping a fistful of Barrington's hair and holding a knife to his scalp, his teeth bared in a savage sneer. He was terrifying.

He was glorious.

"For Nokomis," he growled as he slashed sideways.

Barrington screamed and dropped his pistol to flatten his palm to the top of his head.

Grace sobbed with reaction, stumbling and struggling to stand. The hem of her nightgown ripped and she tripped over the shreds. "Adam! Oh, God! Are you all right?"

He turned to her, his eyes obsidian-hard, and she shrank back from the fierceness there. She could see that he was still locked in some dark self-imposed hell and was struggling to reorient himself.

"Adam," she sighed, lifting her hand in entreaty.

Her voice must have reached him because he blinked and the crazed look was gone. "Ellie…" He dropped the hank of hair he'd taken from Barrington and came toward her like a sleepwalker, his knife dripping at his side.

She fell into his arms. "He was going to kill you," she sobbed. "He said he ordered the attack on your Indian village."

"I know, Ellie," he whispered against her hair. "I know. But it's over. It's finally over."

She heard other horses arriving coupled with shouted instructions. Someone called Adam's name and then the captain's voice rose above the rest.

"You there!" the captain called. "What the—"

Adam spun around, his muscles tensed. Barrington, blood dripping from the top of his head and trickling down the side of his face, had gotten to his feet and was taking aim at Adam with his pistol.

"You should have been as easy to kill as your uncle." He staggered slightly. "Watch your harlot die first." He shifted the pistol slightly to bring Grace into his line of fire.

Grace froze, her eyes riveted to the barrel of the pistol. Hands came out of nowhere and knocked her aside. As she fell, Adam's arm moved and a lightning flash of steel blurred across the distance to make a deep thump as it landed against Barrington's right shoulder.

Barrington spun around with the force of the blow and his pistol misfired as it hit the ground. Barrington followed, crying out in pain.

Dazed, Grace looked around at the sudden burst of activity. Mr. Renquist was there and draped her cloak around her and hurried her to a coach, reassuring her that Dianthe was safe and that he'd taken her to Lady Annica. A moment later Adam came to her and touched her hand through the window. "Go home, Grace. I don't want you here when the police arrive." He slapped the side of the coach and it pulled away, leaving her to look back and pray that Adam would not be far behind.

Adam unlocked the front door and stepped into the foyer. Dawn was not far off, but a candle had been left burning on the foyer table. Grace?

He sat on the steps, unwrapping the thongs around his moccasins. He did not want to panic Mrs. Dewberry in the morning when she saw blood-dabbed footprints in the foyer. Wrapping business up had taken longer than he would have liked, but at least he knew that there would be no more mistakes or omissions. Barrington, after he'd been bandaged from Adam's scalping, had been taken to a surgeon to tend the knife wound, then placed in Newgate to await trial. When the story was told and all the facts known, it would be impossible to save Leland York from a like fate. Grace would hate the notoriety, but at least she'd be safe with Leland locked away.

He looked down at his bloodstained buckskins and knew he'd never wear them again. It was finally over. Nokomis could rest. Mishe-Mokwa could not read the white man's language, but he would receive Adam's beaded wristband and know that the deaths had been avenged. Still, the satisfaction of knowing that his promise had been kept was tainted by the knowledge that Grace had seen the part of him he'd most wanted to hide—the savage beneath his skin.

The memory of her standing on the wharf, barefoot, in a nearly transparent nightgown, had driven him insane. When he thought of what Barrington might have done to her, he had lost any tenuous hold he'd had on his fury. Speed and surprise were his best weapons against a trap, and he'd used those elements to his advantage. God, but he hadn't meant to scalp the man! It was the sight of Grace and the memory of Nokomis that had blocked his self-control.

He climbed the stairs, his feet silent on the treads. When he reached the landing, he glanced at Grace's door. It was ajar, and a soft glow seeped into the darkened hallway. Thank God she had waited up for him. He needed to see her. Hold her. Know that she was safe.

He eased her door open. She was reclining on her chaise before the fireplace, a book in her hands. Her hair was loose and spilled over her shoulders. She'd shed her torn nightgown in favor of a light wrapper. She was so lovely she took his breath away.

She sat up and turned toward him, a smile curving those luscious lips. She dropped her book on the chaise as she stood and came forward, the sway of her hips mesmerizing him.

"Adam," she said, a hint of tension in her eyes.

Odd, how a single word could set his pulse racing. She stopped close enough for him to smell the jasmine scent on her warm skin. He was precariously close to losing what little self-control he'd been able to regain.

"Barrington is in custody," he told her.

She nodded. "Thank you."

He dropped his moccasins and reached out to her, then let his hand drop to his side. He couldn't touch her, couldn't taint her with the savage part of him. She looked down at his hand and frowned.

"Where is your wristband, Adam?"

"In a courier's pouch bound for Canada."

"I thought you would always love Nokomis."

"I will," he said, and suddenly realized what she had thought. "But a child's love is not what I need now."

"Nokomis was a child?"

"In her eighth winter."

A flicker of sympathy and pain passed through her dark eyes and when she gazed up at him again, the tension was gone. The pink tip of her tongue wet her lips and she went around him to lock her door.

He closed his eyes for a moment to collect his wits. When he opened them again, she was fumbling with the strings of his jacket. She said nothing of her intentions, but he knew what she wanted. And, God help him, he wanted her more.

She lifted the bottom of his jacket and he helped her pull it over his head. Then she stepped closer, rose on her toes and pressed her lips to the hollow of his throat as her hands skimmed up his sides and across his chest. Her mouth moved lower, to the light matting of hair on his chest. She breathed deeply and he realized he smelled of sweat and leather and horse, and she seemed even more aroused.

She scraped her fingernails lightly over his nipples and then licked at the hardened nubs. The shock of it made him gasp. Lust, pure and primal, swept through him. He tugged the sash of her wrapper and it fell away to reveal her gloriously naked beneath. He could barely move, he was so aroused.

Her boldness intrigued him, all the more so because he knew how truly innocent she was, and that everything she did to him now was experimentation. How far would she go to find her limits? How long before she realized there *were* no limits? Not for them. Not ever.

No limits, he prayed. Nothing would be forbidden. Nothing held back. He vowed he would devote his life to the search for the things that would give her the most pleasure.

He pushed the buckskin breeches down over his hips and kicked them away, then held her still, his hands gripping her hips as he knelt, trailing kisses down her throat to her breasts and lower to her abdomen. And lower still. He knew she wanted this by her own actions two nights ago.

She tangled her fingers through his hair and swayed as if her knees would give out. He looked up at her. Her head had fallen back, exposing the long column of throat, her eyes were closed and her lips were parted. Her unbound hair swirled around them and he was suddenly reminded of the first time he'd seen her portrait. He'd thought her the most erotic and tightly contained thing he'd ever seen then, but that portrait paled in comparison to the free and unfettered woman standing before him now. This was the vision he'd carry with him through the rest of his life, across continents and oceans, time and space, wherever his duties took him. No matter what happened between them in the future, *this* portrait of Grace would be his touchstone until the day he died.

"I love you, Ellie," he said against her stomach. "I love you. I love you."

She slipped through his hands until she knelt with him. Tears sparkled in her eyes and she lifted her lips to his. "Adam…I've loved you from the moment I saw you."

Her heartbeat hammered against his and it felt as familiar as his own. He'd finally come home.

* * * * *

If you enjoyed what you just read,
then we've got an offer you can't resist!

Take 2 bestselling
love stories FREE!
Plus get a FREE surprise gift!